Table of Contents

Prologue: The Last Keeper 2

Chapter 1: Routine And Disruption 11

Chapter 2: The Discovery 18

Chapter 3: Across the Stone Bridge 28

Chapter 4: The Forest of Whispers 41

Chapter 5: The Archives Below 54

Chapter 6: The Decision 73

Chapter 7: Return to Dravengate 85

Chapter 8: Crystal Training 107

Chapter 9: Progress and Problems 130

Chapter 10: Archives and Answers 157

Chapter 11: Calculations and Connections 176

Chapter 12: The First Restoration 197

....215

....241

....281

M.N.Whitehouse

THE KEEPER OF TIME

Prologue: The Last Keeper

Five hundred years ago

The crossing was failing.

Keeper Elavir could feel it in the erratic pulse of the Timewell, in the violent shuddering of the sigils, in the very air of Dravengate itself, which seemed to tear and mend with each passing moment. Reality flexed around her as she raced through streets that no longer obeyed the normal laws of space, guided by her Guardian, Seren, who bounded ahead in feline form, golden eyes blazing through the chaos.

They had been too late.

The Keeper of Time

"How much time?" she called to Thorne, who ran beside her, his youthful face grim with determination. He was barely a full Archivist then, not yet bearing the weight of centuries that would eventually silver his hair and line his face.

"Minutes at most," he answered, his breathing laboured as they climbed the steps to the Timewell plaza. "The temporal fractures are cascading. The sixth quadrant has already collapsed completely."

Elavir didn't need to ask what that meant. Whole worlds cut off, connections severed, lives disrupted or potentially destroyed as realities separated violently. All because of one Keeper's ambition. All because Marwen couldn't be satisfied with maintaining balance, he had to seek dominion.

The central square was unrecognizable. Where once the ordered beauty of Dravengate's heart had offered peace and stability, now reality itself bucked and warped. The Timewell, that ancient, perfect mechanism, was a storm of chaotic energy, its silver essence spilling upward into the sky in defiance of all natural law. Around it, the six pillars that had stood for millennia were cracked, two already crumbled to dust.

And in the center of it all stood Marwen, his form no longer entirely human, distorted by the temporal energies he had tried to harness.

M.N.Whitehouse

The Keeper of Time

His Guardian was nowhere to be seen, likely destroyed in the initial surge or fled to save itself. The rogue Keeper's hands were raised toward the maelstrom above, his expression a terrible mixture of triumph and terror as the power he had unleashed consumed him from within.

"It's too late to save him," Elara said, suddenly beside them, her silver hair whipping in the temporal winds. She was young then too, not yet the Elder she would become, but already wise beyond her years. "We must focus on containment or all is lost."

Seren growled in agreement, the massive snow leopard's fur standing on end as waves of distorted time washed over them. The Guardian's presence was all that kept them relatively stable in the chaos, her innate ability to anchor temporal energy creating a bubble of calm in the storm.

Elavir gripped her wand tightly, feeling its ancient power responding to her will, connecting her to the broken heart of the crossing. The current Keeper's wand was still in Marwen's possession, presumably lost to the corruption that had overcome him. This one, her predecessor's tool, had been kept in the Archives as a historical artifact, never meant to be used again.

Until today.

"The primary connections must be preserved," Thorne shouted over the howling of the temporal winds. "Even if we lose most of the network, we must maintain at least one stable pathway or Dravengate itself will collapse entirely."

The Keeper of Time

Elavir nodded grimly. One connection. That was all they could hope to save now, one thread in what had once been a vast tapestry linking countless worlds. The question was, which one?

"The western route," Elara decided, her voice carrying a certainty that would later become her hallmark. "It's the most stable, the oldest. If anything can weather this storm, it's that path."

There was no time for debate. Elavir raised the ancient wand, focusing her will through it toward the Timewell. The connection was painful, like plunging her consciousness into boiling oil, but she endured it, using her training to navigate the chaotic currents of temporal energy.

She could sense Marwen now, or what remained of him, no longer a coherent mind but a jumble of fractured consciousness being torn apart by the very forces he had tried to control. There was no saving him, just as Elara had said. All they could do was try to limit the damage his folly had caused.

With Seren's steady presence anchoring her, Elavir began the desperate work of containment. It wasn't true restoration, there was no time for that, but rather a kind of magical triage, sacrificing the many connections to save the few. With each gesture of the wand, another pathway collapsed, another world separated from the crossing, the energy released channelled to reinforce the remaining structures.

"The shadows are coming through," Thorne warned, pointing to the darkening edges of the square where reality had worn thinnest. "The void entities sense the weakness."

The Keeper of Time

Indeed, amorphous shapes were beginning to coalesce in the spaces between moments, drawn to the catastrophic release of temporal energy like predators to blood in water. Formless yet menacing, they pressed against the barriers between dimensions, seeking entry into a realm that should have been closed to them.

Seren roared, the sound carrying power that pushed back against the encroaching darkness. The Guardian's form began to shimmer with golden light as she drew on her deepest reserves of protective energy, creating a perimeter that the shadows could not easily cross.

But it wouldn't last. Already, Elavir could see her Guardian tiring, the constant pressure of the temporal chaos draining even Seren's formidable strength. They had minutes at most before their defences would fail.

With desperate focus, Elavir drove the ancient wand into the heart of the Timewell, using it as a conduit for her own life force, her own temporal signature. It was a forbidden technique, one that would cost her dearly, but there was no alternative. The crossing needed an anchor, a focal point around which the remaining connection could stabilize.

The wand accepted her sacrifice, drawing her essence into itself, using it to create a template for the new, severely limited crossing that would emerge from the ruins of the old. As her consciousness began to fragment, spreading through the temporal currents, Elavir made one final, crucial decision.

The Keeper of Time

"The wand must be hidden," she gasped, her physical form already beginning to dissolve as the temporal energies claimed her.

"It cannot remain here, not with the shadows watching, waiting

It must go where they cannot easily follow."

With the last of her strength, she pulled the wand free from the Timewell and, with a gesture that cost her more than any of them would ever know, opened a narrow portal to the one world they had managed to keep connected, a realm of limited magic but great stability, far from the heart of the crossing.

"Find me when the time comes," she whispered to the wand, the words carrying layers of meaning that extended beyond the moment. Then, before Thorne or Elara could stop her, she cast the wand through the portal, sending it tumbling across time and space to land in a world that knew nothing of Dravengate or Keepers or the delicate balance between realities.

The portal sealed behind it, leaving only the faintest trace of a connection, a thread so thin that even the most sensitive instruments would struggle to detect it, yet strong enough to endure the centuries to come.

"What have you done?" Thorne cried, reaching for Elavir as her form became increasingly translucent, her being dispersing into the temporal currents.

"What was necessary," she replied, her voice now seeming to come from everywhere and nowhere at once.

M.N.Whitehouse

"The crossing will hold, but in diminished form. One day, when the shadows have forgotten us, when they no longer watch so closely, the wand will find its way back. It will find the one who can restore what we have lost today."

Seren moved to her Keeper's side, the Guardian's form also beginning to fade as the bond between them drew her into the same transformation. There was sorrow in those golden eyes, but also acceptance. They had chosen this path together, as Keeper and Guardian always did.

"Watch," Elavir commanded Thorne and Elara as the last of her physical form dissolved into motes of golden light. "Wait. The wand will choose when the time is right. The next Keeper will come, though perhaps not in the form you expect."

And then she was gone, her consciousness dispersed throughout the crossing, becoming part of the very fabric of Dravengate itself. Seren followed a moment later, the massive leopard dissolving into the same golden light, their essences mingling as they passed beyond physical form.

The temporal storm began to subside, the chaotic energies gradually settling into new patterns, greatly diminished from what had existed before, but stable enough to endure. Where once hundreds of connections had flowed outward from Dravengate to countless other worlds, now only a handful remained, and only one at full strength.

In the sudden, eerie quiet that followed the cataclysm, Thorne and Elara stood alone in the ruined plaza, the broken Timewell before them settling into dormancy, its silver essence no longer flowing but merely drifting in slow, tired circles.

Of Marwen, there was no sign. The rogue Keeper had been consumed entirely by the forces he had unleashed, his ambition for dominion over all worlds ending in his own obliteration.

But at the edges of the square, in the deepest shadows, formless entities still lingered, watching, waiting. They had tasted the rich energy of a wounded crossing, and had glimpsed the possibilities that such damage presented. They would not forget. They would not abandon the opportunity that had been created here.

"We should go," Thorne said finally, his young face aged by grief and exhaustion. "There will be chaos throughout what remains of Dravengate. People will need guidance, explanations."

Elara nodded; her gaze still fixed on the spot where Elavir had been. "She said the wand would return. That a new Keeper would come."

"Perhaps," Thorne replied, his voice heavy with doubt. "But how long must we wait? Years? Decades? Centuries? And what will remain of Dravengate by then?"

Elara turned away from the ruined Timewell, her expression settling into the serene determination that would become her hallmark in the centuries to come. "We will preserve what we can. We will maintain the knowledge, the traditions. We will be ready when the wand chooses again."

Together, they walked away from the plaza, leaving behind the dormant Timewell and the broken sigils, monuments to what had been lost and silent sentinels waiting for a restoration that might never come.

In the shadows, the void entities watched them go, their formless awareness already beginning to seep into the cracks that the Cataclysm had left in the fabric of Dravengate. They would be patient. Time meant nothing to creatures that existed between moments.

They would wait, and watch, and when the opportunity came, when some fool attempted to restore what had been broken, they would be ready.

And far away, in another world, a simple piece of driftwood washed up on a distant shore, its true nature hidden, its power dormant but not extinguished, waiting for the time when it would be found by the one it had been sent to find.

Waiting for the next Keeper of Time.

The Keeper of Time

Chapter 1: Routine And Disruption

Dylan Bennett had a habit of keeping his expectations small, which was why summer break never felt particularly thrilling to him. While other kids treated the last day of term like a prison break, rushing from the building with arms raised in victory, Dylan simply walked toward the exit, methodical and quiet, mentally reviewing the schedule he'd already created for the next six weeks.

His classmates' excitement was a wall of noise that Dylan had learned to filter. Too loud. Too unpredictable. Too much. He adjusted his rucksack straps until they were exactly even, then continued his careful navigation through the crowd.

The simple truth was that Dylan liked routine. Predictability was comfortable. It made sense in a world that often didn't.

The summer stretched before him with beautiful potential, not for adventure, but for order. Six weeks of carefully planned days: wake up at 7:30 AM, breakfast at 8:00 AM (cereal on weekdays, pancakes on weekends), mathematics practice from 9:00 to 10:30 AM, gaming from 10:30 AM to noon. The afternoon schedule was equally precise. His mum called it his "summer operating system," and she had long ago stopped suggesting spontaneous activities that might disrupt it.

As Dylan stepped into the June sunshine, squinting slightly at the intensity of the light that was a rare treat in Blackpool, he immediately spotted a familiar figure waiting near the school gates.

Bruno wasn't a classmate. He wasn't even supposed to be here, he was a Rottweiler, broad-chested and powerful, with the kind of warm brown eyes that made people forget he could probably knock them over in one good sprint. His glossy black coat shone in the sunlight as he sat with remarkable patience, tail thumping rhythmically against the pavement when he spotted Dylan.

A small smile tugged at Dylan's lips as he approached, reaching out to scratch behind Bruno's ears. "Let me guess. You escaped again."

Bruno huffed, as if confirming this fact.

"I told him to stay," a voice cut through the summer air.

Dylan turned to see his stepdad Mally standing with his arms crossed, his expression a careful balance of exasperation and fondness. Malcolm Reynolds, Mally to everyone including Dylan's mum, who had finally stopped using his full name after years of gentle teasing, was a solid presence in Dylan's life, steady and undemanding. He wore faded jeans and a well-worn Iron Maiden t-shirt, his dark hair just beginning to show threads of silver at the temples.

"He pulled a Houdini act when I was checking the post," Mally explained. "One minute sitting on the doorstep, the next minute gone. Didn't take a maths genius to figure out where he was headed."

Dylan nodded, unsurprised. It wasn't unusual for Bruno to ignore instructions.

His stepdad had given up pretending he had full control over the dog years ago. Bruno had his own ideas about where he should be, and most of those ideas involved being wherever Dylan was.

"He needed to make sure I survived the last day," Dylan said, his tone matter-of-fact as he ran his fingers through Bruno's thick fur.

Mally snorted. "Yeah, well, mission accomplished, mate." He reached down to pat Bruno's head, his expression softening. "School's officially out. Your mum's making that pasta thing you like for tea."

Dylan nodded again, already mentally adjusting his evening schedule to accommodate this information. "With the garlic bread?"

"Is there any other way?"

This was the kind of change Dylan could handle, a small variation within an established framework. He shifted his rucksack again, preparing to begin the twelve-minute walk home, when Mally cleared his throat.

"We're heading to the beach tomorrow morning," his stepdad announced, his tone casual but his eyes watching Dylan carefully. "And before you say no, you're coming."

Dylan felt his stomach tighten. The beach wasn't in his plans. The beach was sand that got everywhere, unpredictable waves, too many people, and no clear schedule. The beach was a disruption.

"I hadn't planned," he began, voice even despite the anxiety building in his chest.

"That's why I didn't ask," Mally interrupted, throwing an arm over Dylan's shoulder before he could step away. His stepdad's smile was kind but firm. "We're leaving at six. It'll be quiet, hardly anyone there. Your mum needs to get out of the house, and honestly, so do you."

Dylan stared at the ground, counting the cracks in the pavement. One, two, three, four. His fingers tapped against his thigh in the same rhythm. The beach wasn't just unplanned, it was sensory overload waiting to happen. Sand between his toes, the smell of sun cream, the roar of waves, the glare of sun on water.

"I don't have my beach schedule prepared," he muttered, knowing how it sounded but unable to stop himself.

Mally squeezed his shoulder gently. "I know, mate. But sometimes the best days are the ones we don't plan."

Dylan doubted this very much, but he followed without further protest as they began walking home. Bruno trotted beside them, tail wagging in a perfect metronome, seemingly satisfied with himself. The dog bumped against Dylan's leg occasionally, a gentle pressure that always seemed to come just when the anxiety threatened to spike too high.

Twenty-three steps later, Dylan sighed and pulled out his mobile, opening his calendar app. "What time will we be back?"

"Early afternoon," Mally replied, relief evident in his voice. "Home before the heat gets bad."

Dylan nodded and created a new entry for tomorrow: "Beach Excursion – 6:00 AM to 2:00 PM." He stared at the screen, the unfamiliar block of time disrupting the careful pattern he'd planned for his first full day of summer break. With methodical precision, he began moving his other scheduled activities to accommodate this change.

As they walked, Dylan's mind raced ahead, trying to prepare for all the variables the beach trip might introduce. He would need to pack his noise-cancelling earbuds. He'd wear the blue swim shorts, not the red ones with the scratchy waistband. He would bring his own water bottle because the water at the beach always tasted wrong.

The planning helped calm the flutter of unease in his chest. By the time they turned onto Oakridge Drive, he had mentally rearranged tomorrow into something approaching a manageable shape. Still, as he climbed the three steps to the front porch of the semi-detached house he'd lived in since he was four, a sense of uncertainty lingered.

Bruno pressed against his leg again, warm and solid. The dog looked up at him with those deep brown eyes that somehow always seemed to understand exactly what Dylan was feeling, even when Dylan himself struggled to identify it.

"It'll be fine," Dylan told himself as much as Bruno. "Just a minor adjustment to the schedule.

Inside, the house greeted him with familiar scents and sounds. His mum's voice called from the kitchen, asking about the last day of school. Mally answered for him, giving Dylan a moment to hang his rucksack on its designated hook by the door, third from the left, always the third hook.

Dylan took a breath and followed the sounds of his family, Bruno padding faithfully at his heels. He recited prime numbers in his head as he walked, a habit that helped him transition between activities.

Summer had officially begun. The next six weeks stretched before him, most of them carefully plotted in his planner and colour-coded in his digital calendar.

But by the time Dylan went to bed that night, after checking that his alarm was set correctly and that Bruno was settled in his usual spot on the rug beside the bed, he could already tell, it wouldn't be anything like he expected.

Something about tomorrow felt different. Not just the beach trip, but something beyond that. A whisper of change that didn't fit into any of his carefully constructed routines.

Dylan switched off his lamp, plunging the room into darkness broken only by the thin strip of moonlight between his curtains.

"Goodnight, Bruno," he whispered.

From his place on the floor, Bruno huffed softly in response, the sound comfortingly familiar in the quiet room.

The Keeper of Time

Dylan closed his eyes and began counting backward from one hundred, his nightly ritual to help his busy mind settle toward sleep. He didn't know that this would be the last normal night for a very long time. He didn't know that tomorrow would bring more than just sand between his toes and the roar of ocean waves.

He didn't know that his entire carefully constructed world was about to change.

And Bruno, watching in the dark with those knowing brown eyes, couldn't tell him.

Chapter 2: The Discovery

The beach always looked different in the early morning, emptier, quieter, the sky shifting through soft pastels as the waves rolled lazily toward the shore. Dylan had been to Blackpool beach countless times before, but never quite this early, when the famous promenade stood nearly deserted and the tide stretched out so far it seemed to touch the horizon.

Dylan zipped his light jacket up to his chin, protection against the cool morning breeze coming off the Irish Sea. Despite the clear sky promising warmth later, early June in Blackpool still carried a chill. He walked carefully, placing each foot with deliberate precision on the damp sand that had been swept smooth by the retreating tide.

"Not so bad, is it?" Mally asked, gesturing broadly at the empty expanse around them. "Told you we'd have the place to ourselves."

He wasn't entirely wrong. A few dedicated dog walkers dotted the shoreline in the distance, and an elderly man with a metal detector methodically swept an area near the sea wall, but otherwise, the beach was theirs. The usual crowds, noise, and chaos that Dylan associated with Blackpool beach were absent.

His mum walked a few paces ahead, her dyed red hair caught by the breeze, arms wrapped around herself as she gazed out at the water. She looked more relaxed than she had in weeks, Dylan noticed. Perhaps Mally had been right about her needing to get out of the house.

"The light is perfect," she called back to them. "We should have done this ages ago."

Dylan didn't answer, instead focusing on the familiar weight of his backpack. It contained everything he might need for the next eight hours: a spare set of clothes in case his got wet, his noise-cancelling earbuds, a water bottle, sunscreen (despite its smell, he'd accepted its necessity), three protein bars, his backup charger, and a paperback book on advanced calculus. Preparation made unpredictable situations manageable.

Bruno, meanwhile, was experiencing the beach with unbridled enthusiasm, racing in wide circles, his powerful legs kicking up sprays of sand. Bruno was a study in pure joy, stopping occasionally to investigate something interesting before resuming his excited exploration.

"Reckon Bruno's chuffed we came," Mally observed, hands in his pockets as he walked alongside Dylan.

"He likes open spaces," Dylan replied, watching as Bruno paused to sniff at a piece of seaweed, then promptly sneezed. "Less for him to knock over."

Mally laughed. "Fair point. That tail of his is a weapon in confined spaces."

They continued walking, following the curve of the shoreline. Dylan found himself gradually relaxing into the experience.

The rhythmic sound of the waves created a predictable pattern that soothed rather than jarred his senses. The beach was vast enough that he didn't feel crowded, and the cool morning air carried fewer overwhelming scents than the midday beach would.

After they'd been walking for twenty-three minutes, Dylan had been keeping track, his mum suggested setting up their spot. They found a suitable area, and Dylan helped arrange their things with mathematical precision: beach blanket perfectly squared, cooler at the north corner, bags arranged by size along the east edge.

"I'm going for a walk toward the pier," his mum announced, once everything was arranged to Dylan's satisfaction. "Anyone want to join me?"

"I'll stay with Dylan," Mally replied, settling onto the blanket and pulling out a thermos. "We'll hold down the fort."

Dylan nodded, grateful for the lack of pressure. His mum smiled, understanding in her eyes.

"Back in a bit, then," she said, gently ruffling Dylan's hair before setting off.

Once she'd gone, Dylan sat cross-legged on the blanket, watching Bruno, who had now discovered the joy of digging in the damp sand. Bruno attacked this new activity with characteristic enthusiasm, front paws working furiously, sand flying in all directions.

"He's going to Australia if he keeps that up," Mally commented, sipping from his thermos.

Dylan didn't respond immediately, his attention caught by a pattern of small shells embedded in the sand near their blanket. He counted them silently, thirteen in total, arranged in what was almost a perfect Fibonacci spiral. The mathematical precision of it was satisfying.

"Why did you really want us to come here?" Dylan asked suddenly, not looking away from the shell pattern.

Mally was quiet for a moment, then sighed. "Sharp as ever, aren't you?" He set down his thermos. "Your mum's been worried about you. End of term, you've been more withdrawn than usual. Thought a change of scenery might help."

Dylan processed this information. "I haven't been withdrawn. I've been planning my summer schedule."

"Six color-coded charts and a spreadsheet isn't just planning, mate. That's..." Mally paused, searching for the right word. "That's fortifying."

Dylan considered this. He didn't see his planning as excessive, but he'd learned that others sometimes had different perspectives on what constituted "normal" behaviour.

"I like knowing what's coming," he said simply.

"I know you do," Mally replied, his voice gentle. "But sometimes the best bits of life are the ones you don't see coming."

Before Dylan could formulate a response to this dubious wisdom, Bruno's digging activity intensified dramatically.

Bruno was now excavating with single-minded determination, his powerful front legs working at a frantic pace.

"Whoa, slow down there, mate," Mally called. "You're creating a sandstorm."

But Bruno didn't slow down. If anything, his efforts became even more focused, more purposeful. This wasn't his usual playful digging, this was different. His entire body was tense with concentration.

Dylan frowned, setting aside his conversation with Mally to watch Bruno more closely. "What exactly are you looking for?" he asked, though he didn't expect an answer.

Bruno ignored him, digging faster, kicking sand behind him until his claws scraped against something solid.

Bruno froze. He lowered his head, sniffing intently at whatever he had uncovered. Then he made a sound, not a bark, not a whine, but something in between. A sound of curiosity, perhaps, or recognition.

Dylan stood up, brushing sand from his shorts before stepping closer. Mally followed, watching with amused interest.

"Found buried treasure, has he?" Mally jokes.

But as Dylan knelt beside the hole Bruno had created, he saw something protruding from the sand, something that looked like driftwood, worn smooth by the ocean. It was partially exposed, about the length of his forearm, with a slightly curved shape.

Bruno backed away slightly, but remained fixated on the object, his eyes never leaving it, his posture alert but not aggressive.

"It's just a piece of driftwood," Mally said, glancing between the object and Bruno's intense focus. "Though you'd think he'd found a buried bone from the way he's staring at it."

Dylan didn't respond. Something about the object felt off. Not in a threatening way, but in the way that a misaligned picture frame demanded to be straightened. His fingers twitched with the urge to adjust, to correct, to understand.

He reached down and wrapped his fingers around it.

The moment he did, the air shifted.

It wasn't dramatic. There was no flash of light, no crack of thunder, no swirling of magical energy. Just a subtle change, as if the atmosphere had briefly recalibrated itself around him.

Dylan felt it in the way sound seemed to momentarily dampen, like the volume of the world had been turned down for a fraction of a second. The ocean waves seemed to hesitate, their rhythm faltering before resuming its steady pace. Even the breeze paused, as if holding its breath.

Bruno made a soft, alert sound, not quite a bark, but something close. His eyes remained fixed on the object in Dylan's hand, his body completely still except for a slight tremor running through his powerful frame.

"You all right?" Mally asked, frowning slightly. "You've gone a bit pale."

Dylan blinked, looking down at what he now held fully in his hand. It was indeed shaped like a piece of driftwood, smoothed and polished by years in the sea. About fourteen inches long, it tapered slightly from one end to the other. The wood was a rich, dark colour with subtle variations in tone that seemed to shift as he turned it in his hands.

"I'm fine," Dylan replied after a moment, though he wasn't entirely certain this was true. "It's just... interesting."

"What is it?" Mally leaned closer.

Dylan turned the object over in his hands, examining it with the meticulous attention he applied to anything that caught his interest. To anyone else, it might appear to be nothing more than a particularly aesthetic piece of driftwood. But Dylan noticed details that didn't quite fit that explanation.

The weight, for one thing, it was lighter than it should be for its size and apparent density. And although it appeared water-worn, the texture under his fingertips felt more like polished wood that had been crafted rather than eroded. Most significantly, the balance of it was perfect, the weight distributed with mathematical precision.

It was a wand.

Dylan didn't know how he knew this with such certainty, but the knowledge settled in his mind with the satisfying click of a puzzle piece finding its place.

"Just a nice bit of driftwood," he said aloud, not ready to share his actual thoughts. "Bruno must have smelled something interesting on it."

Mally seemed satisfied with this explanation. "Well, since he worked so hard to find it, I suppose it's yours now. A souvenir from our beach day." He checked his watch. "Your mum should be back soon. Want to help me get the sandwiches out?"

Dylan nodded, but didn't immediately move to help. Instead, he carefully slipped the wand, the driftwood, he corrected himself, into the side pocket of his backpack. As he did so, he could have sworn he felt a subtle warmth emanating from it, like it was responding to his touch.

Bruno finally relaxed his stance, shaking sand from his coat before padding over to Dylan and bumping his head against Dylan's arm. His eyes, when Dylan met them, seemed to hold an unusual intensity, as if he was trying to communicate something important.

"What?" Dylan whispered, too quietly for Mally to hear as he busied himself with the cooler. "What is it?"

Bruno simply huffed, in that way dogs do when humans are being particularly dense, and settled down next to Dylan's backpack, next to the pocket containing the wand.

For the remainder of their beach visit, Dylan found himself unusually distracted. He went through the motions of eating lunch, taking a brief walk along the water's edge with his mum, but his mind kept returning to the object in his backpack, to the strange moment when he'd first touched it, to Bruno's uncharacteristic behaviour.

By early afternoon, as they packed up to head home, Dylan had mentally revised his summer schedule to include extensive research on driftwood, ancient artifacts, and, though he felt slightly foolish even thinking about it, magical objects.

The drive home was quiet, with his mum and Mally chatting softly in the front seats while Dylan stared out the window, one hand resting on his backpack, fingers just inches from the wand. Bruno lay with his head on Dylan's lap, apparently exhausted from his morning of excavation, but Dylan noticed how the dog's ears twitched every time Dylan's fingers moved closer to the side pocket.

When they arrived home, Dylan immediately went to his room, citing a desire to "recalibrate" after the beach trip, an excuse his parents accepted without question, familiar with his need to decompress after outings.

Once alone, he carefully removed the wand from his backpack and placed it on his desk, under the direct light of his lamp. He studied it from every angle, making mental notes of its dimensions, weight, and unusual characteristics.

It looked innocent enough, just a smooth wooden shape, nothing flashing or glowing, nothing trying to convince him that it wasn't just a piece of driftwood.

And yet, it felt different.

Bruno lay curled on the floor nearby, his ears twitching as if listening for something unseen, his eyes rarely leaving the wand.

Dylan exhaled slowly. "Fine," he murmured, more to himself than to Bruno. "Let's see what you actually are."

He reached out and grabbed the wand again, holding it properly now, his fingers wrapping around what was clearly meant to be a handle. He gave it a small flick, expecting nothing, maybe hoping for a spark or some confirmation that he wasn't imagining things.

Instead, the air bent.

Not in a way he could fully explain. It just shifted. Thickened. Folded inward.

A swirling portal opened in the middle of his bedroom, deep and endless, curling with starlight and shadow.

Dylan froze, heart pounding.

Bruno didn't hesitate. He leapt through.

Dylan barely had time to call his name before the portal pulled him in, too, and everything changed.

Chapter 3: Across the Stone Bridge

One moment, Dylan was standing in his bedroom in Blackpool, heart hammering against his ribs. The next, he was falling, or perhaps floating, through a tunnel of swirling light and darkness.

The sensation defied every physical law Dylan had ever studied. It wasn't like dropping through air or being submerged in water. It was as if he had been unravelled at a molecular level, his entire being stretched across dimensions he couldn't comprehend.

His mind, desperate for order amidst chaos, tried to count the seconds, but time seemed to fold back on itself, rendering the exercise meaningless. There was no up or down, no forward or backward, just a kaleidoscopic rush through something that wasn't quite space.

And then, abruptly, it ended.

Dylan gasped as his feet hit solid ground, his knees buckling with the impact. He staggered forward, arms windmilling as he fought to regain his balance. The wand was still clutched tightly in his right hand, his fingers locked around it in a death grip.

"Bruno!" he called, his voice sounding strange in the unfamiliar air.

The environment assaulted his senses all at once. The air smelled different, richer, earthier, with undertones of something he couldn't identify. The light had a quality he'd never seen before, neither the harsh fluorescence of indoor lighting nor the clear brightness of sunlight, but something in between, casting everything in a perpetual golden-hour glow.

And the sounds, subtle but wrong. The ambient noise lacked the familiar urban undertones of cars, distant voices, or household appliances. Instead, he heard rustling leaves, the soft bubbling of flowing water, and strange, distant calls that resembled no birds he knew.

Dylan blinked rapidly, trying to process his surroundings while silencing the screaming panic in his mind. He was standing in a meadow of tall grass that rippled in a gentle breeze. The grass wasn't the dull green of English fields but a silvery-blue that seemed to shimmer with its own inner light. Beyond the meadow, dark trees loomed, their shapes twisted and ancient.

"Bruno!" he called again, his voice cracking slightly.

A familiar bark answered him, and relief flooded through Dylan's system as he spotted Bruno about twenty meters ahead. Bruno was standing at the edge of the meadow, his dark form a stark contrast against the luminescent grass. His tail was high, his posture alert but not fearful.

"Stay there!" Dylan commanded, though he was already moving forward, his trainers sinking slightly into the soft earth.

Bruno, predictably, did not stay. Instead, he took off again, heading toward what appeared to be a path leading away from the meadow.

Dylan muttered under his breath, a string of prime numbers that helped calm his frantic thoughts, before breaking into a run. His bare feet pounded against unfamiliar earth; the wand clenched tightly in his hand. Everything felt too real, the crisp night air filling his lungs, the rustle of the strange grass against his legs, the distant hum of voices beyond the hills. It wasn't a dream, and that terrified him.

"Bruno, stop!" Dylan shouted, his voice echoing strangely in the still air.

Bruno didn't stop.

The Rottweiler continued his determined trot along the path, occasionally glancing back as if to ensure Dylan was following, but never slowing his pace. The chase led them through the tall grass, past clumps of flowers that seemed to glow faintly in the dusky light, and toward what appeared to be a small stone bridge arching over a slow-moving stream.

Dylan slowed as he approached the bridge, his breath coming in short gasps. The structure was simple but beautiful, a perfect semicircle of weathered grey stone without railings, spanning a stream that moved with unnatural stillness. The water reflected the stars overhead with such perfect clarity that it was difficult to tell where water ended and sky began, as if the stream were a mirror placed on the ground.

Beyond the bridge, a winding road led upward toward what appeared to be a town nestled in the shadows of towering trees. Distant lights flickered between the buildings, warm and inviting, yet somehow making Dylan even more aware of how far from home he must be.

He hesitated at the foot of the bridge, logical thought finally reasserting itself. He had no idea where he was. He had no phone, no way to contact his parents, no supplies beyond the wand he still gripped in his hand. The sensible thing would be to try to find a way back immediately, to reject whatever madness had brought him here.

Bruno, however, had no such qualms.

He trotted confidently across the bridge, his claws clicking softly against the stone. Halfway across, he paused, turning to look back at Dylan, his brown eyes reflecting the starlight. There was an unspoken challenge in that gaze, something that seemed to say: Follow me. Trust me.

Dylan exhaled sharply, his free hand clenching and unclenching at his side. "This is completely mental," he muttered to himself. "Completely, utterly mental."

But the wand in his hand hummed with a subtle energy that was impossible to ignore, and Bruno was already continuing across the bridge, and really, what choice did he have? Follow the dog. Figure this out later.

He stepped onto the bridge. The instant his foot met the stone, he felt it.

A sensation, deep in his chest, like a whisper threading through his ribs. Not words, not a voice, but something more abstract, a feeling, a knowledge that settled into his consciousness without passing through his ears.

This place had a name: Dravengate.

And something was waiting for him there.

Dylan froze, one foot on the bridge, one still on the soft earth. The feeling was so unexpected, so utterly foreign, that he nearly retreated. But as quickly as it had come, the sensation faded, leaving him standing half-on, half-off the bridge, breathing heavily.

"Right," he whispered to himself. "Right. This is fine. Completely fine. I'm just standing on a magical bridge in another dimension, following my dog to a town called Dravengate. Perfectly normal Tuesday."

The absurdity of his own words helped, somehow. He took another step, and another, until he was walking steadily across the bridge. The stone beneath his feet seemed to warm slightly with each step, as if recognizing his presence, but otherwise, nothing extraordinary happened.

When he reached the other side, Bruno was waiting, sitting patiently, tail sweeping a small arc in the dust of the path.

"You," Dylan said, pointing an accusatory finger at Bruno, "have a lot of explaining to do."

Bruno huffed softly, rising to his feet and shaking himself as if he'd just come in from the rain. Then, with a sideways glance that seemed almost smug, he continued up the path toward the town.

Dylan followed; fingers still wrapped tightly around the wand. The path wound gently uphill, bordered by strange, luminescent flowers that seemed to turn toward him as he passed, like curious observers. The air grew warmer as they climbed, carrying scents of cooking food, burning wood, and something sweet that Dylan couldn't identify.

As they drew closer to the town, details became clearer. The buildings were unlike anything Dylan had seen before, they seemed to have grown rather than been built, with walls that curved organically and roofs that swooped and curled like waves. Windows glowed with warm light, and smoke curled from chimneys in spirals that seemed too perfect to be natural.

And yet, despite the obvious strangeness, there was something oddly familiar about the place. It triggered a sense of déjà vu so strong that Dylan stopped in his tracks, trying to place the memory. Had he dreamed of this town? Read about it in a book? Seen it in one of his games?

Bruno paused, looking back at him with what Dylan could have sworn was impatience.

"I'm coming," Dylan muttered. "Just... trying to make sense of this."

Bruno huffed again, then continued toward the town's entrance, an archway formed by two living trees that had grown together at the top, their branches intertwining to create a natural gateway. Lanterns hung from the lower branches, casting pools of golden light on the path.

As they passed beneath the archway, Dylan felt another shift, subtle but unmistakable. The air here felt different, charged with an energy that made the hairs on his arms stand up. The sounds of the town enveloped them, quiet conversations, distant music, the crackle of fires, and occasionally, laughter.

Dylan tensed, expecting someone to challenge them, to point and shout at the strange boy and his dog who had appeared from nowhere. But the few people visible on the streets paid them little attention. An elderly man nodded as they passed, a woman carrying a basket of what looked like glowing fruit smiled absently, and a group of children playing some complex game with stones and sticks glanced up briefly before returning to their activity.

Their indifference was perhaps the most unsettling thing so far. Either strangers appearing from other dimensions was so commonplace here as to be unremarkable, or there was something else going on that Dylan couldn't begin to understand.

Bruno moved with confidence through the narrow streets, navigating the twists and turns as if he'd walked them a hundred times before. Dylan followed, trying to create a mental map of their route while simultaneously absorbing every detail of this impossible place.

The streets twisted like they had grown rather than been planned, sometimes widening into small squares with fountains or statues, other times narrowing until Dylan could almost touch both walls with outstretched arms. The buildings leaned in close, their rooftops sometimes nearly meeting above the street, creating tunnels of warm, golden light.

They'd been walking for perhaps ten minutes when Bruno suddenly veered left, off the main path. He slipped through a low archway covered in ivy, disappearing from sight.

Dylan hesitated, eyeing the archway warily. It was small, easy to miss if you weren't paying attention, and the ivy covering it shimmered with a faint blue luminescence that definitely wasn't natural. Following Bruno through strange portals had already led him here, did he really want to see where another mysterious passageway might lead?

But the alternative was standing alone in the street of an impossible town, clutching a magical wand and hoping for the best. With a resigned sigh, Dylan ducked through the archway.

He found himself in a garden, small and hidden, enclosed by high stone walls covered in climbing plants that glowed with soft, multi-coloured light. The space was filled with plants unlike any Dylan had seen before, flowers with petals that seemed to be made of glass, bushes with leaves that chimed softly when brushed by the breeze, trees bearing fruit that pulsed with inner light. Stone pathways wound between the plant beds, leading to a central area where a simple wooden bench stood beneath a tree with silver bark and leaves that seemed to be made of thin, translucent crystal.

Seated on the bench was an elderly figure, a woman wrapped in deep blue robes, her silver hair pulled back in an intricate braid that fell to her waist. She was watching Dylan with quiet amusement, her eyes a startling shade of violet that seemed to glow in the garden's magical light.

Bruno sat at her feet, looking for all the world like he belonged there, like this meeting had been pre-arranged.

"You're early," the woman said, her voice melodious and strong despite her apparent age.

Dylan blinked, his mind racing to process this statement. Early for what? How could he be early for something he didn't know about? And more importantly,

"Who are you?" he asked, gripping the wand tighter. "Where am I? What is this place?"

The woman's lips curved into a gentle smile. "So many questions. But then, that's to be expected. You've come a long way, haven't you?"

Dylan frowned. "I don't know where I've come to, so I can't really judge the distance."

This earned him a soft laugh. "A literal mind. That will serve you well here." She gestured to the space beside her on the bench. "Sit, if you wish. Your journey was abrupt, and you may need a moment to gather yourself."

Dylan remained standing, his body tense.
"I'd rather have answers."

The woman nodded, as if his response was exactly what she'd expected. "My name is Elara. You are in Dravengate, a place that exists between places. And that," her gaze shifted to the wand in his hand, ", hasn't been seen in years."

Dylan glanced down at the wand, then back at the woman, Elara. "What is it?"

Her gaze darkened, but not in fear, just in thought. "That depends," she murmured. "On whether you choose to remember."

The cryptic answer made Dylan's frustration spike. "Remember what? I've never been here before. I've never seen this wand before today. I found it buried on a beach in Blackpool."

"Did you?" Elara asked, raising one silver eyebrow. "Or did it find you?"

Before Dylan could respond to this nonsensical question, Bruno rose from his place at Elara's feet and moved to stand beside him, pressing his warm bulk against Dylan's leg in a familiar, comforting gesture.

Elara watched this with interest. "Your guardian seems to think you need grounding. Perhaps he's right." She stood with surprising grace, brushing stray petals from her robe. "There is someone who still remembers what this place once was," she said softly. "Someone who saw its fall, and lived beyond it."

Dylan frowned. "Who?"

"The mage who resides in the forest," she said. "Find him. He will tell you what Dravengate lost."

She turned toward a narrow path that led deeper into the garden, her movements fluid despite her apparent age. "Rest here for a while, if you wish. The garden is safe. When you're ready, follow the path that leads north from the town square. It will take you to the forest."

"Wait," Dylan called as she began to walk away. "How do I get back home? My parents will be worried."

Elara paused, looking back over her shoulder with a smile that held both kindness and mystery. "Time moves differently here. When you return, not a moment will have passed in your world." She gestured to Bruno. "Your guardian knows the way. Trust him."

And with that, she continued down the path, disappearing behind a curtain of glowing vines that parted at her approach and closed behind her.

Dylan stared after her, his mind filled with more questions than before. Guardian? Time moving differently? None of it made sense, and yet... and yet somehow it felt true, like a mathematical theorem that seemed impossible until you worked through the proof.

He looked down at Bruno, who gazed back with those deep brown eyes that suddenly seemed to hold more knowledge than any dog should possess.

"You knew," Dylan said quietly. "Somehow, you knew about this place."

Bruno huffed softly, neither confirming nor denying, but the look in his eyes was enough.

Dylan sank onto the bench, suddenly overwhelmed by everything that had happened. He placed the wand carefully across his knees, studying it in the garden's magical light. It still looked like an ordinary piece of driftwood, and yet it had torn a hole between worlds, bringing him to this impossible place.

"The mage in the forest," he murmured, trying the words out. They sounded like something from one of his fantasy games, not like something that should exist in reality. "And you're supposed to be my... guardian?",

Bruno settled on the ground beside the bench, resting his head on his paws, his eyes never leaving Dylan.

Dylan exhaled slowly, trying to organize his chaotic thoughts. The logical part of his mind, the part that loved mathematics and physics and the beautiful order of the universe, insisted that none of this could be real. It had to be a hallucination, a dream, something that could be explained by rational science.

But the evidence of his senses was overwhelming. The garden around him hummed with life and magic that no dream could replicate. The bench beneath him was solid, the air he breathed carried scents too complex and strange to be imagined, and Bruno, Bruno was undeniably real, a warm, living presence beside him.

If this was real, then he needed to approach it methodically. First, find this mage and get answers. Then, find a way home. After that... well, he'd have to see.

"Alright," he said, standing up and gripping the wand firmly. "Let's find the forest."

Bruno rose immediately, tail wagging once as if in approval.

Together, they left the garden, stepping back through the ivy-covered archway into the streets of Dravengate. The town seemed more awake now, with more people moving about, carrying on the business of a place that shouldn't exist but undeniably did.

Dylan walked with purpose now, Bruno at his side, as they made their way toward the town square and the path that would lead them to the forest, and hopefully, to answers.

Chapter 4: The Forest of Whispers

The path beyond Dravengate felt different.

As Dylan and Bruno left the town behind, the warm glow of lantern-lit streets gave way to a silvery half-light that seemed to emanate from nowhere and everywhere at once. This wasn't the cobbled streets or twisting alleyways of the town, this was untamed land, thick with trees that reached toward the sky, their branches casting shifting shadows on the ground below.

Dylan hesitated at the forest's edge. The trees ahead were unlike any he'd seen in England, taller, more ancient, with bark that shimmered faintly in the strange light. Their leaves were a deep blue-green, and they rustled even when there seemed to be no wind.

He hadn't planned for this. The wand was clutched firmly in his right hand, but otherwise, he was woefully unprepared for a trek through an unknown forest in an impossible world. He wore only his jeans, t-shirt, and trainers, the same clothes he'd had on when he'd followed Bruno through the portal. No backpack. No water. No map. No compass.

The realization sent a spike of anxiety through him. Dylan liked being prepared. He liked having contingency plans. He liked knowing exactly what to expect.

Elara's words still echoed in his mind, "To remember." What did that even mean? Remember what? And why did she speak as if he'd been here before?

Bruno stepped forward without hesitation, his massive frame blending into the dark-green underbrush. He moved with purpose, his ears alert, as if he knew exactly where to go. Bruno paused after a few steps, looking back at Dylan expectantly.

Dylan swallowed hard, gripping the wand inside his sleeve. "I really hope you know where you're going," he muttered.

Then he followed.

The moment they passed beneath the first trees, the atmosphere changed. The air grew thicker, charged with something Dylan couldn't name but could definitely feel, a pressure against his skin, a tingling at the base of his skull. The forest floor was covered in a carpet of moss that seemed to glow faintly with each footstep, illuminating their path for a brief moment before fading back to darkness.

Dylan tried to keep track of their route, mentally marking turns and distinctive features, but the forest seemed to shift subtly around them. A large boulder he was certain they'd passed earlier appeared again from a different angle. A stream they crossed seemed to flow in a direction that defied the laws of gravity. Twice, he was sure they'd walked in a complete circle, only for the path ahead to reveal something entirely new.

"This doesn't make sense," he said aloud, the sound of his voice oddly muffled by the dense foliage. "The topology is impossible."

Bruno didn't respond, obviously, but his confident stride never faltered. Whatever strangeness affected the forest, it didn't seem to confuse him.

As they walked deeper into the woods, the air grew strange.

Not cold. Not heavy. But charged, like something unseen lurked just beyond sight. The quality of silence changed too, it wasn't the absence of sound, but rather a presence of its own, pressing against Dylan's ears.

And then he heard it.

The trees whispered, not in words, but in soft, rustling movements, a pattern that almost sounded like speech. The sound ebbed and flowed around them, sometimes fading to near silence, other times swelling until it seemed to come from every direction at once.

Dylan's breath hitched. "...Do you hear that?" he asked, his voice barely above a whisper.

Bruno didn't answer.

But he changed.

It was subtle at first, a slight bristling of the fur along his spine, a new tension in his powerful shoulders. His stance adjusted, becoming more grounded, more solid. His tail lowered, not in fear but in focus.

And then something extraordinary happened.

The whispering, which had been growing more intense with each step they took, suddenly receded. Not completely, but noticeably, as if something was pushing it back, creating a bubble of relative calm around them.

Dylan hadn't felt the tension in his own body until it faded, like a background noise you don't notice until it stops. His breathing came easier, his shoulders relaxed, and the prickling sensation at the back of his neck subsided.

He stared at Bruno, who continued walking as if nothing unusual had happened. But something had definitely changed. Bruno moved differently now, with a kind of gravity that seemed to bend the space around him. The shadows no longer clung to his dark coat but seemed to shrink away from it instead.

"You're doing this, aren't you?" Dylan murmured, more to himself than to Bruno.

Bruno glanced back, and in the strange half-light of the forest, his eyes seemed to glow with an inner fire that was definitely not natural.

Dylan exhaled slowly, trying to process what he was seeing. Something was happening to Bruno, something beyond logic, beyond the neat categories and explanations that usually governed Dylan's understanding of the world.

They continued deeper into the forest, the path narrowing until it was barely visible beneath the thick carpet of glowing moss.

The trees grew closer together, their branches intertwining overhead to form a canopy that blocked most of the silvery light. In its place, bioluminescent fungi clung to the tree trunks, casting pools of soft blue and green illumination.

The whispering grew louder again, more insistent, and Dylan noticed that Bruno's protective influence seemed to be working harder to keep it at bay. Bruno's movements were more deliberate now, each step placed with careful precision, his body positioned between Dylan and the deeper shadows of the forest.

"What are they saying?" Dylan asked, knowing he wouldn't get an answer but unable to contain his curiosity. The patterns in the whispers were tantalizing, almost mathematical, with rhythms and repetitions that suggested meaning just beyond his comprehension.

As if in response to his question, the whispers surged, becoming almost frantic. The moss beneath their feet flared brighter, and the fungi on the trees pulsed with increased luminosity.

Bruno stopped abruptly, a low growl rumbling in his chest. Not aggressive, but warning. He turned to face Dylan, and now there was no mistaking it, his eyes were definitely glowing, a warm amber light that seemed to come from deep within.

"Bruno?" Dylan whispered, unsure whether to be fascinated or terrified.

Bruno held his gaze for a moment, then deliberately turned to face forward again, his posture making it clear that Dylan should stay close.

They continued onward, but now Dylan was acutely aware of the changes in his companion. It wasn't just Bruno's eyes or his stance, there was something else, something he couldn't quite see but could definitely feel. A kind of energy that emanated from him, pushing back against the strange forces of the forest.

The path began to slope upward, winding around massive tree trunks and over twisted roots that seemed to writhe with a life of their own. The air grew thinner, clearer, the whispering receding with each step they took toward higher ground.

And then, suddenly, the trees parted.

They emerged into a clearing where broken stone structures lay half-buried beneath moss and vines. The ruins were clearly ancient, weathered columns, crumbling walls, archways that led nowhere. At the centre stood what appeared to be a temple or observatory of some kind, its domed roof partially collapsed but still impressive in the eerie light.

Dylan stopped, his pulse quickening.

This was the place. He didn't know how he knew, but the certainty settled over him like a physical weight.

Bruno stepped forward, nose twitching as he sniffed the air, moving toward the largest structure, an old archway, crumbling but still standing, leading into the darkness beyond.

Dylan hesitated. "Are we sure about this?"

Bruno huffed.

Dylan sighed. "Of course you're sure."

Cautiously, he stepped forward, crossing beneath the archway. The air changed again, cooler, thicker, ancient. It carried scents of stone and earth and something else, something metallic and strange that Dylan couldn't identify.

Inside the ruins, the remnants of what must once have been a grand hall spread before him. Columns lined a central pathway, most broken at various heights, creating an uneven colonnade. The floor was paved with stone tiles arranged in complex geometric patterns that, despite centuries of weathering, still hinted at the precision of their original design.

At the far end of the hall, leaning against the farthest wall, sat a man.

He appeared to be in his fifties, though there was something in his eyes that suggested far greater age. His robes were a faded green, patched in places but clean. His hair and beard were more silver than brown, and his hands, resting on his knees, bore the calluses and small scars of someone who worked with them often.

He looked up as Dylan approached.

His gaze met Dylan's, then shifted to Bruno, widening slightly before returning to Dylan.

And then, quietly, he spoke, with a deep husky voice.

"Finally."

The word hung in the air between them, weighted with meanings Dylan couldn't begin to unravel.

"Who are you?" Dylan asked, his voice echoing slightly in the cavernous space.

The man rose to his feet with a fluid grace that belied his apparent age. "My name is Thorne," he said, his voice deep and resonant. "I am, or was, the Keeper of the Archives of Dravengate."

"Elara sent me," Dylan said, unsure what else to offer. "She said you could tell me what Dravengate lost."

Thorne's expression shifted, something like sorrow passing over his features before being quickly masked. "Elara," he repeated. "She always did have a gift for understatement."

He stepped closer, studying Dylan with an intensity that was almost uncomfortable. "What Dravengate lost," he mused, "would take days to recite in full. But I suspect what she meant was that I could tell you about the Keeper of Time."

Dylan's pulse quickened at the phrase. "The Keeper of Time," he repeated. "What does that mean?"

Thorne's gaze dropped to the wand in Dylan's hand. "It means," he said softly, "that you have found something that has been lost for centuries. Something that was once wielded by those who maintained the balance between worlds."

He gestured toward a fallen column that had been positioned to serve as a bench. "Sit," he said. "This is not a short tale, and you look as though you've travelled far."

Dylan hesitated, then moved to the makeshift seat. Bruno followed, settling at his feet, his glowing eyes never leaving Thorne.

The man noticed this and smiled faintly. "Your Guardian is protective," he observed. "As he should be."

"Guardian?" Dylan echoed, looking down at Bruno. "Elara used that word too. What does it mean?"

"It means," Thorne said, returning to his own seat against the wall, "that you are not as alone in this as you might think." He folded his hands in his lap, his gaze steady. "Now, shall I tell you what Dravengate lost? And perhaps, in doing so, help you understand what you have found?"

Dylan nodded, tightening his grip on the wand. "Yes," he said. "Please."

Thorne took a deep breath, as if gathering his thoughts, or perhaps his courage. When he spoke again, his voice had taken on a rhythmic quality, like someone reciting a story that had been told many times before.

"Long ago, when the boundaries between worlds were thinner, Dravengate stood at the centre of a great crossing, a nexus where paths from many realities converged. It was a place of learning, of exchange, of wonders that few now remember..."

The Keeper of Time

As Thorne's words filled the ancient hall, Dylan listened with growing fascination and disbelief. The story he told, of magical crossings, of Keepers who maintained the balance, of a cataclysm that had shattered connections between worlds, should have seemed absurd. And yet, sitting in these impossible ruins, with a wand in his hand and a dog whose eyes glowed with inner fire at his feet, Dylan found himself believing every word.

The Keeper of Time, Thorne explained, had once been the most important of Dravengate's guardians. They alone could navigate the complex web of temporal connections that bound the crossing together, ensuring that travellers could move between worlds without disrupting the flow of time in any reality.

"The last true Keeper vanished during the Cataclysm," Thorne said, his voice growing softer. "Some say they sacrificed themselves to prevent complete collapse of the crossing. Others believe they fled, taking the secrets of time manipulation with them. All we know for certain is that when they disappeared, the wand you now hold disappeared with them."

Dylan looked down at the seemingly ordinary piece of wood in his hand. "And now it's back," he said quietly.

"Yes," Thorne agreed. "Now it's back. And it has chosen you."

"But why?" Dylan asked, the question that had been building since he first touched the wand finally bursting free. "Why me? I'm nobody special. I'm just," he faltered, unsure how to describe himself to this stranger.

"You are exactly who and what you need to be," Thorne said firmly. "The wand would not have chosen you otherwise."

Bruno shifted at Dylan's feet, making a soft sound that might have been agreement.

Thorne studied Bruno thoughtfully. "Your Guardian already knows this," he observed. "They always sense these things before the rest of us."

Dylan frowned, looking down at Bruno. "He's just my dog," he said, though even as the words left his mouth, he knew they weren't entirely true. Bruno had never been "just" anything.

Thorne's smile held a mix of amusement and sympathy. "Is he?" he asked simply.

Before Dylan could respond, a distant sound echoed through the ruins, something between a howl and a whisper, but unmistakably approaching.

Thorne's expression hardened. "The forest grows restless," he said, rising quickly to his feet. "It senses the wand's return." He moved to Dylan's side with surprising speed. "We must go. There are things in these woods that have waited centuries for the crossing to reawaken, and not all of them have benevolent intentions."

Bruno was already standing, his body tense, his glowing eyes fixed on the archway through which they had entered.

"Go where?" Dylan asked, standing as well, his heart beginning to race.

"To a place of safety," Thorne replied, gathering a worn leather satchel from behind where he had been sitting. "Where I can explain more fully what has begun here today." He looked at Dylan seriously. "The return of the wand is only the beginning. What happens next will depend largely on you."

The howling whisper grew louder, and Bruno let out a low growl, positioning himself between Dylan and the entrance.

"Follow me," Thorne said, moving quickly toward a small doorway in the back wall that Dylan hadn't noticed before. "Your Guardian will protect our retreat, but we should not linger."

Dylan hesitated only briefly before following. Whatever was coming, whatever strange turn his life had taken, he had little choice now but to see it through.

As they hurried through the small doorway into a hidden passage beyond, Dylan cast one last glance back at the hall they were leaving. Bruno followed close behind, his glowing eyes the last thing visible as darkness engulfed them.

The passage beyond was narrow and wound downward, deeper into the earth beneath the ruins. Thorne produced a small crystal from his satchel that emitted a pale blue light, illuminating rough stone walls carved with symbols that Dylan didn't recognize but that somehow seemed familiar.

"Where are we going?" Dylan asked, keeping close behind Thorne, Bruno a reassuring presence at his heels.

"To the last safe haven in Dravengate," Thorne replied without slowing. "A place where the old knowledge is preserved, and where, perhaps, we can begin to understand what your arrival means for all of us."

The passage continued to descend, the air growing cooler but surprisingly fresh. The howling whispers faded behind them, replaced by a deep silence broken only by their footsteps and the occasional drip of water from unseen sources.

Dylan clutched the wand tighter, its presence a strange comfort in this unfamiliar darkness. Whatever happened next, whatever this "Keeper of Time" business meant, he was no longer just a boy from Blackpool who liked mathematics and routine.

He was something else now, something he didn't yet understand.

But as Bruno's warm presence pressed against his leg, those glowing eyes occasionally glancing up at him with what could only be described as reassurance, Dylan found that the uncertainty wasn't quite as terrifying as it should have been.

They were in this together, whatever "this" turned out to be.

Chapter 5: The Archives Below

The passage continued downward for what felt like miles, though Dylan's innate sense of distance told him they couldn't have traveled more than a few hundred metres. Time and space seemed to follow different rules in Dravengate, a thought that both fascinated and unsettled his mathematically-inclined mind.

Thorne moved with the confidence of someone who had walked this path countless times, his small blue crystal illuminating just enough of the tunnel for them to see a few meters ahead. Bruno padded silently behind Dylan, his glowing amber eyes providing additional light in the darkness.

Finally, the passage levelled out and widened, eventually opening into a circular chamber that took Dylan's breath away.

The ceiling arched high overhead, supported by carved stone columns that seemed to grow organically from the floor like ancient trees. The walls were lined with shelves carved directly into the rock, each filled with books, scrolls, and strange objects that glowed faintly in the dim light. In the center of the chamber stood a large table of polished stone, its surface inlaid with an intricate map of what Dylan assumed must be Dravengate and its surroundings.

Hundreds of blue crystals embedded in the ceiling cast the entire chamber in a soft azure glow, like stars in an underground sky.

"Welcome," Thorne said, gesturing around them, "to what remains of the Archives of Dravengate."

Dylan turned slowly, taking in the vastness of the underground library. "This was all hidden beneath those ruins?"

"This is merely the central chamber," Thorne replied. "The Archives once extended throughout the entire valley, connecting all parts of Dravengate. Much has been lost, but I've preserved the most essential knowledge here."

Bruno moved past them both, sniffing the air carefully before apparently deciding the space was safe. He circled the chamber once, then settled near the passage they had entered through, his posture alert but relaxed.

"Your Guardian takes his role seriously," Thorne observed with approval. "That's good. You'll need his protection in the days ahead."

Dylan frowned, still struggling with this concept. "You keep calling him that, Guardian. He's my dog. My stepdad got him as a puppy."

Thorne smiled slightly. "And yet he led you to the wand, did he not? He guided you across the bridge to Dravengate, and through the forest to my dwelling." He gestured toward Bruno's glowing eyes. "Those are not the eyes of an ordinary dog, Dylan Bennett."

Dylan couldn't argue with that logic. Nothing about Bruno's behaviour had been ordinary since the moment they'd found the wand. "Then what is he?" he asked quietly.

Thorne moved to one of the shelves and carefully removed an ancient-looking tome bound in dark blue leather. "Every Keeper has a Guardian," he explained, returning to the table and gently opening the book. "They take different forms in different eras, but their purpose remains constant, to protect, to guide, and to anchor."

He turned the book toward Dylan. On the yellowed page was an illustration of a figure much like himself, holding a wand identical to the one Dylan now possessed. Beside the figure stood a large wolf-like creature with glowing eyes.

"The bond between Keeper and Guardian is among the oldest magics of the crossing," Thorne continued. "The Guardian serves as the Keeper's protector, yes, but also as their connection to the physical world when they work with temporal energies."

Dylan studied the illustration, then looked at Bruno, who gazed back with those impossible amber eyes. "So he's... magical? Has he always been?"

"In essence, yes," Thorne replied. "Though his abilities would have remained dormant until activated by your connection to the wand." He closed the book carefully. "The fact that you found each other is no coincidence. Guardians and Keepers are drawn together, even across boundaries between worlds."

Dylan sank into one of the chairs by the stone table, trying to process this information. Bruno, his clumsy, affectionate Bruno who knocked over end tables with his wagging tail and stole socks from the laundry basket, was actually some kind of magical guardian being?

And yet, as he thought about it, certain things began to make sense. The way Bruno always seemed to know when Dylan was feeling overwhelmed, pressing against his leg just when the noise or confusion threatened to become too much. The way he had always been able to calm Dylan during meltdowns when no one else could get through.

"So what does this mean?" Dylan finally asked. "For him? For me?"

Thorne sat across from him, his expression serious. "It means that you have been chosen to play a vital role in the restoration of the crossing. The wand's appearance and your arrival here are not random events, Dylan."

He gestured toward the wand that Dylan still clutched tightly. "The Keeper of Time was once the most important guardian of Dravengate. They maintained the delicate balance of temporal energies that allowed the crossing to function properly."

Dylan looked down at the seemingly ordinary piece of wood in his hand. "And you think I'm supposed to be the new Keeper?"

"The wand has chosen you," Thorne replied simply. "It would not have responded to your touch otherwise."

"But why me?" Dylan pressed, the question that had been nagging at him since this began. "I'm not... special. I'm just," He hesitated, uncertain whether to mention his autism in this strange world where the concept might be meaningless.

Thorne's expression softened. "You see patterns where others see chaos, don't you? You understand the underlying mathematics of reality in a way that most cannot grasp."

Dylan stared at him, startled by the accuracy of the assessment.

"These are precisely the qualities needed in a Keeper of Time," Thorne continued. "The temporal mathematics of the crossing are beyond most minds. They require someone who can perceive the abstract patterns that govern reality." He leaned forward, his gaze intent. "The wand chose you because you can understand what it needs to show you."

Bruno moved from his post by the entrance, coming to sit beside Dylan's chair. He pressed his warm bulk against Dylan's leg, a familiar, comforting gesture that now carried new meaning.

"What happened to the last Keeper?" Dylan asked.

"They disappeared during the Cataclysm, the event that shattered the crossing and isolated Dravengate from many of the worlds it once connected to." Thorne rose and moved to another shelf, returning with a cylindrical case from which he withdrew a rolled parchment. "It happened nearly five hundred years ago, by Dravengate's reckoning."

He unrolled the parchment on the table, revealing what appeared to be a map, but unlike any map Dylan had ever seen. Instead of landmasses and oceans, it showed a complex network of lines and nodes, with Dravengate at the centre represented by a golden circle. Many of the lines were broken or faded, with only a few still glowing with faint light.

"This is the crossing as it exists today," Thorne explained. "Once, every line you see was a vibrant connection to another world, maintained by the power of six great sigils that anchored the crossing to Dravengate."

Dylan studied the map with growing fascination. There was a mathematical elegance to the pattern, a complex geometry that reminded him of advanced topological models he'd studied in his free time. "And these broken lines, they're the connections that were lost?"

"Yes," Thorne confirmed. "When the Cataclysm struck, most of the connections collapsed. The sigils that maintained them went dormant or were damaged. Only a few pathways remained intact, including, it seems, the one that led to your world."

Dylan traced one of the still-glowing lines with his finger. "So, the portal that brought me here, that was one of these connections?"

"Indeed," Thorne said. "Though how the wand found its way to your beach is a mystery even to me. It was thought lost forever when the last Keeper vanished."

A thought occurred to Dylan. "You said there were six sigils that anchored the crossing. What exactly are they?"

Thorne smiled slightly, as if pleased by the question. "The sigils are ancient symbols of power, each representing one aspect of reality that the crossing must maintain balance within: Time,

Space, Matter, Energy, Thought, and Form." He gestured to six points on the map where the lines converged. "They once stood at these nexus points, stabilizing the entire structure of the crossing."

"And now they're... what? Broken?"

"Dormant," Thorne corrected. "Their power still exists, but it lies sleeping, waiting for the touch of a Keeper to reawaken it." He looked directly at Dylan. "Your touch."

The implications of this statement hung in the air between them. Dylan stared at the map, his mind racing as he began to understand what Thorne was suggesting. "You think I'm supposed to restore these sigils. To fix the crossing."

"That is what the return of the wand signifies," Thorne confirmed. "The time has come for the crossing to be restored, and you have been chosen to play a central role in that restoration."

Dylan felt the weight of this responsibility settling onto his shoulders. It was too much, far too much for a sixteen-year-old boy from Blackpool who just wanted his summer holiday to go according to schedule. And yet, a part of him, the part that had always loved complex puzzles and mathematical challenges, was intrigued by the problem presented.

"I wouldn't even know where to begin," he said finally.

Bruno huffed softly, nudging Dylan's hand with his nose.

"Your Guardian disagrees," Thorne observed with a slight smile. "And so do I. You've already begun, whether you realize it or not.

The very fact that you're here, that the wand responded to you, that your Guardian's powers have awakened, these are all the first steps in the restoration."

He rolled up the map carefully and returned it to its case. "The question is not whether you can do this, Dylan. The question is whether you will choose to."

Dylan frowned. "What do you mean, choose? It sounds like I don't have much choice."

"There is always a choice," Thorne replied gravely. "The wand has selected you, yes, but you must accept the role willingly. The power of a Keeper cannot be forced or coerced. It must be embraced."

He moved to another shelf and returned with a small wooden box, which he placed on the table before Dylan. "This is why I brought you here, to the heart of the Archives. So that you might understand what is being asked of you before you decide."

Dylan eyed the box warily. "What's in there?"

"Knowledge," Thorne replied simply. "Specifically, the knowledge of what happened during the Cataclysm, and why the restoration of the crossing carries both promise and peril." He placed his hand atop the box but did not open it. "Before you commit to this path, you should understand the true history of Dravengate's fall."

Bruno moved closer; his eyes fixed on the box with an intensity that suggested he sensed something significant about its contents.

"The choice must be yours," Thorne continued. "If you decide that this burden is not one you wish to bear, I can help you return to your world, and perhaps find a way to suppress the wand's connection to you. You could return to your normal life."

"And if I choose to stay? To try to restore these sigils?"

"Then you accept the role of Keeper, with all the responsibilities and dangers that entails," Thorne said solemnly. "It will not be an easy path. There are forces in Dravengate that do not wish to see the crossing restored, entities that have thrived in the chaos following the Cataclysm. They will resist you. They may even try to harm you."

Bruno growled softly at this, the sound reverberating through the chamber with unexpected power.

"Yes," Thorne acknowledged, glancing at Bruno. "Your Guardian senses the truth of this warning. The dangers are real, Dylan."

Dylan looked down at the wand in his hand, then at Bruno, whose glowing eyes reflected a fierce protectiveness. Finally, he met Thorne's gaze.

"Show me," he said quietly. "Show me what's in the box. I need to understand before I decide."

Thorne nodded, seemingly pleased with this response. He opened the box carefully, revealing what appeared to be a small crystal similar to the ones illuminating the chamber, but with a deeper, more intense blue light emanating from its core.

"This is a memory crystal," Thorne explained. "Created by the last Archivist before the Cataclysm, it contains their direct experiences of those events." He lifted it from the box with reverent care. "To access the memories, you need only hold the crystal and focus your thoughts upon it. The wand will strengthen the connection."

Dylan hesitated, then extended his free hand. Thorne placed the crystal in his palm, where it felt surprisingly warm against his skin.

"Be warned," Thorne said, his voice grave. "What you are about to experience may be disturbing. These are the memories of someone who witnessed the near-destruction of Dravengate and the crossing it protected."

Dylan nodded, tightening his grip on both the crystal and the wand. Bruno pressed closer against his leg, as if lending his strength for what was to come.

"Focus on the crystal," Thorne instructed, his voice growing distant as Dylan's attention narrowed to the glowing blue stone in his hand. "Let it show you what you need to see."

Dylan took a deep breath and concentrated on the crystal. For a moment, nothing happened. Then, as if responding to his intent, the wand in his other hand grew warm, and the crystal's light intensified.

The Archives chamber around him faded from view as new images flooded his mind, vivid, urgent, and terrifyingly real. Dylan gasped as he was plunged into memories that were not his own, witnessing firsthand the catastrophe that had nearly destroyed Dravengate five centuries ago.

He saw the crossing in its full glory, a magnificent network of pathways connecting countless worlds. He saw travellers from a hundred different realities moving freely through the town, exchanging knowledge, goods, and cultural artifacts.

And then he saw the betrayal.

A Keeper, not unlike himself, but older, with eyes that held both brilliance and growing madness, attempting to redirect the crossing's power for personal gain. The horrific backlash as the delicate balance was disrupted. The sigils flickering, failing. Connections shattering like glass. People screaming as reality itself seemed to tear apart around them.

Most disturbing of all, he saw the shadows that emerged from the broken connections, entities of pure chaos that thrived in the destabilized crossing, feeding on fear and confusion, growing stronger as Dravengate weakened.

The memories shifted, showing the desperate efforts to contain the damage. The last Keeper, not the betrayer, but their successor, sacrificing themselves to stabilize what remained of the crossing, using the wand to seal the worst breaches before disappearing into one of the still-functioning pathways, taking the wand with them.

The final memory showed Dravengate as it began its long decline, a shadow of its former glory, isolated from most of the worlds it once connected to, its population dwindling as hope faded.

With a gasp, Dylan returned to the present, the crystal in his hand now dim and cool. He was shaking, his mind reeling from the intensity of the experience.

"Now you understand," Thorne said quietly. "The restoration of the crossing is vital, but it also carries great risk. If done improperly, it could trigger another Cataclysm. And the shadows that emerged during the first disaster, they still exist, growing stronger in the spaces between worlds. They will resist any attempt to restore the order that would constrain them."

Dylan set the crystal carefully back in its box, trying to process everything he had seen. "Those shadow things, what exactly are they?"

"We call them the Void Entities," Thorne replied grimly. "They are not truly living beings as we understand them, but rather manifestations of the chaos that exists between realities. In a properly functioning crossing, they cannot enter our world. But when the Cataclysm damaged the boundaries, they found their way in."

Bruno growled again, the sound deeper and more threatening than Dylan had ever heard from him before.

"Your Guardian senses them," Thorne observed. "The protection of Keepers against such entities is one of the Guardian's primary purposes."

Dylan looked at Bruno with new appreciation. No wonder he had always been so protective of him. On some level, even before the wand had activated their connection, Bruno had been fulfilling his purpose.

"So, what happens now?" Dylan asked. "If I agree to try to restore these sigils, where would I even start?"

Thorne's expression lightened slightly. "Then you are considering accepting the role?"

Dylan looked down at the wand, thinking about everything he had learned. Part of him wanted to hand it back, to ask Thorne to help him return to Blackpool and his normal life of routines and mathematics and gaming. It would certainly be the safer choice.

But another part, the part that had always loved solving complex problems, the part that found beauty in mathematical patterns that others couldn't see, was intrigued by the challenge presented. And beyond that, there was a sense of rightness to it all, as if some part of him had been waiting for this moment without knowing it.

"I'm considering it," he said carefully. "But I need to know more. I need to understand exactly what I'd be getting myself into."

"A wise approach," Thorne approved. "The first step would be to locate the dormant sigils. Some are still in their original locations, while others have been moved or hidden for safekeeping over the centuries. Each must be activated in a specific way, drawing on the power of the wand and your own innate abilities as Keeper."

"And what about going home? You said time moves differently here, does that mean I could go back and forth? Keep living my normal life while also... doing this?"

"Yes," Thorne confirmed. "As the connection to your world is one of the few that remained intact after the Cataclysm, travel between here and there is possible. And as Elara told you, time flows differently between worlds. You could spend days or even weeks here, and return so that only moments have passed in your world."

This was reassuring. Dylan wasn't ready to abandon his family and his entire life, regardless of how compelling this new role might be. "And Bruno? He comes with me? Both ways?"

"Your Guardian will remain by your side," Thorne assured him. "The bond between you is not limited by the boundaries between worlds."

Bruno huffed in what sounded remarkably like agreement, bumping his head against Dylan's arm.

Dylan exhaled slowly, his mind working through the possibilities, the risks, the unknowns. It was overwhelming, but also... exciting, in a way he hadn't expected. This was a puzzle unlike any he'd encountered before, with stakes higher than he could have imagined.

"I don't have to decide right this minute, do I?" he asked.

Thorne smiled slightly. "No, though I would counsel against delaying too long. The very fact that the wand has returned suggests that changes are already underway. The crossing has been dormant for centuries, but something has stirred it back to life."

He gestured to the book in Dylan's hands. "Take this. Study it. Return to your world if you wish, to consider your decision.

But remember, the wand chose you for a reason. And in my experience, such choices are rarely made in error."

Dylan nodded, tucking the book under his arm. "How do I get back? To my world, I mean?"

"The wand can open the pathway," Thorne explained. "Now that you have connected with it, you need only focus your intent upon returning home, and it will create the portal."

Dylan looked at the wand sceptically. "Just like that? I don't need to say magic words or anything?"

Thorne chuckled. "The magic is not in words, Dylan, but in intent and connection. The wand responds to your will, amplified by your natural affinity for the patterns that underlie reality. Focus on home, and it will take you there."

It sounded too simple, but then again, nothing about this situation was following the rules of normal logic. Dylan stood, still clutching the wand and the book, with Bruno immediately rising to stand beside him.

"If I decide to do this, to try to restore the sigils, will you help me?" he asked Thorne.

"I will share what knowledge I have," the mage promised. "Though much of the journey will depend on your own abilities and the guidance of your Guardian."

Dylan nodded, processing this. "And if I decide not to? If I go home and never come back?"

Thorne's expression grew sombre. "Then Dravengate will continue its slow decline, and the crossing will eventually collapse completely. The few remaining connections to other worlds will be severed, and this place will fade from existence, becoming nothing more than a faint memory in the dreams of those who once knew it."

The weight of this possibility settled over Dylan like a physical burden. It seemed unfair that such a monumental decision should rest on his shoulders, and yet, wasn't that exactly what the wand's choice meant?

"I'll think about it," he said finally. "Properly think about it, I mean."

"That is all I can ask," Thorne replied, inclining his head slightly. "When you have made your decision, return to the stone bridge. It will bring you back to Dravengate, and from there, you can find your way to me again."

Dylan nodded, then turned to Bruno. "Ready to go home, boy?"

Bruno's tail wagged once; those glowing amber eyes fixed on Dylan with complete trust.

Taking a deep breath, Dylan raised the wand and focused his thoughts on his bedroom in Blackpool, the precise arrangement of his furniture, the books on his shelves, the view from his window. He pictured it with all the detail he could muster, concentrating on his desire to return there, and the time he wanted to arrive.

For a moment, nothing happened. Then, just as doubt began to creep in, the air before him shimmered and folded, opening into a swirling portal that showed a glimpse of his familiar room on the other side.

"Whoa," Dylan breathed, startled by how quickly and completely the wand had responded to his thoughts.

"Safe journey, Dylan Bennett," Thorne said from behind him. "Remember what you have learned here today. The choice may be yours, but the need is real."

Dylan nodded once more, then stepped forward into the portal, Bruno at his side. The last thing he saw before the swirling energy engulfed them was Thorne's face, watching with an expression that mingled hope and concern in equal measure.

Then they were falling through that strange in-between space again, Dylan clutching the wand and book tightly as reality bent around them. And just as suddenly, they were back, standing in Dylan's bedroom as if they had never left, the portal closing behind them with a soft sound like a sigh.

Dylan staggered slightly, disoriented by the abrupt transition. Bruno shook himself, his eyes no longer glowing but returned to their normal warm brown. The only evidence that their impossible journey had actually happened was the ancient book tucked under Dylan's arm and the wand still clutched in his hand.

He glanced at his bedside clock and blinked in surprise. It read exactly the same time as when they had left, not even a minute had passed. Elara had been right about how time worked between the worlds.

A soft knock at his door startled him from his thoughts. "Dylan?" his stepdad's voice called. "Your mum wants to know if you need anything from the shops. She's making a list."

"Um, no thanks," Dylan called back, hastily tucking the wand and book under his pillow. "I'm good."

There was a brief pause. "You sure you're alright in there? Bruno's been quiet... not his usual clumsy self."

Dylan glanced at Bruno, who was sitting unnaturally still, watching the door with intelligent eyes. "He's fine, just... resting."

Another pause. "If you say so," Mally replied, though something in his tone suggested he wasn't entirely convinced. "tea's at seven."

As his stepdad's footsteps faded down the hallway, Dylan let out a breath he hadn't realized he was holding. Had Mally sensed something different? Could he somehow tell that Bruno had changed, even though his outward appearance had returned to normal?

Bruno padded over to his usual spot on the rug beside Dylan's bed and settled down, watching Dylan with eyes that now seemed impossibly knowing.

"This is mental," Dylan muttered, sitting heavily on the edge of his bed. "Completely mental."

He looked down at the wand he'd pulled back out from under his pillow, then at the book with its ancient leather binding. The choice before him seemed impossible, return to his normal life and pretend none of this had happened, or accept the role of Keeper and undertake a task that seemed far too large for one sixteen-year-old boy from Blackpool.

And yet, as Bruno watched him with those knowing eyes, Dylan couldn't help but feel that the choice had already been made the moment he first touched the wand on that beach.

The only question was whether he would accept it.

Chapter 6: The Decision

Dylan sat cross-legged on his bed, staring at the ancient book splayed open before him. The pages were yellowed with age, the text written in a fluid script that should have been completely foreign to him, and yet, somehow, he could understand it. Whether this was some property of the book itself or an effect of his connection to the wand, he couldn't tell.

Three hours had passed since their return from Dravengate. Three hours of reading about sigils and crossings and the complex magical theories that governed movement between worlds. Three hours of trying to convince himself that it had all been some extraordinarily vivid dream, a task made impossible by the tangible evidence of the book and wand, and by Bruno's watchful presence.

Bruno hadn't left his side since they'd returned, maintaining a quiet vigilance that felt different now that Dylan understood its true nature. Every so often, Bruno would shift his position or huff softly, as if commenting on something Dylan had read.

"This is completely mad," Dylan muttered, running his fingers over a particularly elaborate diagram showing the theoretical structure of the crossing. "Time manipulation, magical sigils, guardians... it's like something from one of my games."

Bruno made a soft rumbling sound, somewhere between a growl and a whine.

"I know, I know," Dylan replied, finding it oddly natural to converse with Bruno as though the dog could understand every word. "Except games have rules that make sense. Clear objectives. Defined parameters." He gestured at the book in frustration. "This is all... abstract. Theoretical. How am I supposed to know if I'm doing it right?"

He turned the page to find an illustration of a previous Keeper, a woman with intense eyes holding the same wand he now possessed, surrounded by swirling energies that the artist had depicted as elaborate spirals. Beside her stood a large feline creature with the same glowing eyes that Bruno had displayed in Dravengate.

Dylan glanced at his own guardian. "Apparently your predecessor was a big cat. Probably less clumsy."

Bruno huffed indignantly, his tail thumping once against the floor.

Despite himself, Dylan smiled. Then his expression sobered as he continued reading. According to the text, the sigil of Time was the first that needed to be awakened, the primary anchor from which all other connections flowed. Its location was described as "the heart of the ancient gateway, where stone meets sky."

"Doesn't exactly give us GPS coordinates, does it?" Dylan muttered.

A knock at his bedroom door made him jump. He hastily closed the book and shoved it under his pillow, hiding the wand beneath his blanket just as the door opened.

His mum poked her head in, her dyed red hair pulled back in a loose ponytail. "You've been awfully quiet in here. Everything alright?"

Dylan nodded, perhaps a bit too quickly. "Just reading. Thinking."

Sam stepped into the room, her eyes warm but concerned. "About the beach? I know it wasn't your favourite outing, but you seemed to enjoy parts of it."

"The beach was... fine," Dylan replied, struggling to reconcile the mundane memory of their family trip with everything that had happened since. Had it really only been that morning that they'd gone to the beach? That Bruno had dug up the wand? It felt like weeks ago.

Sam sat on the edge of his bed, careful to maintain the distance Dylan preferred during conversations. "Mally said you found something interesting? Some driftwood?"

Dylan's pulse quickened. "Yeah, just... a piece of driftwood. Bruno dug it up."

"Always the treasure hunter, aren't you?" Sam said fondly, reaching out to scratch Bruno behind the ears. Bruno leaned into her touch, the picture of an ordinary, affectionate dog. Nothing about him suggested he was a magical guardian being from another dimension.

"It looked cool," Dylan said with a shrug, trying to keep his voice casual. "Smooth. Symmetrical."

Sam smiled. "Another item for your collection of interesting objects, then?"

Dylan nodded, relieved she wasn't asking to see it. His mother had always been understanding of his tendency to collect things that caught his interest, perfect rocks, unusually shaped leaves, objects with pleasing mathematical properties.

"Tea's in twenty minutes," she continued, standing up. "Pasta bake. And Mally's made garlic bread."

"I'll be down," Dylan promised.

After his mum left, closing the door behind her, Dylan exhaled shakily. The mundane reality of family tea felt surreal against the backdrop of everything he'd learned about Dravengate and his supposed role as Keeper.

He retrieved the book from under his pillow and the wand from beneath his blanket, staring at them both. Part of him wanted to hide them away, to pretend none of this was happening. He could just... not go back. Not accept the role. Return to his carefully planned summer of maths practice and gaming and routine.

Bruno moved closer, resting his large head on the edge of the bed, his brown eyes fixed on Dylan with an intelligence that now seemed impossible to miss.

"What do you think?" Dylan asked softly. "Should we do this? Try to fix a magical crossing between worlds? Become the Keeper of Time or whatever?"

Bruno blinked slowly, then deliberately placed one paw on Dylan's knee.

"I'll take that as a yes," Dylan murmured. "But you're biased. This is literally what you were made for, apparently."

He set the book aside and raised the wand, studying its seemingly ordinary appearance. According to the texts, the wand was both a tool and a key, amplifying the Keeper's innate abilities while also providing access to pathways and powers that would otherwise remain locked.

"I'm not even sure what I'm supposed to be able to do," he said, more to himself than to Bruno. "Open portals, yes. But all this talk of 'temporal manipulation' and 'reality anchoring'... what does that actually mean in practice?"

Bruno made a soft sound, then deliberately turned his gaze toward Dylan's desk, specifically, toward the small clock that sat on its corner.

Dylan frowned, then raised the wand tentatively, pointing it at the clock. Nothing happened.

"I don't think it works like that," he said, lowering the wand. "From what I read, it's not about zapping things. It's about... understanding patterns. Seeing the connections between things."

He hesitated, then closed his eyes, trying to focus on the steady ticking of the clock. In his mind, he visualized the movement of its hands, the turning of its gears, the steady progression of seconds into minutes into hours.

Time was a pattern. A rhythm. A mathematical progression.

With his eyes still closed, Dylan raised the wand again, concentrating on that pattern, trying to sense it rather than merely observe it. For a moment, nothing happened.

Then he felt it, a subtle shift, a whisper of connection between himself and the steady flow of time within the clock. The wand grew warm in his hand, responding to his focus.

When he opened his eyes, the clock had stopped.

Dylan stared, his pulse quickening. The second hand was frozen mid-tick, suspended between moments. He hadn't intended to stop it, had merely been trying to sense its rhythm, but somehow, his concentration had interfered with its normal function.

"Did I break it?" he whispered.

Bruno huffed softly, nudging Dylan's arm.

Hesitantly, Dylan focused again, this time trying to visualize the clock resuming its natural pattern. The wand pulsed once in his hand, and immediately the clock began ticking again, as if it had never stopped.

"Okay," Dylan breathed, a strange mix of terror and excitement flooding through him. "Okay. That was... something."

He set the wand down carefully on his bedside table, his thoughts racing. This was real. All of it. The magic, Dravengate, his role as Keeper, it wasn't a dream or a hallucination or an elaborate game. He had just manipulated time, if only in the smallest way.

The implications were staggering. According to the book, the Keeper of Time could do far more than stop a clock. They could adjust the flow of time within limited areas, create temporal bubbles where time moves differently, even glimpse possible futures or echo-images of the past.

But with such power came enormous responsibility. The texts were clear about the dangers of temporal manipulation, paradoxes, fractures in the timeline, ripple effects that could spread far beyond the Keeper's intention. The last Keeper's betrayal had nearly destroyed the entire crossing, damaging connections between worlds that had stood for centuries.

What if he made a mistake? What if he couldn't control the power properly? What if,

Bruno interrupted his spiralling thoughts by placing his head directly in Dylan's lap, those deep brown eyes staring up at him with complete confidence.

Dylan exhaled slowly, finding his centre again. "Right," he murmured, scratching behind Bruno's ears. "One step at a time. We don't have to fix everything at once."

The tea bell rang downstairs, his mum's signal that food was ready. Dylan carefully returned the book to its hiding place beneath his pillow and tucked the wand into the drawer of his bedside table.

"Come on," he said to Bruno. "Let's go pretend everything's normal for a while."

Bruno followed him downstairs, back into the routine domestic world that now felt both comfortingly familiar and strangely incomplete, as if Dylan had always been looking at it through a window, and now that window had opened to reveal a larger reality beyond.

tea was predictably normal, his mum chatting about a commission she was working on (she was a freelance graphic designer), Mally sharing an amusing story about a customer at the record shop where he worked. Dylan went through the motions, answering questions when asked, eating mechanically, while his mind continued to race with everything he'd learned.

Bruno stationed himself under the table, as always, but Dylan noticed how the dog's attention remained focused on him, alert for any sign of distress or danger. Had it always been that way? Had Bruno always been this protective, and Dylan simply hadn't recognized it for what it was?

"Earth to Dylan," Mally's voice broke through his thoughts. "You with us, mate?"

Dylan blinked, realizing he'd been asked a question. "Sorry, what?"

"I asked if you wanted to go to that new exhibit at the science museum this weekend," Mally repeated. "The one about mathematical patterns in nature. Seemed like your kind of thing."

"Oh," Dylan said, momentarily thrown by the collision of his two worlds, mathematical patterns were exactly what he'd been thinking about, but in a context Mally could never imagine. "Yeah, that sounds good."

His mum gave him a thoughtful look. "Are you sure you're feeling alright? You seem distracted."

"Just tired," Dylan lied. "And thinking about... stuff."

"Teenage stuff?" Mally asked with a grin. "The great mysteries of the universe? The meaning of life?"

The irony was almost painful. "Something like that," Dylan managed to reply.

After tea, he helped clear the table, then retreated back to his room, Bruno following close behind. Once the door was closed, Dylan retrieved the book and wand, settling back on his bed to continue reading.

The more he learned about the role of Keeper, the more overwhelming it seemed. According to the text, the Keeper was responsible not only for maintaining the sigils that anchored the crossing, but also for ensuring the stable flow of time across all connected worlds. They served as a living regulatory system, sensing disruptions and correcting them before they could cascade into larger problems.

"No pressure," Dylan muttered, turning the page.

Yet alongside the enormity of the responsibility, there was something undeniably compelling about it. The mathematical beauty of the crossing's design, the elegant way the sigils balanced and supported each other, the complex patterns that governed movement between worlds, it all spoke to the part of Dylan that had always found solace and joy in numbers and systems.

This was the ultimate puzzle. The ultimate pattern.

And maybe, just maybe, he was uniquely suited to understand it.

Dylan closed the book, his decision crystallizing. He would return to Dravengate. He would learn more about the sigils and what it meant to be a Keeper. He didn't have to commit to fixing the entire crossing immediately, but he could at least explore this new role, this new world that had opened to him.

After all, according to both Elara and Thorne, time moves differently between worlds. He could spend days in Dravengate and return to find that only moments had passed here, or even manipulate time to suit himself. He could maintain his normal life, his routines, his family, his summer plans, while also beginning to explore his role as Keeper.

It wasn't an either/or choice. It was a both/and.

Bruno, who had been watching him intently throughout this internal deliberation, stood up and stretched, tail wagging once as if he sensed Dylan's decision.

"We'll go back tomorrow," Dylan told him quietly. "After breakfast. We'll find Thorne again and tell him... tell him I want to learn more. That I'm willing to try."

Bruno huffed softly, something that sounded remarkably like approval.

Dylan set the book on his bedside table and picked up the wand, turning it slowly in his hands. It no longer looked like an ordinary piece of driftwood to him. Now he could see the subtle patterns in its grain, the perfect balance of its weight, the way it seemed to respond to his touch with a warmth that went beyond physical temperature.

"I'm going to need to make a schedule," he said firmly. "Time here, time there. Projects, goals, contingency plans."

Bruno tilted his head, his expression almost amused.

"Don't give me that look," Dylan told him. "If I'm going to be the Keeper of Time, I'm going to be organized about it."

The absurdity of the statement hit him suddenly, and he found himself smiling. Who would have thought that his love of schedules and patterns would turn out to be preparation for managing magical time differentials between worlds?

That night, Dylan lay in bed, the wand carefully placed on his bedside table, the book tucked securely under his pillow. Bruno was in his usual spot on the rug beside the bed, but there was a new alertness to his posture, even in rest.

As Dylan drifted toward sleep, his mind filled with images of sigils and crossings and the strange beauty of Dravengate. Tomorrow would begin a journey unlike anything he could have imagined when he'd reluctantly agreed to the beach trip that morning.

The Keeper of Time

He was Dylan Bennett, sixteen years old, from Blackpool, England. He liked mathematics and gaming and keeping to his carefully constructed routines.

And now, it seemed, he was also the Keeper of Time, or at least, he would be, if he could figure out how to awaken the sigils and restore the crossing. It wasn't the summer holiday he had planned. It was going to be so much more.

Chapter 7: Return to Dravengate

The following morning, Dylan woke before his alarm. He lay still for a moment, his mind immediately racing with everything that had happened the day before. The beach, the wand, Dravengate, Thorne, the Archives, it all came flooding back with such clarity that any lingering hope it might have been a dream evaporated instantly.

Bruno was already awake, sitting at attention beside the bed rather than sprawled out as he usually was in the mornings. His brown eyes fixed on Dylan with an awareness that seemed impossible to miss now that Dylan knew what to look for.

"Right," Dylan murmured, sitting up. "We're doing this."

He reached for his notebook on the bedside table and flipped to a fresh page. If he was going to become the Keeper of Time, he needed a plan. Structure. Organization. That was how he approached any new challenge, and despite the extraordinary nature of this one, he saw no reason to change his methods.

For the next thirty minutes, Dylan created what he called his "Keeper Schedule," allocating specific time blocks for his normal life in Blackpool and his new responsibilities in Dravengate.

He drew up a chart with color-coded sections:

- Blue for family time and obligations in Blackpool

- Green for his regular study schedule and personal projects

- Red for Dravengate training and sigil restoration

- Yellow for contingency time (because even the most careful plans needed flexibility)

Seeing it laid out on paper made the whole thing feel more manageable. More real, but also more structured. Less overwhelming.

Bruno watched this process with what looked remarkably like amusement, his head tilted slightly as Dylan meticulously filled in his chart.

"Don't judge," Dylan told him. "This is how I process things."

Bruno huffed softly, as if to say he wasn't judging at all.

After getting dressed and gathering his essential supplies, notebook, pencils, a small digital camera (to document the sigils), snacks, and a water bottle, Dylan carefully placed everything in his backpack. He hesitated before adding his laptop, wondering if technology from his world would even work in Dravengate. Better not to risk it, he decided. He could always bring it later if needed.

The wand was the last item, which he slipped into an interior pocket of his jacket. He'd read enough fantasy books to know that magical objects shouldn't be casually tossed into backpacks among granola bars and notebooks.

"Ready?" he asked Bruno, who stood by the door, clearly eager to get moving.

Downstairs, Dylan found his mum already at work in her home office, headphones on as she focused on her computer screen. He knocked lightly on the door frame, and she looked up with a smile, sliding the headphones down.

"Morning, love. You're up early."

"Bruno and I are going for a walk," Dylan said, the half-truth making him feel slightly guilty. "Down to the park, maybe along the beach. Is that okay?"

Sam looked pleased. "Of course. That's lovely. It's good to see you getting out more." She glanced at his backpack. "Taking your homework with you?"

"Just some things to read," Dylan replied vaguely. "And snacks."

"Always prepared," his mum said with a fond smile. "Your stepdad's gone to open the shop, but he said to remind you about the science museum this weekend."

"I remember," Dylan assured her. The museum visit was already blocked out in blue on his new schedule. "We shouldn't be gone too long."

After a quick breakfast, Dylan attached Bruno's lead, more for show than necessity, since Bruno rarely needed restraining, and they headed out into the morning sunshine. The plan was simple: find somewhere private to open the portal, then return to Dravengate to speak with Thorne.

The beach seemed the logical choice. Not the main tourist section, but the quieter stretch to the north where the dunes provided some privacy. It felt appropriate, too, since that was where this had all started.

They walked briskly, Dylan's mind churning with questions he wanted to ask Thorne. How exactly did the sigils work? What specific abilities would he develop as Keeper? How did the shadow entities fit into all this? The book had provided some information, but much of it was theoretical or historical rather than practical.

When they reached a secluded area between two large dunes, Dylan unclipped Bruno's lead and took a deep breath. "Okay," he murmured. "Let's give this a try."

He removed the wand from his jacket pocket, feeling it's now-familiar warmth against his palm. According to his reading, creating a portal should be straightforward for a Keeper, simply a matter of focusing on the destination and time, while channelling intent through the wand.

Dylan closed his eyes, picturing the stone bridge that led to Dravengate, remembering its perfect arch over the mirror-still water, the path that led up to the town. He thought of Thorne and the Archives, of the strange beauty of the silvery-blue grass and the twisted trees of the forest.

"Dravengate," he whispered, raising the wand.

For a moment, nothing happened. Then, as if responding to the intensity of his focus, the air before him shimmered and folded, opening into a swirling portal that revealed glimpses of that otherworldly landscape beyond.

"Brilliant," Dylan breathed, both terrified and exhilarated by the power flowing through him. It had worked even more easily than he'd expected.

Bruno made a soft sound of approval, moving to stand beside him, ready to make the crossing.

"Here we go again," Dylan said, and together, they stepped through the portal.

The transition was easier this time, still disorienting, but not as shocking as the first journey had been. When they emerged on the other side, they stood once again at the foot of the stone bridge, the path to Dravengate stretching before them.

Bruno shook himself, and Dylan watched in fascination as a subtle change came over the dog. His posture straightened, his muscles seemed to gain definition, and his eyes shifted from their normal brown to that glowing amber that marked him as a Guardian. It wasn't a complete transformation like Dylan had seen in the forest, but rather an enhancement of Bruno's natural form, as if the magic of Dravengate allowed him to express his true nature more fully.

"That's rather impressive," Dylan told him, and Bruno responded with what could only be described as a proud huff.

They crossed the bridge together, Dylan feeling once again that strange sensation of recognition as his feet touched the stones. The town of Dravengate looked different in what appeared to be morning light, the buildings more clearly defined, the colours more vibrant, the streets busier with people going about their day.

As before, no one seemed particularly surprised by their presence. A few people nodded in greeting as they passed, but there was no sense of alarm at strangers appearing from another world. Perhaps, Dylan reasoned, in a place like Dravengate, such comings and goings were commonplace, even after centuries of decline.

Their destination was clear, they needed to find Thorne again, to tell him Dylan had decided to accept the role of Keeper, at least provisionally. But instead of heading directly back toward the forest ruins, Dylan felt a pull toward the centre of town. Something there was calling to him, a faint but insistent tug that seemed connected to the wand in his pocket.

"This way," he murmured to Bruno, who followed attentively as they wound through the narrow streets toward what appeared to be the town square.

Unlike the quiet, empty space he'd glimpsed on their first visit, the square was now bustling with activity. A market of some kind was in progress, with stalls selling goods that ranged from the mundane to the fantastical, fruits that glowed with inner light, fabrics that shifted colours as they moved, devices that seemed to float above the vendors' tables.

But it wasn't the market that had drawn Dylan. His attention fixed immediately on the structure at the centre of the square, a circular stone platform raised about a meter above the ground, surrounded by six pillars that arched inward to meet at the top, forming a domed lattice of intricate stonework.

"The Timewell," a voice said beside him, and Dylan turned to find Elara standing there, her silver hair braided elaborately, her deep blue robes replaced with a simpler grey outfit that made her look more like an ordinary elder than the mysterious figure from the garden.

"The what?" Dylan asked, his gaze drawn back to the structure.

"The Timewell," she repeated. "Once, it was the heart of Dravengate, a place where the flow of time could be seen, studied, and when necessary, adjusted." She smiled slightly at Dylan's expression. "Yes, it's one of the sigil locations you seek. The primary one, in fact."

Bruno moved closer to Elara, his manner respectful but watchful, his glowing eyes assessing her with careful attention.

"Your Guardian remembers more than you might think," she observed. "They always do."

Dylan looked from Elara to the structure and back again. "Why did you send me to Thorne first, if this is right here in the town square?"

"Because information without understanding is dangerous," she replied simply. "You needed to learn what this place is, what it means, before you could approach the Timewell." Her violet eyes studied him carefully. "And have you decided? Will you accept the role of Keeper?"

Dylan hesitated, then nodded. "I want to try. I don't know if I can fix everything, but... I want to learn. To understand."

Elara's expression warmed. "A wise approach. Too many come to power seeking to wield it before they comprehend it." She gestured toward the Timewell. "Shall we inform Thorne of your decision? He'll be waiting for us there."

"He's here?" Dylan asked, surprised. "I thought he stayed in the forest."

"He emerges on market days," Elara explained as they began walking toward the central structure. "When there are enough people that one more face won't draw attention."

As they approached the Timewell, Dylan could see Thorne standing near one of the pillars, looking much as he had in the ruins except that his faded green robes had been replaced with simpler clothing that helped him blend with the townspeople. He looked up as they approached, his expression brightening with what looked like cautious hope.

"You've returned," he said to Dylan. It wasn't a question.

"I have questions," Dylan replied. "A lot of them. But I want to learn. To understand what this Keeper thing is about."

Thorne's smile deepened. "And this is precisely why the wand chose you," he said. "Not because you already know all the answers, but because you ask the right questions."

Dylan glanced at the Timewell, feeling the wand in his pocket warming in response to its proximity. "Elara called this the Timewell. She said it's one of the sigils."

"The primary one," Thorne confirmed, echoing Elara's words. "The sigil of Time, from which all other connections flow." He gestured for Dylan to come closer to the structure. "Look, but do not touch, not yet."

Dylan approached the edge of the raised platform, peering at the intricate stonework. Up close, he could see that the pillars were covered in carved symbols similar to those he'd noticed in the underground passages of the Archives. The platform itself was inlaid with a complex pattern of lines and circles that seemed to shift subtly if he looked at them too long, as if they existed in more than three dimensions.

But the most fascinating feature was at the centre of the platform, beneath the arched lattice of the pillars, a circular depression about a meter across, which appeared to be filled with a silvery substance that wasn't quite liquid and wasn't quite gas. It moved in slow, complex patterns, occasionally forming shapes that almost resembled letters or numbers before dissolving back into formless motion.

"What is that?" Dylan asked, unable to hide his fascination.

"Distilled time," Thorne replied quietly. "Or more accurately, a medium through which the flow of time can be perceived, studied, and influenced. In the days before the Cataclysm, the Keeper would use the Timewell to monitor the temporal currents of the crossing, ensuring that all connected worlds remained in proper alignment."

Dylan frowned, studying the swirling silver substance. "How does it work? I mean, time isn't a physical thing you can look at, is it?"

"Isn't it?" Elara asked with a small smile. "Time leaves physical traces, the rings of trees, the layers of rock in a cliff face, the decay of elements, the movement of stars. What you see here is a concentration of those traces, filtered through the magic of the crossing to create a medium that responds to temporal currents."

Dylan's scientific mind struggled with this explanation, but he couldn't deny the evidence before his eyes. The silver substance was clearly responding to something, its patterns shifting in ways that suggested purpose rather than randomness.

"The Timewell has been dormant since the Cataclysm," Thorne continued. "The sigil that powered it was damaged, and without a Keeper to repair and maintain it, it has been little more than a monument, a reminder of what Dravengate once was."

"And I'm supposed to fix it?" Dylan asked, feeling the enormity of the task.

"You're supposed to try," Elara corrected gently. "The wand chose you, but the outcome is not predetermined. The future of the crossing depends on many factors, of which you are just one, albeit a crucial one."

Bruno moved beside Dylan, pressing against his leg in that familiar, comforting way, his glowing eyes fixed on the Timewell with intense focus.

"Your Guardian senses the connection," Thorne observed. "They always had a special relationship with the Timewell, even before the Cataclysm. Some believed that Guardians could perceive time differently, seeing not just the present moment, but echoes of what has been and what might be."

Dylan looked down at Bruno with new appreciation. "Is that why he always seems to know when something's about to happen? Like when I'm about to have a meltdown, or when someone's at the door before they knock?"

Thorne nodded. "The Guardian's perception extends beyond ordinary senses. It's one of the qualities that makes them such effective protectors for Keepers, who are often... absorbed in their work with time and may not notice more immediate concerns."

Dylan could relate to that. When he was focused on a mathematical problem or deeply engaged in one of his games, the outside world tended to fade away. Having Bruno as a sort of early warning system had been helpful long before he knew about Guardians and Keepers.

"So, what now?" he asked, looking back at the Timewell. "Do I just... touch it with the wand or something?"

Elara and Thorne exchanged glances. "Not quite so simple," Thorne said carefully. "The sigil must be awakened gradually, with proper preparation and understanding. A misstep could have serious consequences, affecting the flow of time not just here but in connected worlds, including your own."

"Before you attempt to awaken the sigil," Elara added, "you must learn to control your own abilities as Keeper. The wand responds to your will, but that will must be disciplined, focused, and informed by knowledge of temporal principles."

"Like when I stopped my alarm clock?" Dylan asked, remembering his experiment from the previous night.

Thorne looked surprised. "You've already begun experimenting?"

"Just a small test," Dylan explained. "I wanted to see if any of this was real. I focused on my clock, trying to sense its pattern, and it... stopped. Just for a moment, until I let it go again."

Thorne's expression shifted to one of cautious approval. "That's actually quite impressive for a first attempt. Most new Keepers require weeks of practice before achieving even that level of temporal manipulation."

"It's because of how his mind works," Elara said with certainty. "He perceives patterns more directly than most. This will be both a strength and a challenge for him."

Dylan wasn't sure how to feel about them discussing him this way, but he couldn't deny the accuracy of Elara's assessment. His autism did give him a different perspective on patterns, he often saw connections and structures that others missed, but could also become overwhelmed by too much sensory input or unexpected changes.

"So, I need training," he summarized, bringing the conversation back to practical matters. "Before I can even try to awaken the sigil."

"Yes," Thorne confirmed. "But we can begin immediately, if you're willing. The market provides good cover for us to work here without drawing too much attention."

Dylan glanced around at the busy square, where people moved about their business seemingly oblivious to the fact that a crucial magical ritual was being discussed in their midst. "Won't they notice if we start doing... magic... right in the middle of everything?"

Elara smiled. "Dravengate exists in a state of... selective awareness. Most of its inhabitants see what they expect to see. Unless we do something truly dramatic, they'll simply perceive three people and a dog having a conversation near the old monument."

This was both reassuring and slightly unnerving. Dylan wondered what other magical activities might be happening around Dravengate that he wasn't perceiving because he didn't expect to see them.

"Alright," he said, making his decision. "Where do we start?"

"With the fundamentals," Thorne replied. "Understanding the nature of time as it exists within the crossing."

He gestured for Dylan to sit on a nearby bench that offered a clear view of the Timewell while remaining a respectful distance from it. Bruno settled at Dylan's feet, his posture alert but relaxed, his glowing eyes occasionally scanning their surroundings as if looking for potential threats.

For the next hour, Thorne explained the basic principles of temporal magic as it related to the crossing. Much of it was theoretical, occasionally veering into areas that resembled advanced physics or higher mathematics, but presented in terms of magical energy rather than scientific principles. Dylan found himself taking mental notes, making connections to concepts he'd studied in his own world, quantum theory, string theory, relativity.

"Time isn't linear," Thorne emphasized. "Not really. We perceive it that way because our minds are designed to experience reality in sequence, but the actual structure of time is more... branching. Flowing. Like a river with currents and eddies and backwaters."

"And the Keeper's job is to make sure the river stays within its banks?" Dylan suggested, trying to fit this into a conceptual framework he could understand.

"A fair analogy," Thorne agreed. "Though perhaps more accurately, the Keeper ensures that the various tributaries and branches remain properly connected to the main flow, that no section becomes dammed or diverted in ways that would cause damage to the overall system."

Elara, who had been listening quietly, added, "The crossing exists because these temporal rivers, these flows of time from different worlds, naturally intersect at certain points. Dravengate was built at one such intersection, and the sigils were created to stabilize and maintain these connections."

Dylan frowned, processing this information. "So, when the Cataclysm happened, it was like... a flood? Or maybe a drought? Something that disrupted the natural flow?"

"Both, in a way," Thorne replied. "The rogue Keeper attempted to redirect too much of the flow to serve their own purposes. This caused a backlash, some connections flooded with temporal energy while others were drained almost completely. The system as a whole nearly collapsed."

This made a kind of sense to Dylan, whose mathematical mind was already translating these magical concepts into equations and models he could work with. "And awakening the sigils would... what? Reestablish the proper flow patterns?"

"Precisely," Elara said, her violet eyes approving. "Each sigil governs one aspect of the crossing's stability. Time, Space, Matter, Energy, Thought, and Form. Together, they create a balanced system that allows for controlled connection between worlds."

"The sigil of Time is primary," Thorne continued, "because without proper temporal alignment, the other connections become dangerous or impossible. Two worlds operating at dramatically different temporal rates cannot safely interact without a buffer, a regulated interface that the Timewell once provided."

Dylan glanced at the circular platform with new understanding. It wasn't just a fancy magical device, it was a crucial regulatory system, a control mechanism for forces that could potentially cause immense damage if left unchecked.

"This is a lot of responsibility," he said quietly.

"It is," Elara acknowledged. "But remember, you're not being asked to take it all on at once. The restoration of the crossing will be a gradual process, with each step building on the last."

Bruno nudged Dylan's hand with his nose, as if sensing his growing anxiety and offering reassurance.

"The first task," Thorne said, "is simply to learn to perceive the temporal currents directly. You've already demonstrated an aptitude for this with your clock experiment. Now we need to develop that ability further."

He produced a small object from his pocket, a crystal similar to the ones that had illuminated the Archives, but smaller and with a paler blue light.

"This is a training tool," he explained, handing it to Dylan. "A simplified version of the memory crystals, designed to help novice Keepers develop their temporal perception. Hold it in one hand, the wand in the other, and try to sense the patterns within the crystal."

Dylan accepted the crystal, which felt cool against his palm, and retrieved the wand from his pocket. As instructed, he held them separately, one in each hand, and focused his attention on the crystal.

The Keeper of Time

At first, he perceived nothing beyond its physical properties, weight, temperature, the faint light it emitted. But as he continued to concentrate, allowing his mind to settle into the same state he'd achieved with the clock, a new awareness began to unfold.

There was a pattern within the crystal, a rhythm, a pulse, a cycle of energy that wasn't quite physical and wasn't quite magical, but something in between. It reminded him of the steady beat of music, or perhaps the oscillation of a wave function in quantum physics.

"I can feel it," he murmured, his eyes half-closed as he focused on the sensation. "It's like... a heartbeat, almost. But more regular. More precise."

"Good," Thorne said quietly, careful not to break Dylan's concentration. "That's the baseline temporal signature of the crystal. Now, using the wand, try to align your own temporal perception with that rhythm."

Dylan frowned slightly, uncertain what this meant in practical terms. But he allowed his instincts to guide him, focusing on the wand in his right hand while maintaining his awareness of the crystal's rhythm in his left.

Gradually, he felt the wand warming, responding to his intent. There was a subtle shift in his perception, as if his consciousness were adjusting its frequency to match that of the crystal. The rhythm became clearer, more defined, and he could now perceive nuances within it, minor variations, subtle harmonics.

"It's changing," he reported, fascination overriding his uncertainty. "Or maybe I'm perceiving more detail? It's like... when you adjust the focus on a microscope and suddenly see all the structures that were blurry before."

"Excellent," Thorne said, his voice betraying genuine pleasure. "You're demonstrating a natural aptitude for temporal atonement. This is precisely the skill needed to work with the Timewell."

Dylan continued the exercise, alternately focusing and relaxing his attention, discovering that he could adjust his perception like tuning a radio to different frequencies. Each subtle shift revealed new aspects of the crystal's temporal signature.

After about twenty minutes, Thorne gently suggested they end the session. "It's important not to overextend yourself when beginning these practices," he explained. "Temporal perception can be draining, especially as your mind and body adjust to the experience."

Dylan reluctantly disengaged his focus from the crystal, blinking as his awareness returned fully to his physical surroundings. He was surprised to find that he felt tired, not exhausted, but with the pleasant fatigue that comes after intense mental effort.

"That was... amazing," he admitted, returning the crystal to Thorne. "It's like having a new sense."

"In a way, you do," Elara said. "The ability to perceive temporal currents directly is uniquely developed in Keepers. With practice, you'll become more sensitive to these patterns in everything around you, not just in specialized tools like the crystal."

Bruno, who had remained vigilant throughout the exercise, now moved closer to Dylan, pressing against his leg as if offering support. His glowing eyes seemed to assess Dylan's condition, checking for signs of strain or distress.

"I'm okay," Dylan told him, finding it increasingly natural to speak to Bruno as if the dog fully understood him, which, he was beginning to realize, might actually be the case.

"Your Guardian is right to be attentive," Thorne noted. "The early stages of a Keeper's training can sometimes trigger unexpected side effects, heightened sensitivity to temporal anomalies, disorienting shifts in perception, even brief glimpses of potential futures or echoes of the past."

"That sounds... unsettling," Dylan said, not entirely sure he was ready for spontaneous visions or time slips.

"It's why the Guardian bond is so important," Elara explained. "They provide an anchor, a fixed point of reference when the Keeper's perception begins to expand beyond normal limitations."

Dylan scratched behind Bruno's ears, grateful for the dog's steady presence. "So what's next? More exercises with the crystal?"

"For now, yes," Thorne confirmed. "Daily practice will help you develop the necessary control and sensitivity. I suggest alternating between different crystals with varying temporal signatures to expand your range of perception."

He handed Dylan a small pouch containing several crystals of different sizes and shades of blue. "These are calibrated to different frequencies. Begin with the palest ones, which have the simplest signatures, and gradually work your way to the deeper blues, which contain more complex patterns."

Dylan accepted the pouch, tucking it carefully into his backpack. "And once I've mastered this? Then we try to awaken the sigil?"

"Not immediately," Elara cautioned. "The next step would be to observe the Timewell directly, using your enhanced perception to understand its current state. Only then can we determine the proper approach to awakening the sigil."

This seemed reasonable to Dylan, whose methodical mind appreciated a step-by-step process rather than rushing into something as significant as reactivating an ancient magical device.

"I should probably head back soon," he said, glancing at the position of the sun, which seemed to be nearing mid-morning in Dravengate time. "I told my mum I'd only be gone for a walk, and I don't want her to worry."

"Of course," Thorne said. "Maintaining your life in your own world is important. The balance between worlds is reflected in the balance of your own existence."

This resonated with Dylan, who had already been thinking in terms of carefully scheduled time between his two lives. "When should I return?"

"That depends on your world's time," Elara replied. "For you, perhaps tomorrow? That would give you opportunity to practice with the crystals in your own space, while allowing a full day here for your next lesson."

Dylan nodded, mentally adjusting his schedule. "Tomorrow morning, then. Same place?"

"Meet me at the garden where we first spoke," Elara suggested. "It's more private, and there are aspects of your training better conducted away from public spaces, even with Dravengate's selective awareness."

With their next meeting arranged, Dylan prepared to depart. Creating the return portal was even easier this time, a simple matter of focusing on the dunes in Blackpool while channelling his intent through the wand. The swirling gateway appeared before him, offering a glimpse of his familiar space on the other side.

"One last thing," Thorne said before Dylan stepped through. "The crystals are safe to use in your world, but be cautious with any temporal manipulation there. Your world's natural laws are less... flexible... than Dravengate's. The consequences of disruption could be unpredictable."

"I'll be careful," Dylan promised, appreciating the warning. The last thing he needed was to accidentally create some kind of time anomaly in his bedroom.

With a final nod to Thorne and Elara, Dylan stepped through the portal with Bruno at his side. The transition was smoother now, almost familiar, and then they were standing on the dunes in Blackpool once more.

Dylan checked his phone and was relieved to find that only forty-five minutes had passed since they'd left the house, plenty of time for a reasonable morning walk. Bruno shook himself, his eyes returning to their normal warm brown, the subtle enhancements to his physique fading until he was once again just an ordinary Rottweiler.

Except, of course, he wasn't ordinary at all.

"Well," Dylan said, removing the pouch of crystals from his backpack, "I guess we have homework."

As soon as they got home and had gone upstairs, Bruno settled beside him and Dylan carefully arranged the crystals in order from palest to deepest blue, ready to begin his first official training session as the Keeper of Time.

Chapter 8: Crystal Training

For the next three days, Dylan devoted every spare moment to practicing with the training crystals. He established a routine: one hour before breakfast, thirty minutes after lunch, and two hours in the evening before bed. Each session was carefully logged in a notebook designated specifically for his Keeper training, with detailed observations about the different temporal signatures.

The pale crystals contained the simplest patterns, regular, rhythmic pulses that reminded Dylan of sine waves. These were easiest to attune to, requiring only basic concentration. By the end of the first day, he could align with these patterns almost instantly.

The medium-blue crystals proved more challenging. Their temporal signatures contained overlapping rhythms, like interference patterns of overlapping ripples. These required more intense focus, but by the third day, Dylan had mastered them as well.

It was the darkest crystals that continued to challenge him. Their patterns shifted unpredictably, like a mathematical equation that kept rewriting itself. He could attune to them briefly, but maintaining the connection left him mentally exhausted.

Bruno observed every practice session with unwavering attention. Though his eyes remained their normal brown in this world, there was a new alertness to his posture, a subtle vigilance that suggested his Guardian nature was becoming more active even outside of Dravengate.

On the morning of the fourth day, Dylan woke early, feeling both nervous and excited. Today he would return to Dravengate for his next lesson with Elara and Thorne. According to his Keeper Schedule (now neatly pinned to the wall above his desk), he had allocated four hours in Dravengate, which might equate to several days there given the temporal differential between worlds.

After breakfast, Dylan packed his backpack with his notebook, several granola bars, and a bottle of water. He'd also added a small first aid kit, because even in a magical realm, he believed in being practical.

"Ready?" he asked Bruno, who was waiting patiently by the door, clearly aware of their plans.

His mum was in her home office, working on a deadline for a client. Dylan popped his head in to let her know they were heading out for another walk.

"Again?" she asked, looking up from her computer with a mixture of surprise and pleasure. "That's three times this week. You're turning into a regular outdoorsman."

Dylan shrugged, trying to appear casual. "It helps me think. And Bruno enjoys it."

At the mention of his name, Bruno padded into the office, tail wagging as Sam scratched his ears. "Well, I'm not complaining.

Fresh air and exercise are good for both of you." She glanced at Dylan's backpack. "Planning a longer expedition today?"

"Maybe," Dylan replied vaguely. "Depends on the weather. I might do some reading at the park."

"Just be back for tea. Mally's making his famous lasagna tonight."

With promises to return on time, Dylan and Bruno set off. They headed for the same secluded spot between the dunes where they'd opened the portal before. It was becoming their regular transition point, and Dylan appreciated the consistency.

Once they were certain no one was around, Dylan took out the wand. Creating the portal was becoming almost second nature, a simple matter of clear visualization and focused intent.

The swirling gateway appeared before them, and Dylan took a deep breath before stepping through with Bruno at his side. The journey between worlds was smoother now, less disorienting, and then they were standing once again at the foot of the stone bridge that led to Dravengate.

As they crossed the bridge, Dylan took a moment to observe his surroundings more carefully than he had on previous visits. The air felt different, not just in scent but in some quality he couldn't quite define. Bruno underwent his now-familiar transformation, his form becoming more defined, his eyes shifting to that glowing amber that marked his Guardian nature.

Dravengate was quieter today, with fewer people in the streets than during the market day. Those they did pass gave them curious glances but no outright stares. Dylan wondered if the town's inhabitants were becoming accustomed to seeing him, or if the "selective awareness" that Elara had mentioned was simply filtering him into the background of their perception.

The ivy-covered archway to Elara's garden was exactly where Dylan remembered it, though he suspected he might have had trouble finding it without Bruno's guidance. Bruno led the way with confidence, ducking through the low entrance with Dylan following close behind.

The garden seemed different in the daytime, brighter, more vibrant, with the glowing plants now competing with natural sunlight that filtered down through the crystal-like leaves of the silver-barked tree at its centre. Elara was already there, seated on the wooden bench, but this time she wasn't alone. Thorne stood nearby, examining one of the glass-petaled flowers with scholarly interest.

"Right on time," Elara said with approval as Dylan approached. "Punctuality is a good trait in a Keeper of Time."

"I like schedules," Dylan replied simply.

"How have you found the crystal exercises?" Thorne asked, turning from his examination of the flower.

Dylan removed his backpack and took out his notebook. "I've been practicing three times a day," he explained, opening to the pages where he'd recorded his observations. "The pale and medium crystals are manageable now, but the darkest ones are still difficult to maintain connection with for more than a few minutes."

Thorne took the notebook, scanning Dylan's meticulous notes with evident interest. "These are remarkably detailed observations for a beginner. Most novice Keepers struggle to articulate what they perceive in the temporal currents."

Dylan shrugged slightly. "I like patterns. Numbers. The temporal signatures are complex, but they follow mathematical principles. Once I realized that, it became easier to track them."

"This is precisely why the wand chose you," Elara said, gesturing for Dylan to sit beside her on the bench. "The temporal mathematics of the crossing are beyond most minds, but yours is uniquely suited to comprehend them."

Dylan sat, feeling a mix of pride and uncertainty at her words. His autism had often made life more challenging in some ways, but here, it seemed to be an advantage. The thought was both empowering and slightly overwhelming.

"Today," Thorne said, returning Dylan's notebook, "we will advance your training in two significant ways. First, you'll learn to perceive temporal currents without the aid of the training crystals. And second, you'll begin to understand how to influence these currents, not just perceive them."

Bruno settled at Dylan's feet, his posture alert but relaxed, those glowing eyes watching the proceedings with intelligent interest.

"Before we begin," Elara said, "show us what you've learned. Demonstrate your atonement to one of the crystals."

Dylan nodded and removed the pouch of crystals from his backpack. He selected a medium-blue one that he'd worked with extensively over the past days, holding it in his left hand while taking the wand in his right. Closing his eyes, he focused his attention on the crystal, allowing his perception to shift into the state he'd been practicing.

The crystal's temporal signature bloomed in his awareness, a complex rhythm of overlapping pulses, like multiple heartbeats slightly out of sync. With practiced ease, Dylan aligned his focus through the wand, synchronizing with the pattern until it felt as though the crystal's rhythm and his own consciousness were moving in perfect harmony.

"Very good," Thorne murmured. "Now, without opening your eyes, try to extend your awareness beyond the crystal. Reach out with your temporal perception."

Dylan frowned slightly in concentration. This was new territory. He tried to imagine his awareness expanding, like ripples spreading from a stone dropped in water.

At first, there was nothing, just the familiar rhythm of the crystal in his hand. But then, gradually, he began to sense something else. Fainter patterns, more distant, but definitely present. Multiple signatures, each with its own distinct rhythm and character.

"I can feel... something," he said softly. "Other patterns. Different from the crystal. All around us."

"Those are the temporal signatures of everything in the garden," Elara explained, her voice equally soft. "Every living thing, every object, has its own relationship with time, its own temporal fingerprint."

Dylan expanded his awareness further, fascinated by this new perspective. He could sense the distinct patterns of the plants around them, some fast and fluttering, others slow and deep. He could perceive the steady, solid presence of the stone bench beneath him, almost unchanging compared to the living things.

And most distinctly of all, he could sense Bruno. The Rottweiler's temporal pattern was unlike anything else in the garden, powerful, complex, but with a familiar quality that resonated with Dylan's own pattern, as if their signatures were harmonics of the same fundamental frequency.

"Bruno feels... connected to me," Dylan said, surprised by the discovery.

"The Guardian bond," Thorne confirmed. "It creates a temporal resonance between Keeper and Guardian, allowing them to work in synchronization even across different planes of existence."

Slowly, Dylan opened his eyes, allowing his perception to return to normal. The experience left him slightly dizzy but exhilarated. "That was... incredible," he admitted. "Like seeing with a completely different sense."

"This perception is the foundation of a Keeper's power," Elara said. "To understand the flow of time, one must first be able to perceive it directly."

"The next step," Thorne continued, "is learning to influence these patterns. Not just to observe, but to adjust when necessary."

He approached a flowering bush near the bench, one with blossoms that opened and closed in a rhythmic pattern, like time-lapse photography of flowers blooming and fading in rapid succession.

"This is a chronoblossom," he explained. "Its lifecycle is accelerated, completing what would take a normal plant months in the span of minutes. This makes it an ideal subject for your first attempt at temporal manipulation."

Dylan watched the plant with fascination as the flowers repeatedly bloomed and withered before his eyes, each cycle taking perhaps thirty seconds to complete.

"What I want you to do," Thorne instructed, "is focus on the plant's temporal signature, just as you did with everything in the garden a moment ago. Once you have a clear sense of its pattern, try to slow it down, not stopping it completely, but extending each cycle to perhaps twice its natural length."

Dylan nodded, understanding the concept but uncertain about the execution. He raised the wand, focusing his attention on the chronoblossom. Its temporal signature was easy to discern after his previous exercise, a rapid, pulsing rhythm that matched the visible cycle of its flowers.

"Now," Thorne said quietly, "visualize that rhythm slowing down. Use the wand not to force the change, but to suggest it, like adjusting the tempo of music rather than halting it completely."

Dylan concentrated, imagining the plant's temporal signature stretching out, each pulse elongating while maintaining the same basic pattern. The wand grew warm in his hand, responding to his intent. For a moment, nothing visible happened, though Dylan could feel something shifting in the pattern he perceived.

Then, gradually, the chronoblossom's cycle began to change. The flowers moved more slowly, their blooming and fading extending over a longer period. What had been a thirty-second cycle stretched to forty seconds, then fifty, finally settling at around one minute per complete bloom-and-fade sequence.

"Well done," Elara said, genuine approval in her voice. "Especially for a first attempt."

Dylan maintained his focus, finding that once established, the adjusted rhythm required less active concentration to maintain. "It's like... setting a new equilibrium," he observed. "Once the pattern is changed, it wants to stay in the new configuration unless disturbed."

"Precisely," Thorne confirmed. "This is why temporal manipulation doesn't require constant effort from the Keeper. Once established, the new patterns tend to maintain themselves until another force acts upon them."

After a few minutes, Thorne suggested Dylan release his influence, allowing the chronoblossom to return to its natural rhythm. This proved easier than the initial adjustment, simply a matter of withdrawing his focus and letting the plant's inherent pattern reassert itself.

"The key principle here," Thorne explained as the chronoblossom resumed its rapid cycle, "is that you're not creating or destroying time, merely adjusting its flow within a localized area. This is fundamental to understanding how the sigils work, they don't generate temporal energy, they regulate its distribution and flow."

Dylan nodded, the concept making sense to his mathematically inclined mind. "Like diverting a river rather than creating water," he suggested.

"An apt analogy," Elara agreed. "And like water, time seeks its own level. Push too hard in one direction, and it will eventually push back, sometimes with devastating consequences, as we saw in the Cataclysm."

For the next couple of hours, Dylan practiced on various plants in the garden, each with different temporal signatures requiring different approaches. Some responded easily to his influence, while others resisted, requiring more focused concentration or subtler adjustments.

Bruno remained at Dylan's side throughout these exercises, occasionally shifting position when Dylan worked with particularly resistant subjects, as if lending his own strength to the effort. Dylan began to notice that when Bruno was in direct contact with him, a paw on his foot, or leaning against his leg, the more difficult manipulations became slightly easier, the connection between them somehow amplifying his abilities.

"You're developing a good instinct for this," Thorne observed as Dylan successfully adjusted the growth rate of a vine that curled around one of the garden's stone columns. "Many novice Keepers try to force changes, which creates instability. You're working with the existing patterns, not against them."

"It's like solving equations," Dylan explained. "You can't just change one variable without accounting for how it affects the others. Everything has to balance."

Elara smiled. "Exactly so. And this understanding will be crucial when you begin working with the sigils, which are essentially massive equations written into the fabric of reality."

After another half hour of practice, Thorne suggested they take a break. Dylan realized he was mentally tired. He sat on the bench, taking a drink from his water bottle and one of the granola bars from his backpack.

Bruno settled beside him, those glowing eyes watching the garden with alert interest. Dylan broke off a piece of his granola bar and offered it to the dog, who accepted it with surprising delicacy given his enhanced size in this realm.

"Your Guardian has adapted well to this transition," Elara observed, watching them with a thoughtful expression. "Some take longer to acclimate to their dual nature."

"He's always been adaptable," Dylan replied, scratching behind Bruno's ears. "More than me, honestly."

"Don't underestimate your own adaptability," Thorne said, joining them near the bench. "Many would find the revelation of other worlds and magical responsibilities overwhelming. You've approached it with remarkable composure."

Dylan considered this. "I suppose... it all follows certain patterns. Rules. Even the magic has logic to it, once you understand the principles." He shrugged slightly. "I like understanding how things work. This is just... more complex than most things I've studied."

"After you've rested," Elara said, "we should visit the Timewell again. Now that you've developed basic temporal perception, you'll be able to observe it more meaningfully."

Dylan nodded, finishing his snack. The prospect of examining the Timewell with his new abilities was both exciting and slightly intimidating. According to Thorne's explanations, it was the most significant of the sigils, the primary anchor for the entire crossing.

When they were ready, the three of them (four, counting Bruno) left the garden and made their way through Dravengate's winding streets toward the central square. The town felt different to Dylan now, not just in appearance but in the subtle temporal currents he could now perceive flowing through it. Some buildings seemed to exist in slightly slower time than others, while certain areas pulsed with more rapid frequencies.

"You're noticing the temporal variations," Thorne observed, seeing Dylan's attentive gaze moving across their surroundings. "Dravengate was built at a nexus of temporal currents. Even in its diminished state, those currents still flow through the town in complex patterns."

"It's like... seeing the wind," Dylan tried to explain. "Not directly, but by its effects on things."

When they reached the central square, Dylan immediately focused on the Timewell. The circular platform with its domed latticework of pillars stood empty today, no market stalls or townspeople nearby. It seemed as though the area was deliberately being given space, treated with a reverence that even Dravengate's seemingly oblivious residents observed.

As they approached, Dylan felt a subtle pressure against his newly developed temporal senses, not painful, but intense, like stepping from a dimly lit room into bright sunlight. The Timewell radiated temporal energy at a level far beyond anything he'd encountered in his training so far, its patterns infinitely more complex than even the darkest of the training crystals.

"It's... overwhelming," he admitted as they stopped a few meters from the platform.

"Focus on your breathing," Elara advised. "Let your perception adjust gradually. Don't try to comprehend the entire pattern at once."

Dylan followed her guidance, deliberately slowing his breathing while allowing his senses to adapt to the Timewell's powerful emanations. Gradually, the overwhelming impression resolved into discernible patterns, still complex beyond anything he'd encountered, but no longer a featureless wall of sensation.

"Better?" Thorne asked after a few minutes.

Dylan nodded. "I can... sort of see it now. There are layers to it. Rhythms within rhythms."

"What you're perceiving is the residual function of the Timewell," Thorne explained. "Even in its dormant state, it continues to process a fraction of the temporal energies it was designed to manage. When fully activated, its capacity would be many times greater."

With careful steps, they approached the platform, climbing the three shallow steps that led to its surface. Up close, Dylan could now see details he'd missed before, intricate symbols carved into the stone beneath his feet, forming concentric circles around the central depression where the silver substance flowed in its hypnotic patterns.

Bruno stayed close to Dylan's side, his posture more alert now, eyes scanning their surroundings as if watching for potential threats.

"Your Guardian senses something," Elara noted quietly. "The Timewell's activation, even in this preliminary stage, may draw attention we'd prefer to avoid."

"The shadow entities?" Dylan asked, remembering Thorne's warnings.

"Possibly," Thorne confirmed. "Or others who might have their own interests in the crossing's restoration. Not all in Dravengate welcome the prospect of change, even positive change."

This was a sobering reminder that their work wasn't occurring in isolation. There were other forces at play, some potentially hostile to their efforts.

"What exactly am I looking for?" Dylan asked, focusing back on the Timewell.

"The sigil itself," Thorne replied. "The physical structure you see is merely the housing. The actual sigil is a pattern embedded in the temporal energy, visible only to those with the ability to perceive it."

Dylan concentrated, focusing his attention on the swirling silver substance at the centre of the platform. At first, he saw only the hypnotic flow of its surface, but as he extended his temporal perception, much as he had in the garden, deeper patterns began to emerge.

Beneath the seemingly random movements, there was structure, a complex geometric form that pulsed with its own rhythm, like a heartbeat slowed to near hibernation. The shape reminded Dylan of the fractals he'd studied in his mathematics books, infinite patterns repeating at different scales, but with a three-dimensional quality that no computer-generated fractal could match.

"I can see it," he said softly, almost afraid that speaking too loudly might disrupt his perception. "It's like... a geometric shape. But alive somehow. Pulsing."

"That is the sigil of Time," Elara confirmed. "The primary anchor of the crossing, currently in a state of dormancy."

"And I'm supposed to... wake it up?" Dylan asked, the enormity of the task suddenly very real.

"Eventually," Thorne said. "But not today, and not alone. The awakening of the Time sigil will require careful preparation and the combined efforts of all of us, including your Guardian."

Bruno made a soft sound, almost a purr despite his canine nature, his eyes fixed on the swirling silver substance with an intensity that suggested he was perceiving even more than Dylan.

"For now," Elara continued, "we want you to simply observe. To understand its current state and begin to form a connection with it, as you've done with the training crystals."

Dylan nodded, returning his attention to the sigil. Now that he could perceive its basic structure, he began to notice details, rhythmic variations in its pulsing, areas where the pattern seemed stretched or compressed, places where the elegant geometry was disrupted or damaged.

"It's... broken in places," he observed. "Like a gear with missing teeth."

"The damage from the Cataclysm," Thorne confirmed. "The sigil was not destroyed, but significant portions of its structure were disrupted when the rogue Keeper attempted to redirect its power."

Dylan continued his examination, mentally mapping the sigil's current state, noting where the damage seemed most severe and where the original pattern remained intact. His mathematical mind automatically began analysing the structure, identifying the underlying principles that governed its design.

"It's a quaternion array," he murmured, almost to himself. "A four-dimensional geometric structure projected into three-dimensional space."

Thorne looked at him with surprise. "That's... remarkably accurate.

Dylan shrugged slightly. "I like studying higher-dimensional mathematics. This looks like some of the projection models I've seen, just... vastly more complex."

After about twenty minutes of observation, Elara suggested they withdraw. "It's unwise to remain too long near the Timewell in its current state," she explained. "Even dormant, it affects those around it in subtle ways. Too much exposure can lead to temporal dissonance, a disconnection from normal time flow that can be disorienting or even dangerous."

They descended from the platform and moved to a small seating area at the edge of the square, where they could discuss their observations without being too close to the Timewell's influence.

The Keeper of Time

"What you've done today," Thorne said once they were settled, "is the first step toward eventually awakening the sigil. By observing and understanding its current state, you begin to form the connection necessary to influence it."

"It seems impossibly complex," Dylan admitted. "The training crystals are like... like single notes compared to an entire symphony."

Elara agreed. "But remember, you won't be expected to conduct the entire symphony at once. The awakening process is gradual, focusing on one section of the pattern at a time, slowly bringing the whole back into harmony."

"And I won't be doing it alone?" Dylan confirmed.

"No," Thorne assured him. "Your Guardian will provide essential support, and both Elara and I will lend our knowledge and whatever power we can offer. The Keeper is central to the process, but not isolated in it."

This was reassuring. The prospect of single-handedly repairing something as vast and complex as the Time sigil had seemed overwhelming, even with his growing abilities.

"What's next, then?" Dylan asked, always preferring to have a clear plan of action.

"Continue your training with the crystals," Thorne instructed. "But add two new exercises. First, practice extending your temporal perception to everyday objects in your world, as you did with the garden here. Start with simple, mechanical things like clocks or watches, then progress to more complex systems."

"And second," Elara added, "begin working with your Guardian to strengthen your connection. The exercises I'll show you will help you synchronize your temporal awareness with Bruno's, amplifying both your abilities."

She demonstrated a series of focused meditation techniques designed to enhance the bond between Keeper and Guardian. These involved both physical contact and mental visualization, creating what she called a "resonance loop" that allowed their energies to flow more freely between them.

After practicing these techniques under Elara's guidance for about half an hour, Dylan could already feel a difference in his connection with Bruno. The Rottweiler's presence in his awareness was stronger, more defined, like a clear note cutting through background noise.

"With practice," Elara explained, "this connection will allow you to draw on each other's strengths. Your analytical precision will help focus Bruno's intuitive power, while his natural affinity for temporal currents will enhance your ability to perceive and manipulate them."

The sun was beginning to lower in Dravengate's sky, casting long shadows across the square. Dylan realized they had been training for several hours, though it had felt like much less time.

"I should probably head back soon," he said, checking his watch, which continued to show Blackpool time despite their location in another realm. "I promised my mum I'd be home for tea."

"Of course," Thorne said. "Maintaining balance between your worlds is important, especially at this early stage of your training."

Before they parted, Elara handed Dylan a small leather pouch. "These are more advanced training crystals," she explained. "They contain more complex temporal signatures that will help prepare you for working with the sigil."

Dylan accepted the pouch, adding it to his backpack alongside the original crystals. "When should I return?"

"Give yourself three days to practice with the new crystals and connection exercises," Thorne suggested. "Then come back, and we'll assess your progress."

With a plan established, Dylan prepared to depart. Creating the portal back to Blackpool was becoming almost routine now, a simple matter of focused visualization and intent channelled through the wand.

As the swirling gateway formed before them, Elara placed a hand lightly on Dylan's shoulder. "You've made impressive progress today," she said. "The path ahead is challenging, but you're showing a natural aptitude that gives us hope."

Dylan nodded, appreciating her encouragement but also feeling the weight of expectation it carried. "I'll do my best," he promised, not wanting to commit to more than that.

The Keeper of Time

With a final nod to Thorne and Elara, Dylan stepped through the portal with Bruno at his side. The transition between worlds was smoother each time, and then they were standing once again in the secluded spot between the dunes, the familiar sounds and smells of Blackpool surrounding them.

Dylan checked his watch and was pleased to see that only about two hours had passed since they'd left, plenty of time to get home for tea. Bruno shook himself, his eyes returning to their normal brown, the enhanced aspects of his physique fading as they returned to their home reality.

As they walked back toward home, Dylan found his mind still processing everything he'd learned. The temporal perception exercises had changed something in him, he now noticed subtle patterns in the world around him that he'd never been aware of before. The rhythmic swaying of trees in the breeze, the pulsing flow of traffic at intersections, even the varied pace of pedestrians on the sidewalk, all seemed to form part of a complex temporal tapestry that he was only beginning to understand.

Bruno trotted beside him, outwardly just an ordinary Rottweiler again, but Dylan could still feel the enhanced connection between them, a resonance that persisted even in this world, where magic seemed to follow different rules.

When they arrived home, the smell of Mally's lasagna already filled the house. Dylan found his stepdad in the kitchen, carefully layering the pasta dish before it went into the oven.

"Good timing," Mally said, glancing up with a smile. "tea's in forty-five minutes." He paused, studying Dylan for a moment longer than usual. "You look... different. Good walk?"

"Yeah," Dylan replied, trying to sound casual despite his surprise at Mally's observation. "Just exploring the dunes."

Mally nodded, though his gaze lingered on Bruno, who was drinking noisily from his water bowl. "He seems different too. Calmer. More... I don't know. Present?"

Dylan felt a flicker of alarm. Could Mally somehow sense the change in Bruno? In himself? "He's just tired from all the walking," he said, hoping his voice sounded normal.

"Hmm," Mally responded noncommittally, returning his attention to the lasagna. After a moment, he added, "Whatever you're doing on these walks, it seems good for both of you. You seem more... centred. Less anxious about your routines."

There was something in his stepdad's tone, not suspicion exactly, but awareness that something had changed. Dylan wasn't sure how to respond, so he simply nodded and headed upstairs to wash up before tea, Bruno following at his heels.

In his room, Dylan carefully stored the advanced crystals in his desk drawer, alongside the original training set. "We need to be more careful," he murmured to Bruno. "Mally's noticing something." Bruno made a soft sound that might have been agreement, settling on his rug with a watchful gaze fixed on Dylan.

"We've got a lot of practicing to do," Dylan said, checking his schedule for the evening. "And I still need to finish that game level I was working on before all this started. Plus, that maths assignment for summer study."

Bruno huffed softly, bumping against Dylan's leg in what felt like reassurance.

"You're right," Dylan agreed, as if the dog had spoken. "One thing at a time. We've got a schedule."

And for now, that schedule included Mally's lasagna, followed by an evening of crystal practice and perhaps, if time permitted, a few rounds of his favourite game. Being the Keeper of Time, Dylan was discovering, didn't mean abandoning his normal life, it just meant fitting new responsibilities into the careful structure he'd always maintained.

As they headed back downstairs for tea, Dylan couldn't help but wonder if Mally's observations would continue. His stepdad had always been perceptive in an understated way, noticing things that others missed. If he was already seeing changes in Dylan and Bruno after just a few Dravengate visits, what would he notice as their training progressed? It was another variable to account for in an increasingly complex equation, but then, managing complex equations was exactly what Dylan did best.

Chapter 9: Progress and Problems

Mally's lasagna tea had been a success, with Dylan managing to participate in the family conversation despite his mind occasionally drifting to temporal signatures and sigil patterns. Neither his mum nor Mally seemed to notice anything unusual, though Dylan caught Bruno watching him attentively whenever the conversation veered close to topics that might reveal his secret.

The next three days passed in a carefully structured rhythm of normal life and magical training. Dylan maintained his schedule with mathematical precision, dividing each day into color-coded blocks on his chart: blue for family time, green for his own projects and studies, red for Keeper training, and yellow for unexpected events, though so far, the yellow blocks had remained reassuringly empty.

The advanced training crystals that Elara had given him proved significantly more challenging than the first set. Their temporal signatures were not just complex but sometimes seemingly contradictory, patterns that folded back on themselves or abruptly shifted direction in ways that defied Dylan's initial attempts to track them.

"It's like trying to follow a Möbius strip," he muttered to Bruno during their second evening practice session. "Just when I think I understand the pattern, it twists into something else."

Bruno, lying on the rug beside Dylan's bed, tilted his head slightly as if considering this assessment. In the days since their training with Elara, Dylan had noticed subtle changes in their connection even in this world. He couldn't see Bruno's eyes glow amber here as they did in Dravengate, but he could feel a deeper awareness flowing between them, especially during their practice sessions.

Following Elara's instructions, Dylan had been practicing the resonance exercises designed to strengthen their bond. These involved sitting quietly with Bruno, one hand resting on the dog's head or shoulder, while visualizing their energies as complementary patterns flowing between them. At first, it had felt somewhat silly, just Dylan sitting with his dog, imagining coloured light flowing between them, but by the third day, the results were undeniable.

During these connection moments, Dylan found he could perceive faint echoes of what Bruno was sensing, not visual images or sounds, but impressions, feelings, awareness of things beyond his normal perception. Bruno's senses were acutely attuned to shifts in the environment that Dylan would never notice on his own, creating an early warning system for unexpected disruptions.

This proved particularly useful when his mum nearly walked in on him practicing with the crystals. Bruno had grown suddenly alert, his attention shifting to the door several seconds before any sound of approaching footsteps. Dylan had just enough time to tuck the crystals and wand under his pillow before his mum knocked and entered to ask about their plans for the weekend.

On the morning of the fourth day, Dylan woke feeling both excited and nervous. Today they would return to Dravengate to continue his training, and according to his schedule, it was also the day they might begin preliminary work with the Timewell itself.

As he got dressed, Dylan mentally reviewed everything he'd learned about temporal manipulation. He'd made significant progress with the advanced crystals, managing to attune to even the most complex signatures for brief periods. He'd also practiced extending his perception to everyday objects, starting with his alarm clock and gradually working up to more complex systems like his laptop and the television downstairs.

The results had been fascinating. Electronic devices had temporal signatures that were precise but shallow, lacking the rich complexity of living things. His laptop's signature was a rapid, steady pulse, almost metronomic in its regularity. The old grandfather clock in the hallway, by contrast, had a deeper, more resonant pattern, as if its long existence had given it a more substantial relationship with time.

Most interesting of all had been his mother's houseplants. Like the chronoblossom in Elara's garden, but much subtler, each plant had its own distinctive rhythm, some quick and fluttering, others slow and steady. Dylan had spent nearly an hour just observing the variations between different species, noting how their temporal signatures seemed to correlate with their growth patterns and life cycles.

"Ready for today?" he asked Bruno, who was already sitting attentively by the bedroom door, clearly aware of their plans.

Bruno's tail thumped once against the carpet in what Dylan had come to recognize as affirmation.

After breakfast, during which Dylan informed his mum that he and Bruno would be "exploring the shore north of town" (technically true, as that was where they accessed the portal), they set off with Dylan's backpack fully stocked for what might be a longer stay in Dravengate than their previous visits.

"We'll be back for tea," Dylan promised as they left, maintaining the careful balance between his two lives.

The morning was overcast, typical Blackpool weather replacing the previous days' sunshine. A light drizzle had left the pavements damp, and the air carried the distinctive scent of the sea mixed with approaching rain. Despite the gloomy conditions, Dylan felt a growing excitement as they approached their usual portal spot between the dunes.

Creating the gateway to Dravengate had become almost second nature now, a simple matter of focused visualization and intent channelled through the wand. As the swirling portal formed before them, Dylan took a deep breath and stepped through with Bruno at his side.

The contrast between Blackpool's grey morning and Dravengate couldn't have been more striking. Here, the sky was a vibrant blue streaked with puffy white clouds, the air warm and fragrant with unfamiliar blossoms. As always, Bruno underwent his subtle transformation as they crossed over, his form becoming more defined, his eyes shifting to that glowing amber that marked his Guardian nature.

They crossed the stone bridge and made their way through Dravengate's winding streets toward Elara's hidden garden. Dylan found himself noticing details he'd overlooked on previous visits, the way certain buildings seemed to have grown rather than been constructed, the subtle glow that emanated from some of the stones in the street, the occasional shimmer in the air that suggested magic was being worked nearby.

Most interesting was his growing awareness of the temporal currents flowing through the town. With his newly developed perception, he could sense how time moved differently in various parts of Dravengate, flowing more quickly in busy areas like the marketplace, moving more slowly in quiet courtyards and gardens. It wasn't a dramatic difference, but it was noticeable to his enhanced senses.

When they reached the ivy-covered archway to Elara's garden, Dylan paused, extending his perception before entering. He could sense two presences within, the familiar signatures of Elara and Thorne, both waiting for him.

"They're already there," he told Bruno, who huffed softly in acknowledgment.

As they ducked through the low entrance, Dylan was surprised to find not just Elara and Thorne, but a third person he hadn't met before. A young woman perhaps a few years older than himself stood near the central tree, examining one of the crystal-like leaves with scholarly interest. She wore simple clothes, sturdy trousers and a loose tunic in deep green, but carried herself with a confidence that suggested she was more than a casual visitor.

"Ah, right on time," Elara said, rising from her seat on the wooden bench. "Dylan, I'd like you to meet Rowan, the Archivist's apprentice."

The young woman turned, offering Dylan a brief but genuine smile. She had dark hair pulled back in a practical braid and intelligent eyes that assessed him with open curiosity.

"So, you're the new Keeper," she said, her accent different from the others Dylan had met in Dravengate, sharper, more clipped. "Or potential Keeper, I should say. The wand's chosen you, but the sigils haven't confirmed it yet."

"Rowan," Thorne said, his tone gently chiding, "we discussed approaching this with tact."

She shrugged, unapologetic. "Just stating facts. No point dancing around it." She extended a hand to Dylan in what he recognized as a gesture from his world rather than a Dravengate custom. "Rowan Veller. I help maintain what's left of the Archives and translate the old texts when this one's eyes are too tired." She nodded toward Thorne with what seemed like affectionate disrespect.

Dylan shook her hand, finding her directness oddly refreshing after Elara and Thorne's sometimes cryptic manner. "Dylan Bennett. And this is Bruno." He gestured to Bruno, who was watching Rowan with careful attention.

Rowan's eyes widened slightly as she took in Bruno's glowing eyes and enhanced form. "A canine Guardian," she murmured. "Interesting choice. The records show most recent Guardians manifested as felines or birds of prey." She crouched down, meeting Bruno's gaze without flinching. "But I can see the strength in this form. Loyalty. Persistence. Good qualities for uncertain times."

Bruno made a soft sound, somewhere between a growl and a purr, that might have been approval.

"Rowan has been studying the original instructions for the sigil awakening ritual," Thorne explained. "Her expertise in ancient languages and ceremonial protocols will be invaluable as we prepare for the next phase of your training."

"Which text did you find it in?" Dylan asked, his natural curiosity engaged.

Rowan looked up, seeming pleased by the question. "The Codex Temporis, primarily, though I cross-referenced with Keeper Elavir's journals for the practical applications. The theoretical structure was there, but Elavir actually performed several reactivations during the Lesser Disruption, so her notes provided crucial context."

Dylan nodded, filing away these references for future investigation. "And what did you learn? About the awakening ritual, I mean."

"It's more complex than the historical accounts suggested," Rowan replied, straightening up. "Not just a matter of applying power through the wand, but a precise sequence of adjustments to the sigil's internal structure, essentially rebuilding it from the inside out while maintaining its overall integrity."

She reached into a satchel hanging at her side and withdrew a rolled parchment, which she spread on the small stone table near the bench. "I've diagrammed the sequence here. It's essentially a mathematical progression, each step building on the last in a specific pattern."

Dylan moved closer to examine the diagram. It was an intricate representation of what he recognized as the Time sigil, but broken down into component sections, each labelled with symbols he didn't recognize but that clearly indicated a sequence.

"This is remarkable," he said, genuinely impressed. "It's like an algorithm for rebuilding the sigil's structure."

Rowan nodded, seeming pleased by his understanding. "Exactly. Each section must be reactivated in the correct order, or the entire structure becomes unstable. It's why previous attempts to revive the crossing have failed, they approached it as a single unit rather than a complex system of interdependent components."

"Which is where your mathematical thinking will be particularly valuable," Thorne added, joining them at the table. "The sequence follows patterns that might seem counterintuitive to most, but I suspect will make perfect sense to your mind."

Dylan studied the diagram more closely, his thoughts already working through the implied progression. It reminded him of certain fractal generation algorithms he'd studied, where complex structures emerged from relatively simple iterative processes.

"It builds from the centre outward," he observed, tracing the sequence with his finger. "But not in concentric circles, more like a spiral, with each new section anchoring to multiple previous points."

"Precisely," Rowan confirmed, eyebrows raised slightly in approval. "Each activation creates connection points for subsequent sections, forming a self-reinforcing network that grows stronger with each addition."

Bruno moved beside Dylan, those glowing eyes fixed on the diagram with an intensity that suggested he understood more than an ordinary dog should. Dylan had noticed this before, Bruno seemed to comprehend complex concepts despite having no way to verbally engage with them.

"Your Guardian perceives the pattern as well," Elara observed from where she still sat on the bench. "This is good. For the ritual to succeed, both Keeper and Guardian must understand the sequence, even if in different ways."

"So, when do we start?" Dylan asked, looking up from the diagram.

"Today we begin the preparation," Thorne replied. "The actual awakening will require several sessions, each focusing on a different section of the sigil, with rest periods between to allow the newly activated portions to stabilize."

"Think of it like physical therapy for someone recovering from an injury," Rowan suggested. "Push too hard too fast, and you cause more damage. Work methodically with proper rest intervals, and the recovery is more complete."

This analogy made sense to Dylan, whose mind always worked best with concrete comparisons. "So what's our first step?"

"A detailed assessment of the sigil's current state," Thorne said. "Now that you've developed your temporal perception, you'll be able to map the damage more precisely than our previous observations allowed."

"And while you're doing that," Rowan added, "I'll be setting up the monitoring equipment to track the sigil's responses to initial stimulus."

Dylan blinked, surprised by the mention of equipment. "You have technology here? Like, actual devices?"

Rowan smiled, a hint of mischief in her expression. "Not like what you're thinking of. No electronics or digital systems. But we have instruments designed to detect and measure temporal fluctuations, essentially mechanical sensors that respond to changes in the flow of time."

"They're artifacts from before the Cataclysm," Thorne explained. "Created by earlier Keepers to help monitor the crossing's stability. Rowan has been restoring them for our use."

This was a fascinating new aspect of Dravengate that Dylan hadn't considered before, the blend of magic and mechanical ingenuity that had gone into building and maintaining the crossing. It made sense that a civilization advanced enough to create connections between worlds would have developed specialized tools for working with such complex forces.

After a brief period of preparation, gathering the necessary equipment and materials, they set off for the town square where the Timewell stood. As they walked, Rowan fell into step beside Dylan, her curiosity apparently overcoming any initial reservations.

"So, you're from one of the connected worlds," she said, her tone conversational. "What's it like there? The texts describe many different realms, but firsthand accounts are rare since the Cataclysm."

"It's..." Dylan paused, trying to think how to describe his world to someone who may never had experienced it. "More structured, in some ways. Less magical, obviously. We have technology instead, machines and computers and networks that connect people and information."

"Like a mechanical version of the crossing?" Rowan suggested.

"Sort of, yes," Dylan agreed, finding the comparison apt. "But most people don't think about how it all works, they just use it without understanding the systems behind it."

"That sounds familiar," Rowan said with a wry smile. "Most people in Dravengate have forgotten what this place truly is.

The Keeper of Time

They live their lives surrounded by remnants of incredible magic without ever questioning or exploring it."

They reached the town square, which was quieter today than during their previous visits. The Timewell stood isolated in the centre, the space around it respectfully empty as always. As they approached, Dylan could sense the powerful temporal currents emanating from the structure, but this time he was prepared for the intensity and able to adjust his perception accordingly.

Rowan immediately set to work arranging her instruments around the perimeter of the Timewell platform, delicate devices of brass and crystal that reminded Dylan of antique scientific equipment he'd seen in museums, though clearly designed for purposes beyond anything in his world.

Meanwhile, Thorne guided Dylan through a more detailed examination of the Time sigil, now that his perception had developed beyond their initial assessment. With Bruno at his side, Dylan focused his attention on the swirling silver substance at the centre of the platform, extending his awareness into its depths to perceive the complex pattern beneath.

"Map the damage as precisely as you can," Thorne instructed. "Note where the pattern is weakest, where connections have been severed, where the flow is disrupted."

Dylan concentrated, allowing his mathematical mind to analyse the structure systematically. The sigil's pattern was incredibly complex, but the damage followed discernible patterns, areas where the geometric harmony was broken, where energy flowed erratically or not at all.

"It's most damaged here," he said after several minutes of careful observation, indicating a section toward what he perceived as the southwestern quadrant of the pattern. "The connections are almost completely severed, and the flow is redirected in a way that puts stress on adjacent sections."

"Excellent observation," Thorne said, genuinely impressed. "That aligns with our historical records of where the Cataclysm's effects were most severe."

"And there's something else," Dylan continued, focusing on a different area. "This section here, it's not exactly damaged, but... altered. Like someone deliberately rewrote the pattern rather than it being broken by accident."

Thorne and Elara exchanged glances. "That would be the emergency modification implemented during the Cataclysm," Elara explained. "A temporary measure to prevent complete collapse of the crossing."

"It wasn't meant to last centuries," Thorne added. "It's like a tourniquet, effective at stopping immediate catastrophe, but harmful if left in place too long."

Dylan nodded, understanding the analogy. "We'll need to undo that modification as part of the restoration?"

"Eventually," Elara confirmed. "But carefully, and only after strengthening the surrounding sections."

The Keeper of Time

For the next half hour, Dylan worked with Bruno to create a detailed map of the sigil's current state, noting every area of damage, every altered section, every point where energy flowed incorrectly. Rowan's instruments recorded fluctuations in the temporal field as they worked, providing data that would help them plan the restoration sequence.

By the time they finished, Dylan had a comprehensive understanding of the Time sigil's condition, far more detailed than what he'd perceived during their earlier visits. It was daunting, seeing the full extent of the damage, but also encouraging to recognize that the basic structure remained intact beneath the broken sections.

"This is invaluable information," Thorne said as they reviewed the maps and notes they'd created. "With this level of detail, we can create a much more precise restoration plan."

"What happens next?" Dylan asked, glancing at the Timewell, which continued its slow, hypnotic swirling beneath the domed lattice of pillars.

"Now," Rowan said, checking one of her instruments, "we test your ability to influence the sigil on a very small scale. Not awakening or restoration, just a minor adjustment to see how it responds to your connection through the wand."

This was both exciting and intimidating. Working with training crystals and garden plants was one thing; attempting to influence the primary sigil of the crossing, even in a small way, was quite another.

"Is it safe?" Dylan asked, not embarrassed to voice his concern.

"We've established safety parameters," Elara assured him. "Rowan's instruments will alert us to any unexpected reactions, and we've chosen the most stable section of the sigil for this initial test."

Thorne pointed to an area of the sigil that Dylan had noted as relatively undamaged. "Focus your attention here," he instructed. "This section regulates the basic rhythm of the Timewell, its heartbeat, if you will. A slight adjustment to its tempo would be noticeable in our measurements but wouldn't disrupt the overall structure."

Dylan took a deep breath, mentally preparing himself. Bruno moved closer, pressing against his leg in that reassuring way that seemed to stabilize their connection.

"Remember the resonance exercises," Elara reminded him softly. "Draw on your Guardian's strength to help maintain focus."

Dylan nodded, taking the wand from his pocket. As always, it warmed to his touch, responding to his intent even before he consciously directed it. He closed his eyes briefly, focusing on the connection with Bruno, feeling the resonance between them strengthening as they synchronized their awareness.

Then, opening his eyes, he extended his perception toward the Timewell, focusing specifically on the section Thorne had indicated. Its pattern was relatively simple compared to the more complex areas of the sigil, a steady, pulsing rhythm that reminded Dylan of a metronome.

"I see it," he murmured. "The base rhythm."

"Good," Thorne said quietly. "Now, very gently, try to increase that rhythm, just a slight acceleration, as if turning a dial one small increment."

Dylan raised the wand, focusing his intent through it while maintaining his awareness of the sigil's pattern. He visualized the rhythm speeding up slightly, the pulses coming just a fraction faster than before. The wand grew warmer in his hand, channelling his will toward the Timewell.

For a moment, nothing seemed to happen. Then, gradually, he felt the pattern responding, the rhythm accelerating precisely as he'd envisioned, the pulses coming closer together in perfect mathematical progression.

"It's working," Rowan reported, watching her instruments with intense focus. "The temporal frequency in that sector is increasing exactly as anticipated."

Dylan maintained his concentration, carefully holding the adjustment steady without pushing further. Bruno remained pressed against his leg, those glowing eyes fixed on the Timewell, his presence somehow amplifying Dylan's control over the delicate procedure.

"Excellent," Thorne said after about a minute. "Now, just as carefully, return it to its original rhythm and then withdraw your influence completely."

This proved somewhat more challenging than the initial adjustment. Slowing the rhythm back down required a different kind of control, like easing off an accelerator rather than pressing it. Dylan focused intently, visualizing the pattern returning to its original state in gradual, controlled increments.

When he sensed it had returned to its baseline, he slowly withdrew his influence, allowing his connection with the sigil to fade gently rather than breaking it abruptly.

"Perfect," Elara said as he lowered the wand. "A clean adjustment and withdrawal, with no residual disturbance."

Rowan was checking her instruments, a look of genuine surprise on her face. "The readings are remarkably stable," she reported. "Usually, even minor adjustments leave fluctuations in the field, but this... it's as if the sigil accepted your influence as natural."

"That's a very positive sign," Thorne explained to Dylan. "It suggests the wand's choice was correct, your connection with the Time sigil is harmonious rather than forced."

Dylan felt a mixture of relief and accomplishment. He'd actually manipulated the Timewell, even if only in a small, controlled way, and it had responded positively to his influence.

"Can we try another section?" he asked, his confidence growing.

Thorne and Elara exchanged glances. "Perhaps one more small test," Thorne conceded. "But we must be cautious not to overtax either you or the sigil at this early stage."

He indicated another relatively stable section of the pattern, this one controlling what he described as the "amplitude" of the temporal flow rather than its frequency. "This regulates the strength of the pulses rather than their timing. See if you can increase the amplitude slightly, then return it to normal as before."

Dylan nodded, raising the wand again and focusing his perception on the new section. Its pattern was different from the first, more like waves than pulses, with distinct crests and troughs flowing in a steady sequence. He could see how adjusting the amplitude would make these waves taller and deeper without changing their frequency.

With Bruno's steady presence supporting him, Dylan focused his intent through the wand, visualizing the waves growing slightly larger while maintaining their rhythm. The wand grew warm again, channelling his will toward the sigil.

This time, the response was faster, as if the Timewell had already recognized and accepted his influence. The waves in the pattern began to increase in size, their peaks rising higher and troughs dipping lower, while maintaining perfect mathematical proportion.

"Remarkable," Rowan murmured, watching her instruments. "The amplitude is increasing in precise, controlled increments."

Dylan held the adjustment steady for about thirty seconds, then began the careful process of returning it to its original state. As before, this required a different kind of control, but he found it easier this time, his confidence building with experience.

When he had withdrawn his influence completely, lowering the wand and taking a step back from the Timewell, he felt a curious mixture of exhilaration and fatigue. The mental focus required for such precise manipulation was demanding, even with Bruno's support.

"You've done extremely well," Elara said, studying him with approval. "Few potential Keepers achieve such fine control in their initial attempts."

"The sigil responds to him naturally," Thorne observed. "This bodes well for the restoration process."

Rowan was comparing readings from her instruments, her expression thoughtful. "There's something else," she said after a moment. "During the second adjustment, there was a faint response in one of the damaged sections, not directly influenced, but somehow resonating with the changes you made."

She showed them the readings on one of her devices, which displayed curves and symbols that meant nothing to Dylan but clearly indicated something significant to the others.

"That's unusual," Thorne admitted. "Typically, damaged sections remain inert until directly addressed in the restoration sequence."

"It suggests a greater degree of natural affinity than we anticipated," Elara explained to Dylan. "The sigil isn't just accepting your influence, it's actively responding to it, even in areas you weren't directly targeting."

"Is that good or bad?" Dylan asked.

"Good, potentially," Thorne replied. "It may make the restoration process more efficient. But it also means we need to be even more careful with the sequence, if one adjustment can affect multiple sections, the potential for unintended consequences increases."

As they discussed the implications of these observations, Dylan became aware of a subtle change in Bruno's demeanour. The Rottweiler had moved slightly away from him, his attention focused not on the Timewell but toward the edge of the square, his posture shifting from relaxed to alert.

Dylan followed his Guardian's gaze but saw nothing unusual, just the empty square with its scattered benches and planters, the street beyond leading back into town.

"Bruno?" he said softly, recognizing the warning signs in the dog's body language. "What is it?"

Bruno made a low sound, not quite a growl but a clear indication of concern. His glowing eyes remained fixed on something Dylan couldn't see, his powerful body tensing as if preparing for action.

Thorne noticed this change immediately. "Your Guardian senses something," he said, his voice dropping to a near whisper. "

And given their particular atonement, it's likely related to the temporal field."

"I don't see anything," Dylan said, still scanning the area where Bruno was focused.

"You wouldn't, necessarily," Elara explained, also speaking quietly. "Guardians perceive threats on levels beyond ordinary sight. It could be a disturbance in the temporal currents, or perhaps an entity that exists partially in another phase of reality."

"The shadow entities?" Dylan asked, remembering Thorne's warnings from their first meeting.

"Possibly," Thorne acknowledged. "Or simply a natural fluctuation in the crossing's structure, responding to our work with the sigil."

Rowan had moved to check one of her instruments that was positioned in the direction of Bruno's focus. "There's definitely something," she confirmed. "A distortion in the temporal field, small, but growing."

Bruno's growl deepened, his form beginning to shift subtly, muscles expanding, fur bristling, his presence becoming more imposing. It wasn't the complete transformation Dylan had glimpsed in the forest during their first journey to Dravengate, but it was heading in that direction.

"We should conclude for today," Elara decided, her tone making it clear this wasn't merely a suggestion. "Pack up the instruments, Rowan. Dylan, prepare to withdraw with your Guardian."

Dylan nodded, but found himself reluctant to leave without understanding what had triggered Bruno's response. "Can we at least try to see what's causing this? If it's something that might interfere with the restoration, shouldn't we know what we're dealing with?"

Thorne hesitated, then nodded slowly. "A valid point. But we approach with extreme caution, and at the first sign of genuine danger, we retreat immediately. Agreed?"

"Agreed," Dylan confirmed.

With Bruno leading the way, they moved carefully toward the edge of the square where the Rottweiler's attention was focused. Rowan brought one of her smaller instruments, a brass device that resembled a compass but with multiple needles that swung in different directions, apparently tracking temporal fluctuations.

As they drew closer to the spot, Dylan began to sense what had alerted Bruno. There was a disturbance in the temporal currents, subtle but growing, like ripples spreading from an unseen stone dropped into still water. It felt wrong somehow, discordant with the natural patterns he'd been learning to perceive.

"I can feel it now," he said quietly. "It's like... interference. Static in the patterns."

"That's a good description," Thorne acknowledged. "This is typical of unauthorized incursions into the temporal field, entities attempting to access or influence the crossing without proper atonement."

They stopped about five meters from the source of the disturbance, which remained invisible to ordinary sight but increasingly evident to Dylan's enhanced perception. It was as if reality itself was thinning at that point, the boundary between dimensions becoming permeable.

Bruno positioned himself directly between Dylan and the disturbance, his transformation continuing, his size increasing, his muscles more defined, those glowing eyes now burning with protective intensity.

"Your Guardian is preparing to defend against whatever may emerge," Elara observed. "This suggests the disturbance is indeed hostile rather than merely natural."

As if in response to her words, the air at the focal point of the disturbance began to visibly shimmer, like heat rising from pavement on a hot day. Within that shimmer, shadows moved, not physical darkness, but an absence of light that seemed to have substance and form.

"Void entities," Thorne murmured, his voice tense. "Just as I feared."

The shimmering intensified, the shadows within it coalescing into more defined shapes, vaguely humanoid but with proportions that seemed wrong, limbs too long or bent at impossible angles, forms that shifted and flowed as if struggling to maintain coherence in this reality.

Bruno's growl deepened into something that resonated beyond ordinary sound, his form now fully transformed into the enhanced Guardian state, larger, more powerful, radiating a golden light that contrasted sharply with the darkness trying to manifest before them.

"Dylan," Thorne said urgently, "you should prepare to open a portal back to your world. If these entities fully materialize, the situation could become dangerous very quickly."

But even as Dylan reached for the wand to comply, something unexpected happened. The shadow entities, now partially visible within the shimmering distortion, seemed to recoil from Bruno's transformed presence. Their shapes wavered, losing cohesion, the darkness fragmenting like smoke dispersed by wind.

"They're retreating," Rowan said, watching her instrument with fascination. "The incursion is collapsing."

"It's the Guardian's influence," Elara explained. "They were not prepared for a fully bonded Keeper-Guardian pair. Most recent restoration attempts lacked this protection."

Within moments, the shimmering distortion had faded entirely, the shadows retreating to whatever space between dimensions they had emerged from. The temporal currents gradually returned to their normal patterns, the disturbance dissipating without further incident.

Bruno remained in his enhanced form for several minutes longer, watchful and alert, before gradually shifting back to his normal appearance, though his eyes retained their golden glow, a reminder that they remained in Dravengate where his Guardian nature was fully expressed.

"That was... informative," Thorne said once it was clear the threat had passed. "And concerning. The void entities are aware of our work with the Timewell, as we suspected they might be, but they appear more organized in their response than previous encounters suggested."

"Organized how?" Dylan asked, still processing what they'd just witnessed.

"This wasn't a random incursion," Rowan explained, checking readings on her instrument. "The temporal signature suggests a deliberate probe, testing our defences, assessing our capabilities."

"Like reconnaissance," Dylan suggested, drawing on his knowledge of gaming strategies.

"Precisely," Thorne agreed. "They're gathering information before committing to a more substantial incursion."

"Which means they consider our restoration efforts a significant threat to whatever goals they're pursuing," Elara added.

"Or opportunity," Rowan countered. "Don't forget that the void entities thrive on instability in the crossing. Our work with the Timewell creates fluctuations they might attempt to exploit or expand."

This was a sobering thought. Dylan had been focused on the challenges of restoring the sigils themselves, not considering that the very process might attract opposition from forces that preferred the crossing remain damaged.

"So what do we do?" he asked. "Abandon the restoration?"

"Absolutely not," Thorne replied firmly. "If anything, this confirms the importance of our work. The crossing's current state is vulnerable to these incursions. Only by restoring it to full functionality can we secure it against such threats."

"But we must proceed with even greater caution," Elara cautioned. "And perhaps accelerate certain aspects of your training, Dylan. your Guardian proved remarkably effective at repelling this probe, but more substantial incursions may require active defence rather than mere presence."

This led to a revised training plan, with Rowan offering to teach Dylan some basic protective measures that earlier Keepers had developed specifically to counter void entities. These weren't offensive magics, the Keeper's role was fundamentally creative rather than destructive, but rather techniques for stabilizing reality against attempts to distort it.

By the time they finished discussing these adjustments to their approach, the sun was lowering in Dravengate's sky. Dylan checked his watch, which continued to track Blackpool time despite their location in another world, and was relieved to see he still had plenty of time before he needed to be home for tea.

"We should conclude today's work with the Timewell," Thorne decided. "But perhaps move to the Archives for the remainder of our session. It's more secure against temporal disturbances, and there are resources there that might help prepare you for potential future encounters."

Dylan agreed, feeling a mixture of excitement and apprehension about this new dimension to his training. The appearance of the void entities had made the stakes of their work more concrete, this wasn't just about restoring magical connections between worlds, but protecting those worlds from forces that would exploit weaknesses in those connections.

As they gathered their equipment and prepared to leave the square, Bruno remained vigilant, occasionally turning to scan the area where the disturbance had occurred, his posture making it clear he considered the threat postponed rather than eliminated.

Dylan placed a hand on the Rottweiler's broad shoulder, feeling the residual energy of his Guardian transformation still humming beneath the surface. "Good job," he said quietly

Chapter 10: Archives and Answers

The journey to the Archives took them through parts of Dravengate that Dylan hadn't explored before. Leaving the central square behind, they followed Thorne and Rowan down narrower streets that wound away from the main thoroughfares, gradually ascending toward what appeared to be an older section of the town. The buildings here had a weathered quality, their stone facades covered in trailing vines and intricate carvings worn smooth by time.

Bruno remained vigilant throughout their walk, occasionally pausing to scan their surroundings, his enhanced senses alert for any hint of the disturbance they'd encountered at the Timewell. Dylan found himself grateful for the Rottweiler's protective presence, especially now that he'd seen firsthand the kind of threats that might be drawn to their work.

"The Archives weren't always hidden away like this," Rowan explained as they navigated the increasingly complex network of alleys and courtyards. "Before the Cataclysm, they were housed in a grand building at the heart of Dravengate, a repository of knowledge from all connected worlds, open to scholars and travellers alike."

"What happened to it?" Dylan asked, ducking under a low archway as they turned down a particularly narrow passage.

"Destroyed during the initial temporal shock waves," Thorne replied, his voice carrying a hint of old sorrow. "Many irreplaceable texts and artifacts were lost. What remains is what could be salvaged and relocated to the backup facilities, primarily records related to the crossing's maintenance and history."

They emerged into a small, secluded courtyard dominated by what appeared to be an ancient tree. Its trunk was massive, easily four meters in diameter, with bark the colour of burnished copper. Instead of spreading outward, its branches curved upward, forming a natural canopy that arched over the entire courtyard.

"The Archive Tree," Elara explained, seeing Dylan's wondering expression. "One of the oldest living things in Dravengate, and one of the few structures that survived the Cataclysm relatively intact."

"The tree is the Archives?" Dylan asked, confused.

Rowan smiled, her eyes lighting up with enthusiasm that transformed her usually serious expression. "Not exactly, but it's a good guess. The tree guards the entrance."

She approached the massive trunk and placed her palm against the coppery bark, closing her eyes briefly in what appeared to be a moment of concentration. The tree responded immediately, a vertical seam appearing in the previously solid surface, widening to reveal a doorway leading into the hollow interior.

"That's brilliant," Dylan said, genuinely impressed by the living security system.

"It only responds to those it recognizes," Thorne explained. "An inheritance from the days when Dravengate connected to worlds with less-than-friendly intentions. The tree remembers those it's granted access to, sometimes across generations."

"Will it recognize me?" Dylan asked, hesitating at the threshold.

"The wand grants you passage," Elara assured him. "As a potential Keeper, your access is guaranteed regardless of prior introduction."

Bruno showed no such hesitation, padding forward through the doorway ahead of the humans, his glowing eyes adjusting instantly to the dimmer light within. Dylan followed, with Rowan close behind him and Thorne and Elara bringing up the rear.

Inside, the tree's hollow core opened into a circular chamber much larger than should have been possible given the tree's external dimensions. Soft, amber light emanated from globes suspended from the curved ceiling, illuminating a space that blended natural and constructed elements seamlessly. The inner walls were lined with shelves that appeared to have grown directly from the living wood, each filled with books, scrolls, and strange objects that Dylan couldn't immediately identify.

"This is just the central hub," Rowan said, noting Dylan's awed expression. "The actual Archives extend underground, with specialized chambers for different categories of knowledge. This is where we catalogue and organize materials before storing them in their proper sections."

A large wooden table dominated the centre of the room, its surface inlaid with the same map of the crossing that Thorne had shown Dylan during their first meeting. Around it were arranged several chairs, each carved from the same coppery wood as the tree itself, with cushions of soft green fabric that looked surprisingly comfortable.

"Please, sit," Thorne invited, gesturing to the chairs. "After the excitement at the Timewell, a moment of rest before continuing would be advisable."

Dylan didn't argue, suddenly aware of the mental fatigue that had been building since their work with the sigil. The chair was indeed as comfortable as it looked, seeming to adjust subtly to accommodate his posture as he sat down. Bruno settled on the floor beside him, still alert but visibly more relaxed now that they were within the protected space of the Archives.

Rowan disappeared briefly into one of the side passages, returning moments later with a tray holding several steaming cups. "Restoration tea," she explained, placing the tray on the table. "Traditional remedy for temporal fatigue. Tastes terrible but works wonders."

She handed Dylan a cup of deep green liquid that smelled faintly of mint and something else he couldn't identify, something almost metallic. Their fingers brushed briefly during the exchange, and Dylan noticed Rowan's hand lingered a moment longer than strictly necessary before withdrawing.

"Fair warning," she added with a hint of amusement in her eyes, "it's an acquired taste. Best to drink it quickly rather than sip."

Taking her advice, Dylan downed the tea in three large gulps. The flavour was indeed unusual, bitter and sharp, with an aftertaste that reminded him oddly of the smell of old books. But the effect was almost immediate, a refreshing clarity washing through his mind, dispelling the fog of fatigue that had been gathering.

"That's... intense," he said, blinking as the sensation spread through his body.

"But effective," Rowan replied with satisfaction, finishing her own cup. "Traditional Keeper remedy. The plants it's made from only grow in areas with high temporal flux, absorbing and stabilizing the energy. When consumed, they transfer that stability to the drinker."

"Medicinal properties tied to magical conditions," Dylan observed. "That's fascinating."

"You should see our medical texts sometime," Rowan said, her expression brightening with scholarly enthusiasm. "Whole sections on chronobotany, plants that interact with temporal energy in ways your world's science would find impossible."

"I'd like that," Dylan replied honestly, finding her excitement contagious.

Elara and Thorne exchanged a brief glance, a subtle smile passing between them that Dylan didn't notice, his attention focused on

Rowan as she began describing some particularly unusual temporal plants.

"Before we delve into botanical curiosities," Thorne interjected gently, "perhaps we should address the more pressing matter of the void entity incursion."

"Right," Rowan said, straightening in her chair, her professional demeanour returning. "Sorry. I get carried away with the research aspects."

"It's fine," Dylan assured her, oddly disappointed by the shift back to business. "But yes, we should probably focus on the... what did you call them? Void entities?"

Thorne nodded, his expression grave. "Creatures from the spaces between realities. Not truly alive as we understand life, but conscious in their own way, drawn to disruptions in the normal fabric of existence."

"Like sharks sensing blood in water," Rowan added, her earlier enthusiasm replaced by serious focus.

"Precisely," Elara agreed. "The damage to the crossing creates a kind of... wound... in reality. The void entities are attracted to such wounds, feeding on the chaotic energy that leaks through."

"And they're intelligent?" Dylan asked, remembering how the shapes had seemed to retreat strategically rather than simply dissipating.

"In a manner of speaking," Thorne replied. "They possess a form of collective awareness rather than individual minds as we understand them. They can learn, adapt, and coordinate their actions toward common goals."

"Which makes them dangerous," Rowan concluded. "Especially when those goals conflict with our efforts to restore the crossing."

Dylan frowned, processing this information. "But why would they oppose restoration? If the crossing is repaired, wouldn't that close the 'wounds' they're feeding on?"

"That's exactly why they resist," Elara explained. "For centuries, they've been sustaining themselves on the energy leaking from the damaged crossing. Our efforts threaten their food source."

"It's not malice, exactly," Thorne added. "More like a preservation instinct. But the effect is the same, they will attempt to disrupt our work if they can."

Bruno made a soft growling sound, as if expressing his opinion on these entities. Dylan placed a hand on the Rottweiler's head, feeling the residual energy of his Guardian transformation still humming beneath the surface.

"They retreated when Bruno transformed," he observed. "Does that mean they're vulnerable to Guardian magic specifically?"

"Guardian energy directly counters void energy," Rowan confirmed, leaning forward with an intensity that Dylan was beginning to recognize as her default state when discussing technical matters. "It's one of the primary reasons Keepers have

Guardians, to shield them from void incursions during sensitive temporal work."

She rose from her chair and moved to one of the shelves, returning with a large, leather-bound volume that she placed on the table. Opening it to a marked page, she revealed an intricate illustration of what appeared to be a Guardian in feline form facing off against shadowy entities similar to what they'd witnessed at the Timewell.

"This is from Keeper Marwen's journals, approximately three hundred years ago," she explained. "One of the last documented major void incursions before today. Note how the Guardian's energy, represented by these gold lines, creates a barrier that the void entities cannot penetrate."

Dylan studied the illustration with interest. The artist had depicted the Guardian's protective energy as a network of golden lines forming a dome-like structure around a central figure he assumed was the Keeper, while the void entities appeared as amorphous shadows pressing against this barrier but unable to breach it.

"So, Bruno was creating a shield like this?" he asked, trying to reconcile the illustration with what he'd witnessed.

"In essence, yes," Thorne confirmed. "Though likely on a smaller scale, given that you're both still developing your connection. With practice, this protective capacity will grow stronger and more extensive."

"Which brings us to the next phase of your training," Elara said. "Now that we know the void entities are actively monitoring our work with the Timewell, you need to learn defensive techniques more quickly than we had originally planned."

Rowan closed the book and moved back to her chair, sitting down with a thoughtful expression. "I think we should start with the resonance barrier," she suggested to Thorne. "It's relatively simple but effective against minor incursions, and it builds naturally on the connection exercises they've already been practicing."

Thorne nodded in agreement. "A good place to begin. And perhaps also the temporal anchor technique, as a precaution in case they need to stabilize reality during a more significant disturbance."

For the next two hours, Dylan and Bruno practiced these defensive techniques under the careful guidance of their three mentors. The resonance barrier involved an extension of the connection exercises they'd already mastered, with Dylan and Bruno synchronizing their awareness to create a protective field around them both. The temporal anchor was more complex, a method for stabilizing a small area of reality against attempts to distort or disrupt it, essentially "locking" the natural flow of time in place temporarily.

Both techniques drew heavily on Dylan's mathematical mind. The resonance barrier required precise calculation of harmonics between his energy and Bruno's, while the temporal anchor involved what Rowan described as "differential temporal geometry", a concept that would have been incomprehensible to most but that Dylan found intuitively familiar, like a more complex version of calculus.

"You're picking this up remarkably quickly," Rowan observed after Dylan successfully created a small temporal anchor that stabilized a test object, a special crystal that normally pulsed with an erratic rhythm but that now maintained a steady, controlled pattern under the influence of his technique.

"It makes sense mathematically," Dylan explained, trying to articulate his intuitive grasp of the process. "It's like... solving four constants in a system of differential equations, except the variables include temporal coordinates as well as spatial ones."

Rowan's eyes lit up with unmistakable interest. "Exactly! That's precisely what's happening, though most Keepers conceptualize it more abstractly." She leaned closer, her enthusiasm evident. "Have you studied multivariable calculus formally, or is this intuitive for you?"

"Bit of both," Dylan admitted. "I've worked through some university-level texts on my own, but I also just... see patterns in things. It's hard to explain."

"You don't need to explain," she said with unexpected gentleness. "Some minds are simply attuned to certain types of patterns. It's a gift, especially for a Keeper."

There was something in her expression that Dylan couldn't quite interpret, an intensity beyond mere scholarly interest, but he wasn't sure what it signified. Before he could consider it further, Thorne cleared his throat, drawing their attention back to the training.

"While these defensive techniques are important," he said, "they are ultimately precautionary. Our primary focus remains the restoration of the Time sigil, which brings us to the next phase of preparation."

Elara nodded, rising from her seat. "We should show him the models," she suggested.

Thorne agreed, and they all followed as Elara led them deeper into the Archives, down a spiral staircase that descended below the tree's massive root system. The passage opened into a large circular chamber with a domed ceiling that mirrored the architecture of the Timewell above ground.

At the centre of this chamber stood a complex three-dimensional model of what Dylan immediately recognized as the Time sigil, rendered in metal and crystal with incredible detail. Unlike the actual sigil, which was partially visible only to those with temporal perception, this model made the entire structure visible in physical form.

"This is amazing," Dylan said, circling the model slowly, taking in its intricate construction. "It's exactly how the sigil appears to my perception, but... externalized."

"That's precisely the purpose," Rowan explained, stepping up beside him. "It allows us to study and plan interventions without directly interacting with the actual sigil. The model is magically linked to the Timewell, any changes in the real sigil are reflected here, allowing us to monitor its condition."

Dylan noticed coloured sections throughout the model, with damaged areas highlighted in red and stable sections in blue. The section they had worked with earlier that day glowed with a subtle golden light, indicating recent activity.

"We'll use this model to plan the restoration sequence," Thorne explained. "Working from the most stable areas outward toward the most severely damaged sections, rebuilding the connections in a precise order to maintain overall stability."

Time went on as they discussed the restoration plan in detail, with Rowan taking particular care to explain the mathematical principles underlying the sequence. Dylan found himself deeply engaged in these discussions, his mind readily grasping concepts that would have seemed impossibly abstract just days ago.

Bruno remained close throughout, occasionally offering his own form of input by directing attention to specific sections of the model with pointed looks or subtle gestures that Dylan was learning to interpret. His understanding of the sigil's structure seemed to operate on a different level than Dylan's, less analytical, more intuitive, but no less valid.

"Your Guardian perceives the energy flows directly," Elara observed, watching Bruno indicate a particular junction in the model with focused attention. "While you comprehend the mathematical structure, he senses the actual currents of power that flow through that structure."

"Together, you provide the perfect balance of precision and intuition required for the restoration," Thorne added. "Neither alone would be sufficient, but in combination, formidable."

As the planning session continued, Dylan became aware of Rowan's increasing proximity. She had begun the discussion maintaining a professional distance, but as they delved deeper into the mathematical complexities, she had gradually moved closer, occasionally brushing against him as they both pointed out features in the model. Dylan, focused entirely on the technical discussion, didn't register anything unusual about this, but Elara observed the dynamic with quiet amusement.

When they finally concluded the session, Dylan checked his watch and was surprised to find they had been in the Archives for nearly three hours. "I should probably head back soon," he said reluctantly. "My parents will be expecting me for tea."

"Of course," Thorne agreed. "You've made excellent progress today, both with the Timewell itself and in your defensive training. We'll continue in three days' time, if that suits your schedule?"

Dylan nodded, mentally checking his carefully planned Keeper Schedule. "Three days works. Same time?"

"Actually," Rowan interjected, "I was thinking we might start a bit earlier. There are some preliminary calculations I'd like to work through with you before we attempt the next phase with the sigil."

There was something in her tone, a slight hesitation, perhaps, that caught Dylan's attention, though he couldn't pinpoint why it seemed significant. "That's fine," he agreed. "I can adjust my schedule."

"Excellent," Thorne said. "Rowan will meet you at the bridge when you arrive and bring you directly to the Archives. The calculations she mentions are indeed important preparation for our next steps."

As they made their way back up to the main chamber, Rowan fell into step beside Dylan. "I'm really impressed with how quickly you're grasping these concepts," she said, her usual direct manner softened slightly. "Most apprentice Keepers struggle for months with principles you're mastering in days."

"It helps that I enjoy mathematics," Dylan replied simply. "This is just... a different application of patterns I already understand."

"Still," she insisted, "you have a natural aptitude that's rare. It's... refreshing to work with someone who thinks in similar ways."

There was something in her expression that Dylan couldn't quite interpret, a warmth beyond professional approval, but his limited experience with social cues left him uncertain of its meaning. He defaulted to his usual response when faced with ambiguous social situations: polite acknowledgment without presumption.

"Thanks," he said. "I'm enjoying learning all this. It's fascinating."

Rowan looked as if she might say something more, but they had reached the main chamber where Elara and Thorne were waiting. The moment passed, and she stepped back, resuming her more professional demeanour.

After brief farewells and confirmation of their next meeting time, Dylan prepared to open the portal back to Blackpool. Creating the gateway had become almost effortless now, a simple matter of focused visualization channelled through the wand. As the swirling portal formed, he turned to thank his mentors once more.

"Before you go," Rowan said suddenly, stepping forward. "Here," She handed him a small leather-bound book. "Some additional notes on the temporal mathematics we discussed. I thought you might find them interesting."

Dylan accepted the book with genuine appreciation. "Thanks. I'll definitely read through this."

"I've added some of my own annotations," she continued, a hint of colour appearing in her cheeks. "Questions and observations that... well, I thought you might have unique insights on."

"I'll let you know what I think," Dylan promised, tucking the book carefully into his backpack.

With a final nod to everyone, he stepped through the portal with Bruno at his side. The transition between worlds was now familiar, almost comfortable, and then they were standing once again between the dunes on Blackpool's shore, the sound of waves replacing the quiet ambience of the Archives.

As always, Bruno shook himself, his form returning to normal, eyes shifting from glowing amber back to their usual warm brown. Dylan took a moment to reorient himself to his home reality, the mathematical complexities of temporal magic still swirling in his mind.

The walk home gave him time to process everything that had happened, their work with the Timewell, the encounter with the void entities, the defensive techniques they'd practiced, and the detailed planning for the sigil restoration. It was a lot to absorb, yet he found his mind readily organizing it all into coherent patterns that made sense within his established understanding of the world.

Bruno trotted beside him, outwardly just an ordinary dog again but with that new awareness between them that persisted even in this world. Dylan found comfort in their strengthened connection, especially after witnessing how effectively Bruno had responded to the potential threat at the Timewell.

When they arrived home, Dylan's mum was in the kitchen preparing tea, the familiar scent of her specialty chicken curry filling the house. She looked up with a smile as Dylan and Bruno came in.

"Good walk?" she asked. "You were gone quite a while."

"Yeah, it was good," Dylan replied, settling into the practiced rhythm of these conversations. "We went all the way up the north shore. Bruno had a brilliant time chasing seagulls."

The Rottweiler, hearing his name, padded over to Sam for his customary ear scratch, playing his part in their domestic routine with perfect naturalness.

The Keeper of Time

"Mally called," she said as she stirred the curry. "He's running late at the shop, some special delivery of vintage vinyl that needs cataloguing. Said not to hold tea, he'll grab something there."

Dylan nodded, heading upstairs to wash up before tea. In his room, he carefully placed his backpack on the bed and removed Rowan's book, examining it more closely now that he had privacy.

It was small but densely packed with information, the pages covered in neat handwriting with different coloured inks indicating various levels of notes and annotations. Flipping through it briefly, he could see that the content was indeed focused on temporal mathematics, but with a particular emphasis on the theoretical underpinnings rather than just practical applications.

What caught his attention, though, were Rowan's personal annotations in the margins. Unlike the main text, which was formal and academic, these notes were conversational, almost as if she were having a dialogue with the original author, and, by extension, with Dylan as the new reader.

"These explanations overcomplicated," one note read beside a particularly dense paragraph. "Think of it as nested frequencies rather than layered dimensions." Another, beside a diagram of temporal flow patterns: "Reminds me of Fibonacci spirals in nature, wonder if Dylan would see the same connection?"

The direct reference to him was surprising. Clearly, she had prepared this book specifically with him in mind, tailoring her comments to what she anticipated would interest or resonate with him. It was thoughtful in a way that went beyond mere professional courtesy.

Dylan wasn't sure what to make of this. His experience with friendship was limited, and romance was an even more bewildering territory that he generally avoided due to the complex and often unspoken social rules involved. Was Rowan simply being a dedicated mentor? Or was there something more to her attention?

Bruno, who had followed him upstairs, nudged his hand with his nose, as if sensing his confusion.

"What do you think, boy?" Dylan asked quietly. "Is she just being helpful, or is it something else?"

Bruno tilted his head, those brown eyes somehow conveying both wisdom and amusement, but offering no clear answer to Dylan's question.

With a slight shrug, Dylan set the book aside for later study. Regardless of Rowan's intentions, the material itself would be valuable for his training, and that was what mattered most at the moment. The rest, the social complexities, the potential meanings behind certain looks or gestures, could wait until he had more data to analyse.

"Tea!!" his mum called up, tea was ready, and Dylan headed back downstairs, Bruno following faithfully behind. As they sat down to eat, Dylan found his thoughts alternating between the mathematical challenges of sigil restoration and the unexpected puzzle of human interaction that Rowan presented.

Oddly enough, between the two, it was the latter that seemed more daunting to decode.

Chapter 11: Calculations and Connections

The next three days passed in a carefully structured rhythm that Dylan found both productive and comforting. His Keeper Schedule was working brilliantly. The schedule now included a new green block specifically for studying Rowan's book, which he found himself returning to with increasing interest.

The book itself was fascinating, not just for its content on temporal mathematics, which was challenging even for Dylan's advanced understanding, but for the insights it provided into Rowan's thinking. Her annotations revealed a mind that approached problems from unexpected angles, making connections that were both creative and logically sound. More than once, Dylan found himself reaching for a pencil to add his own comments in response to her questions, before remembering this wasn't his book to write in.

"She thinks differently," he told Bruno during an evening study session. "Not like Thorne or Elara, they see patterns, but they follow established rules. Rowan questions everything, looks for exceptions, finds new approaches."

Bruno, lying on the rug beside Dylan's desk, made a soft huffing sound that might have been an agreement. The Rottweiler had taken to positioning himself strategically during these study sessions, sometimes beside Dylan, sometimes by the door, as if maintaining a subtle protective perimeter even in the safety of their home.

The day before their scheduled return to Dravengate, Dylan received an unexpected text message on his phone. The number was unfamiliar, but the content immediately identified the sender:

"Found another reference to nested temporal frequencies in the eastern archives. Matches your observation about harmonic resonance. Thought you'd find it interesting. See you tomorrow. - R"

Dylan stared at the message in confusion. How had Rowan, presumably the "R", gotten his phone number? And more importantly, how was she texting him from Dravengate? He hadn't thought the magical realm had anything resembling mobile phone technology.

After considering for a moment, he typed a reply:

"How are you texting me from Dravengate?"

The response came almost immediately:

"Not in Dravengate. Working in a connected research station in your world. Part of my apprenticeship involves fieldwork in adjacent realms."

This was surprising new information. Dylan hadn't considered that people from Dravengate might regularly cross over to his world for research purposes. The implications were fascinating, how many others might be here, moving among ordinary people while studying aspects of this reality?

"Where exactly are you?" he texted back.

"UCL Library, special collections. Ancient texts section. Keeper apprentices have maintained a research presence in your academic institutions for centuries."

Dylan smiled at the thought of magical researchers from another realm quietly working alongside oblivious university professors and students. It made sense as a strategy, where better to hide unusual research than in institutions already dedicated to pursuing obscure knowledge?

"That's brilliant," he replied. "How long have you been doing fieldwork here?"

"Two years. Mostly London, occasionally Edinburgh. Usually work with Thorne, but he's busy with crossing maintenance."

Their text conversation continued for nearly an hour, with Rowan explaining more about how Dravengate maintained connections to key locations in Dylan's world despite the damaged crossing. These connections were narrow and specific, focused on places with high concentrations of historical and scientific knowledge, universities, libraries, research centres.

"Think of them as specialized capillaries rather than major arteries," Rowan explained. "Limited but functional."

Eventually, their conversation turned back to the temporal mathematics they'd been discussing at the Archives. Dylan found it remarkably easy to communicate with Rowan in this text-based format, without the complications of interpreting facial expressions or tone of voice, he could focus entirely on the exchange of ideas. He surprised himself by how much he enjoyed their back-and-forth, losing track of time until Bruno nudged his leg, reminding him of the time.

"Have to go, tea time," he texted reluctantly.

"Of course. See you at 9am your time tomorrow. Bridge as planned."

Dylan put his phone away with an odd sense of anticipation for tomorrow's session that went beyond the usual excitement about his Keeper training. There was something about Rowan's direct communication style and sharp intelligence that resonated with him in a way he wasn't entirely familiar with.

The next morning dawned bright and clear, a rare perfect summer day in Blackpool. Dylan woke earlier than usual, spending extra time organizing his backpack and checking that he had everything he might need for what would likely be a full day in Dravengate. Along with his usual supplies, he packed a notebook with questions and observations from his study of Rowan's book, thinking she might appreciate his perspectives.

"Going for another walk?" his mum asked as Dylan and Bruno prepared to leave after breakfast.

"Yeah," Dylan replied, trying to sound casual. "Thought we'd explore a bit further up the coast today. There's some interesting geology north of the main beach."

Sam smiled, seeming pleased by his continued interest in outdoor activities. "That's wonderful, love. You've been so active this summer, it's good to see you getting out more."

There was a moment of guilt as Dylan recognized the irony, his mum was happy because she thought he was becoming more engaged with the ordinary world, when in fact he was spending increasing amounts of time in an entirely different reality. But he consoled himself with the knowledge that he was maintaining a good balance between his responsibilities, just as his Keeper Schedule dictated.

"We might be gone most of the day," he added. "I've packed lunch."

"That's fine. Just be back for tea, Mally's sister is visiting, remember? She's dying to see how much you've grown since Christmas."

Dylan had completely forgotten about his aunt's planned visit, and he quickly recalculated his timing. "Right, yes. I'll definitely be back by six."

With promises made, Dylan and Bruno set off for their usual portal spot between the dunes. The morning was quiet, with few people about despite the perfect weather, most tourists would arrive later, once the shops and attractions opened.

Creating the portal had become almost automatic now, a simple matter of focused intent channelled through the wand. As the swirling gateway formed, Dylan felt the now-familiar anticipation of crossing between worlds, a mixture of excitement and scientific curiosity that never seemed to diminish no matter how many times he made the journey.

They stepped through together, the disorientation of transit lasting only moments before they emerged on the other side. As always, Dravengate's atmosphere enveloped them immediately, the quality of light different, the air carrying scents that had no equivalent in Dylan's world. Bruno underwent his subtle transformation, his form enhancing as his Guardian nature expressed itself fully in this realm.

As promised, Rowan was waiting for them at the foot of the stone bridge, though not alone. Beside her stood a figure Dylan hadn't met before, a young man perhaps a few years older than Rowan, dressed in what appeared to be a uniform of sorts, with a distinctive insignia on his shoulder that resembled a stylized shield.

"Right on time," Rowan said by way of greeting, her direct manner unchanged from their previous interactions. "Dylan, this is Lysander. He's Captain of the Guardian Division, essentially Dravengate's protective forces."

Lysander stepped forward, extending a hand in the same gesture from Dylan's world that Rowan had used during their first meeting. He was tall and broad-shouldered, with close-cropped dark hair and alert eyes that immediately assessed Bruno with professional interest.

"You're the new Keeper candidate, right?" he said as they shook hands, his voice carrying a faint accent Dylan couldn't place. "Thorne has spoken highly of your progress."

"Thanks," Dylan replied, not entirely sure how to respond to this unexpected introduction. "This is Bruno, my Guardian," he added, feeling it important to acknowledge Bruno's role formally.

Lysander's attention shifted fully to Bruno, his expression changing from polite interest to focused assessment. "A canine form," he observed. "Unusual in recent centuries, but historically significant. The First Keeper's Guardian manifested as a wolf, according to the oldest records."

Bruno met Lysander's gaze steadily, neither challenging nor submissive, his glowing eyes reflecting a quiet confidence in his role. After a moment of this mutual assessment, Lysander nodded as if coming to a decision.

"May I?" he asked Dylan, gesturing toward Bruno.

Understanding that he was asking permission to examine Bruno more closely, Dylan nodded, though he looked to Bruno for confirmation as well. The Rottweiler moved forward slightly, indicating his acceptance of the scrutiny.

Lysander crouched, bringing himself to eye level with Bruno. He didn't touch the dog, but instead extended his hand palm up, just short of physical contact. For a moment, nothing seemed to happen, then Dylan perceived a subtle shift in the energy between them, a resonance similar to what he'd been practicing in their connection exercises, but with a different quality.

"Remarkable strength," Lysander commented, rising back to his full height. "The bond between you is developing exceptionally well for such a new pairing." He turned to Rowan with a nod. "Your assessment was accurate. They're advancing far more quickly than projected."

Rowan's expression brightened with what might have been pride, though whether for the accuracy of her assessment or for Dylan and Bruno's progress wasn't clear. "Told you," she said simply. "Mathematical aptitude correlates strongly with temporal synchronization capacity."

Dylan glanced between them, feeling slightly excluded from a conversation that was clearly about him. "Sorry, but why exactly are you evaluating us?" he asked Lysander directly.

"Apologies," Lysander replied. "I should have explained. After the void entity incursion at the Timewell, Thorne requested a Guardian Division assessment of your defensive capabilities. Standard protocol when a new Keeper pair encounters hostile entities."

"And?" Dylan prompted when Lysander didn't immediately continue.

"And I'm impressed," Lysander said with surprising candor. "Most Guardians take months to develop the level of protective resonance your Bruno demonstrated during that encounter. It suggests either exceptional natural aptitude or..." he paused, glancing at Rowan.

"Or previous experience," Rowan finished for him, her expression thoughtful. "Which raises interesting questions about Bruno's origins."

Dylan frowned. "Bruno's just a normal dog from my world. My stepdad got him as a puppy from a breeder in Manchester."

"Perhaps in form," Lysander acknowledged. "But Guardians have ways of finding their Keepers across worlds and lifetimes. Sometimes they're drawn to potential Keepers long before either is aware of their true nature."

This was a new and somewhat startling concept. Dylan had been thinking of Bruno's Guardian nature as something activated by their connection to Dravengate, not as an inherent quality that might have drawn them together in the first place.

"You're suggesting Bruno somehow chose us? Even as a puppy?" he asked sceptically.

"It's not a conscious choice as you might understand it," Lysander explained. "More like... magnetic attraction. Certain souls are drawn to each other across time and space, particularly those with complementary magical signatures."

Dylan wasn't entirely comfortable with this slightly mystical explanation, preferring the more concrete mathematical frameworks that Thorne and Rowan typically used. But Bruno seemed untroubled by the theory, his posture relaxed as he watched Lysander with what appeared to be agreement.

"Regardless of how you came together," Lysander continued, "what matters now is that your bond is strong and developing rapidly. Which brings me to the second reason for my presence today." He reached into a small pouch at his belt and withdrew what appeared to be a medallion of some kind, cast in bronze with intricate symbols etched into its surface.

"This is a Guardian Marker," he explained, holding it out for Dylan to see. "It serves both as identification and as a focus for certain protective enchantments. All registered Guardian pairs carry one, it allows access to secure areas of Dravengate and serves as a distress signal in emergencies."

He handed the medallion to Dylan, who examined it with interest. The symbols around its edge reminded him of the markings on the Timewell, though simplified, and at its centre was an emblem that combined elements reminiscent of both a clock face and a shield.

"Thank you," Dylan said, not entirely sure of the protocol for receiving such an item. "Should I... wear it, or...?"

"It's for Bruno, actually," Rowan interjected, a hint of amusement in her voice. "Usually attached to a collar or harness."

"Most Guardians manifest in forms that can wear it more conventionally," Lysander added with a slight smile. "But we've adapted for canine Guardians before."

From another pouch, he produced a simple leather collar with a mounting bracket clearly designed to hold the medallion.

"This will adjust to fit comfortably," he explained. "And the medallion will bond to Bruno's energy signature once placed."

Dylan looked to Bruno for approval, unwilling to make such a decision without his Guardian's acceptance. Bruno stepped forward, head held high, clearly understanding the significance of the moment. With careful movements, Dylan removed Bruno's ordinary collar, a simple blue nylon band with a tag bearing his name and their home address, and replaced it with the leather one Lysander had provided.

The moment he attached the medallion to its bracket, there was a brief flash of golden light as the metal seemed to meld seamlessly with the leather. Bruno stood very still during this process; his glowing eyes fixed on Lysander as if participating in some unspoken ritual.

"It is done," Lysander said formally. "Bruno is now officially recognized as an active Guardian within the Dravengate registry. This grants certain protections and responsibilities under our ancient codes."

The medallion now appeared as if it had always been part of the collar, its bronze surface gleaming with a subtle inner light that matched the glow of Bruno's eyes. Dylan felt a surge of pride mixed with a deepening sense of responsibility. This was another step toward accepting his role as Keeper, not just as a temporary arrangement but as a fundamental part of his identity.

"Now," Rowan said, breaking the solemnity of the moment with her characteristic directness, "we should get to the Archives.

We have calculations to complete before the preliminary sigil work this afternoon."

"Of course," Lysander agreed. "I've taken enough of your time. I'll report my assessment to Thorne, he'll be pleased with your progress." He turned to Bruno, offering a formal bow that seemed remarkably natural despite being directed at a dog. "Guardian Bruno, may your watch be vigilant."

Bruno responded with what could only be described as a dignified nod, completing the formal exchange. With a final nod to Dylan and Rowan, Lysander departed, heading back across the bridge toward the centre of Dravengate.

"Well," Dylan said after a moment, still processing the unexpected ceremony, "that was... official."

"Lysander takes the traditions seriously," Rowan replied as they began walking toward the Archive Tree. "The Guardian Division is one of the oldest institutions in Dravengate, they maintain protocols that predate the Cataclysm."

"Is he always so formal?" Dylan asked.

"Only for official functions," Rowan said with a slight smile. "He's actually quite different when off duty. Terrible sense of humour, ridiculous sweet tooth, unbeatable at strategic board games."

There was something in her tone, a familiarity that suggested more than casual acquaintance. "You know him well?" Dylan found himself asking.

"We grew up together," Rowan explained. "His family and mine have both served Dravengate for generations, his as Guardians, mine as Archivists. We used to get into all sorts of trouble exploring the old ruins as children."

Dylan tried to imagine Rowan as a child, scrambling through ancient structures with a young Lysander. The image was both amusing and somehow poignant, a reminder that Dravengate was more than just a magical realm he visited; it was home to people with their own histories and connections.

"Did you always know you'd be an Archivist?" he asked as they continued toward their destination.

"Pretty much," Rowan replied. "The aptitude runs in families, generally. My mother was Lead Archivist before the accident that... well, before she passed. My father works in the Boundary Division, they monitor the remaining stable connections to other worlds."

There was a brief shadow across her expression at the mention of her mother, quickly controlled but not before Dylan noticed it. He wasn't always adept at reading emotional cues, but this one seemed clear enough.

"I'm sorry about your mother," he said quietly.

Rowan glanced at him, seeming surprised by his perception. "Thank you," she said after a moment. "It was five years ago. A research expedition to an unstable sector of the crossing. There was a temporal surge that no one anticipated."

She fell silent for a few steps, then continued with deliberate lightness, "Anyway, that's partly why I'm so focused on the restoration work. The crossing's instability affects everything in Dravengate, including research safety protocols."

Dylan nodded, understanding more about her dedication now. It wasn't just academic interest driving her involvement, there were personal stakes as well. He found himself wanting to offer some comfort but unsure how, so he defaulted to his strength: practical engagement with the task at hand.

"You mentioned calculations we need to complete before the sigil work?" he prompted gently.

Rowan seemed grateful for the shift back to their mission. "Yes, critically important ones. We need to model the resonance patterns for the first section of the restoration sequence. I've been working on the base equations, but I need your perspective on the multidimensional aspects."

By the time they reached the Archive Tree, they were deep in discussion about temporal wave functions and harmonic coefficients, the brief moment of personal connection giving way to shared intellectual engagement. Bruno padded beside them, his new medallion gleaming in the morning light, occasionally joining their conversation with meaningful looks or subtle gestures that Dylan was becoming increasingly adept at interpreting.

The tree recognized Rowan immediately, the vertical seam appearing in its coppery bark to grant them access to the hollow interior. Inside, the Archives were quieter than during their previous visit, with no sign of Thorne or Elara.

"They're preparing at the Timewell," Rowan explained, seeing Dylan's questioning look. "Setting up the protective perimeter and specialized monitoring equipment. We'll join them this afternoon once our calculations are complete."

She led them to a different area of the Archives than they'd worked in before, a small chamber off the main room that appeared to be a dedicated workspace. A large table dominated the centre, covered with papers, open books, and what looked like mechanical calculating devices of intricate design. Crystal globes suspended from the ceiling provided bright, clear light perfect for detailed work.

"My personal research space," Rowan explained with a hint of self-consciousness. "It's a bit chaotic, but there's an order to it, I promise."

Dylan surveyed the apparent disorder and immediately recognized the underlying system, materials grouped by subject, with current projects positioned for easiest access, reference materials arrayed in a semicircle within arm's reach. It was exactly how he would have organized his own workspace given similar resources.

"It makes perfect sense," he said honestly. "Very efficient arrangement."

Rowan looked surprised, then pleased. "Most people just see the mess," she admitted. "Thorne is always telling me to 'establish a more coherent organizational protocol.'" Her imitation of Thorne's formal speaking style was affectionate rather than mocking.

"It is organized," Dylan insisted. "Just not in a way that's immediately obvious to others."

"Exactly!" Rowan exclaimed, with more enthusiasm than the observation might normally warrant. "The arrangement reflects the connections between concepts, not arbitrary categories."

There was a moment of shared understanding between them, the recognition of a kindred approach to information management that went beyond conventional systems. Dylan felt an unexpected warmth at this connection, a sense that Rowan truly understood an aspect of his thinking that many found peculiar or difficult to follow.

Bruno settled himself near the door, assuming his now-familiar guardian position while remaining attentive to their work. His new medallion seemed to enhance his presence somehow, the bronze catching and reflecting the crystal light in subtle patterns across the room.

For the next several hours, Dylan and Rowan worked through the complex calculations necessary for the first phase of sigil restoration. The work was challenging even for Dylan's mathematical abilities, involving systems of equations that operated in more dimensions than could be easily visualized. Rowan had developed a specialized notation system to help manage these complexities, which Dylan quickly adapted to his own understanding.

They fell into a productive rhythm, with Rowan focusing on the theoretical frameworks while Dylan applied his pattern recognition skills to identify efficient solution paths. Their collaboration was remarkably smooth, each anticipating the other's needs without extensive explanation, passing calculations back and forth with minimal verbal communication needed.

"It's like you're reading my mind," Rowan commented during a brief break, looking up from a particularly complex set of equations they'd just solved together.

"Not really," Dylan replied, taking her comment literally. "I'm just following the logical progression of the work. When you're approaching a problem from a specific angle, there are only so many optimal paths forward."

Instead of being put off by his literal interpretation, Rowan smiled. "That's exactly it, though. Most people don't see those optimal paths, they get distracted by conventional approaches or secondary considerations. You cut straight to the mathematical core."

There was genuine admiration in her voice, and something else, a warmth that seemed to go beyond professional appreciation. Dylan wasn't entirely sure how to respond to this, so he focused on the practical aspects of their success.

"We make a good team," he offered. "Your theoretical framework is brilliant, and I can help find the most efficient solutions within it."

"We do, don't we?" Rowan agreed, her smile widening. "I haven't worked this effectively with anyone since..." she hesitated, then finished, "well, ever, actually."

There was a brief, charged moment of silence between them, broken when Bruno rose suddenly from his position by the door, ears alert, attention focused outward toward the main chamber of the Archives.

"Someone's coming," Rowan said, also noticing the change in Bruno's demeanour. "Probably Thorne checking on our progress."

But it wasn't Thorne who appeared in the doorway a moment later, but Elara, her expression more serious than usual. "We have a situation," she said without preamble. "The void incursion wasn't an isolated event. There have been three more attempts at different points around Dravengate in the past hour."

Rowan was immediately on her feet. "Coordinated probes?"

"It appears so," Elara confirmed. "Lysander's division has contained them, but they're growing bolder. And more concerning, they seem to be targeting locations along the restoration sequence path we've been planning."

"They know," Rowan breathed, the implications sinking in. "Somehow they've discovered our restoration plans."

Dylan stood as well, Bruno moving to his side, the Rottweiler's posture shifting to alert readiness, the medallion on his collar glowing with increased intensity. "How would they know?" he asked. "I thought void entities couldn't access this realm directly except through instabilities in the crossing."

"They shouldn't be able to," Elara agreed, her brow furrowed with concern. "Which suggests either the crossing is more compromised than we realized, or..."

"Or they have help," Rowan finished grimly. "Someone in Dravengate working against the restoration."

The idea that there might be deliberate sabotage from within Dravengate itself added a new and troubling dimension to their challenges. Dylan had been thinking of the void entities as external threats, strange forces from between dimensions drawn to the damaged crossing. The possibility of internal opposition, of someone actively working to prevent their efforts, was something he hadn't considered.

"What does this mean for today's work?" he asked, trying to focus on the immediate implications.

"Thorne wants to proceed, but with enhanced security," Elara replied. "Lysander is arranging a protective detail for the Timewell. The preliminary activation of the first restoration segment is too important to delay, especially if opposition is organizing."

"Our calculations are nearly complete," Rowan reported, gathering the most critical papers from their workspace. "We've mapped the resonance patterns for the initial sequence and identified the optimal harmonization approach."

"Good," Elara said with a nod of approval. "Bring everything to the Timewell. We'll need to adapt the procedure to account for the increased security presence, but the fundamental approach remains valid."

As they prepared to leave, Dylan felt a curious mixture of excitement and apprehension. The stakes of their work had suddenly become more immediate, the opposition more concrete. Bruno seemed to sense his mood, pressing against his leg briefly in that reassuring way that had become so familiar.

"Ready?" Rowan asked, her arms full of their calculation sheets and reference materials.

Dylan nodded, reaching out to take some of the papers from her before they could slip from her grasp. Their hands brushed in the exchange, and for a moment, Rowan's fingers lingered against his, the contact brief but deliberate. Her eyes met his with an expression he couldn't quite interpret, concern mixed with something warmer, more personal.

"We'll be fine," she said quietly. "Your Guardian is stronger than they anticipated, and our calculations are solid. They won't stop us."

There was a confidence in her voice that Dylan found reassuring, not just in her assessment of their chances but in her apparent faith in his abilities. With Bruno at his side and the wand securely in his pocket, he followed Rowan and Elara out of the Archives and toward what would be their first major test as Keeper and Guardian, not just against the technical challenges of sigil restoration, but against active opposition from forces that preferred the crossing remain broken.

The afternoon promised to be far more eventful than their careful planning had anticipated.

Chapter 12: The First Restoration

The Timewell plaza had been transformed since Dylan's last visit. A perimeter of glittering silver-blue energy now encircled the ancient structure, maintained by Guardian Division members standing at regular intervals around its circumference. Each carried a staff tipped with a crystal that matched the energy barrier's hue.

Lysander himself stood at the entrance to the perimeter, his posture alert but controlled as he directed the security operations. He nodded in greeting as Dylan, Bruno, and the others approached.

"The protective boundary is established," Lysander reported. "We've created a temporal isolation field that should mask our activities from outside perception."

"Should?" Rowan questioned; her directness undiminished by the formal atmosphere.

"No security measure is absolute," Lysander acknowledged with a slight grimace. "Especially where void entities are concerned. They perceive reality differently, looking for inconsistencies, gaps in the normal flow of time."

"But this will make their job harder," Elara interjected, her tone reassuring. "Which is all we need for this initial phase."

Dylan studied the barrier with interest, extending his temporal perception to understand its structure. It was unlike anything he'd encountered in his training so far, a complex weave of energies that seemed to fold time back on itself.

"It's like... temporal camouflage," he observed. "Instead of blocking observation completely, it creates a pattern that looks unremarkable from outside."

Lysander looked impressed. "Precisely. Most defensive measures establish solid barriers, which paradoxically make them more noticeable to entities that hunt for anomalies. This approach is subtler."

Bruno examined the barrier as well, his glowing eyes tracking the energy patterns. The medallion at his collar seemed to resonate slightly with the boundary, pulsing with the same silvery-blue light.

"Your Guardian's medallion is synchronized with our security field," Lysander explained. "It grants you both passage while maintaining the field's integrity."

He gestured toward the perimeter, and Dylan felt a subtle shift in the energy flowing from Bruno's medallion. "You may proceed when ready. Thorne awaits you at the Timewell."

As they approached the barrier, Dylan felt a moment of resistance, like walking through heavy curtains, before the energy parted to allow them passage. Bruno experienced no such resistance, the medallion creating a perfect synchronization that allowed him to move through as if the barrier weren't there.

Inside the perimeter, the Timewell stood as before, but with significant additions surrounding it. Monitoring equipment was arranged in a precise pattern around the circular platform, each device humming with quiet energy. Thorne moved between these instruments, making careful adjustments and noting readings.

He looked up as they approached, his expression both serious and expectant. "Ah, good. You've arrived. Did you complete the resonance calculations?"

Rowan nodded, holding up the sheaf of papers they'd brought. "Full harmonic mapping for the primary node and connecting filaments. We've identified the optimal frequency progressions for the stabilization sequence."

Thorne accepted the papers, scanning them quickly. "Excellent work. The approach is elegant, simpler than I had anticipated."

"That was Dylan's contribution," Rowan said with unmistakable pride. "He found a unified pattern underlying what we thought were separate harmonic sequences. It reduced the complexity by nearly forty percent."

Dylan felt a flush of pleasure at the recognition, though he tried to downplay it. "It was just a matter of viewing the system differently. The underlying mathematics were already there in Rowan's theoretical framework."

Thorne glanced between them with a subtle smile before returning to business. "This simplified approach may be a significant advantage. A more streamlined procedure leaves less opportunity for disruption."

He gestured for them to follow him onto the Timewell platform, where additional preparations had been made. An intricate pattern had been traced on the stone surface using luminescent powder that glowed with a soft golden light. The pattern corresponded to the mathematical model they had been working with, a physical representation of the temporal resonance they hoped to establish.

"The resonance diagram will help focus and direct the energies," Thorne explained as they carefully stepped over the pattern. "It provides additional structure for this first attempt."

At the centre of the platform, the silver substance in the Timewell's basin moved in its usual hypnotic patterns, but Dylan noticed subtle changes from his previous observations. The flow seemed more purposeful, as if responding to their presence and preparations.

"It senses what we intend," Elara said quietly, noticing Dylan's focused attention. "The sigil may be dormant, but it retains awareness of its purpose. On some level, it wants to be restored."

This was a new perspective, the idea that the magical constructs they were working with might possess a form of consciousness. Dylan found the concept both fascinating and slightly unsettling.

"Not in the way you're thinking," Elara added, seeming to read his concerns. "It's not independently sentient, but responsive to its intended function. Like a plant turning toward sunlight, it naturally orients toward restoration of proper temporal flow."

Bruno moved to the edge of the central basin, studying the swirling silver substance with intense focus. His medallion glowed more brightly in proximity to the Timewell, creating a visual harmony between Guardian and sigil that seemed to stabilize the surrounding energies.

"Your Guardian recognizes his role in this," Thorne observed. "The medallion is enhancing his natural protective capacity, creating a buffer zone that will help isolate our work from outside interference."

Dylan nodded, feeling a surge of pride in Bruno's evident competence. From ordinary dog to magical guardian, Bruno had adapted to each new development with remarkable ease, as if he had always been meant for this role.

"So," Dylan said, focusing on the task at hand, "what exactly am I doing in this first restoration phase? The calculations give us the patterns, but how do I implement them?"

"This is where theory meets practice," Thorne replied. "The wand will channel your intent, but you must visualize the patterns with absolute clarity."

"Think of it like a musical score," Rowan suggested, stepping closer to Dylan. "The calculations provide the notes, but you're the conductor who brings them to life, setting the tempo, emphasizing certain elements, creating the overall interpretation."

This analogy helped, giving Dylan a framework he could understand. He'd never been particularly musical himself, but he understood the mathematical relationships between notes, the patterns and progressions that created harmony.

"Where do I start?" he asked, removing the wand from his pocket. As always, it warmed to his touch, responding to his intention even before he consciously directed it.

"Here," Thorne said, indicating a specific section of the Timewell's basin. "This is the most stable node in the sigil's current structure, the point from which the restoration should emanate outward."

Dylan positioned himself as directed, with Bruno settling beside him, their bodies aligned with the golden pattern traced on the platform. Rowan moved to a monitoring station a few feet away, while Elara and Thorne took positions at other points around the basin, ready to provide support if needed.

"Begin by establishing connection with the sigil," Thorne instructed. "As you did during our test session, but deeper, not just observing, but actively engaging with its patterns."

Taking a deep breath, Dylan raised the wand and focused his perception on the swirling silver substance before him. With his now-practiced temporal sense, he could perceive the complex geometry beneath the surface movement, the true form of the sigil, currently fragmented and dormant but still retaining its essential structure.

The Keeper of Time

He focused on the node Thorne had indicated, extending his awareness into its patterns, feeling the subtle rhythms and harmonics that defined its current state. The wand grew warmer in his hand, channelling his perception and amplifying his connection to the sigil.

"Good," Elara murmured, her voice sounding oddly distant as Dylan's consciousness became increasingly immersed in the temporal patterns. "Now, introduce the first harmonic sequence from your calculations. Start slowly, allowing the sigil to recognize and respond to the pattern."

Dylan visualized the mathematical progression they had developed, focusing on the primary frequency that would serve as the foundation for the restoration. The wand pulsed in his hand, transmitting this pattern to the sigil with precision that would have been impossible through physical manipulation alone.

For a moment, nothing seemed to happen. Then, gradually, the silver substance began to respond, its swirling patterns shifting subtly to align with the frequency Dylan was projecting. The node at the centre of his focus began to glow with a faint golden light, similar to the pattern traced on the platform but emerging from within the sigil itself.

"Excellent," Thorne said softly. "The sigil is accepting the harmonic. Now, begin the progressive expansion as planned, extending the pattern to the connecting filaments."

This was the more complex part of the procedure. Dylan needed to maintain the primary harmonic while simultaneously introducing additional frequencies that would extend the restoration effect to surrounding areas. It required a level of mental multitasking that would have been challenging under any circumstances, but was particularly demanding given the precise mathematical relationships involved.

Bruno pressed closer against his leg, and Dylan felt a surge of supportive energy flowing from the Guardian. The medallion at Bruno's collar pulsed in rhythm with the sigil's response, creating a resonance that amplified Dylan's ability to maintain multiple patterns simultaneously.

"The Guardian is enhancing his capacity," Elara observed with approval. "This is exactly the synergy we hoped to see."

With Bruno's support, Dylan was able to extend the harmonic pattern as planned, carefully introducing each new frequency in the precise sequence they had calculated. The golden glow within the sigil spread accordingly, flowing outward from the central node along pathways that corresponded exactly to their mathematical model.

"Readings are stable," Rowan reported from her monitoring station. "Temporal coherence is increasing in the target sectors. No sign of disruption or resistance."

Dylan maintained his focus, guided by the calculations but increasingly relying on intuition as he sensed how the sigil responded to each adjustment. It was like a conversation of sorts, he introduced a pattern, the sigil responded, and that response informed his next adjustment. The wand seemed to facilitate this exchange, acting as translator between his intent and the sigil's ancient magic.

As the restoration pattern extended further, Dylan became aware of a growing warmth throughout his body, not uncomfortable, but noticeable. It was as if the energy flowing through the wand was resonating with something within him, awakening an aspect of his being that had been dormant until now.

"Your Keeper essence is activating," Thorne explained, noticing the subtle glow that had begun to emanate from Dylan's skin. "The sigil recognizes you now, not just the wand, but you personally as its caretaker."

This was an unexpected development, though not an unwelcome one. Dylan could feel the connection strengthening, his awareness of the sigil's patterns becoming clearer, more intuitive. What had required careful calculation and conscious effort before now flowed more naturally, as if he were remembering rather than learning.

The restoration continued to progress, the golden glow spreading through approximately a quarter of the sigil's structure, exactly the section they had targeted for this initial phase. As the final connections stabilized, Dylan felt a sense of completion, a harmonic resolution that suggested this portion of the work had reached its natural conclusion.

"I think it's done," he said, his voice sounding strange to his own ears after such deep immersion in the temporal patterns. "This section feels... balanced now."

"Confirmed," Rowan called from her station. "Temporal coherence at 94% in the target sectors, far better than our projected outcome. The sigil is holding the new configuration stably."

Thorne approached the basin, studying the results with evident satisfaction. "Indeed. You've successfully restored the first segment of the Time sigil, Dylan. A significant achievement, especially for your first formal attempt."

Dylan lowered the wand, feeling a curious mixture of exhilaration and fatigue. The process had been mentally demanding but deeply satisfying, like solving a complex mathematical puzzle, but with tangible, visible results.

Bruno remained close at his side, the Guardian's medallion gradually returning to its normal state as the active restoration phase concluded. Bruno looked up at Dylan with those glowing amber eyes, a clear pride evident in his posture and expression.

"Well done, both of you," Elara said, approaching from her position at the edge of the platform. "The synchronization between Keeper and Guardian was exemplary. It significantly enhanced the efficiency of the restoration."

As the immediate work concluded, Dylan became aware once more of their surroundings, the protective barrier still shimmering around the perimeter, the Guardian Division members maintaining their vigilant positions, the subtle tension in the air that spoke of ongoing concerns about possible interference.

"No sign of void activity during the procedure," Lysander reported, joining them on the platform. "The isolation field appears to have been effective, at least for now."

"We shouldn't become complacent," Thorne cautioned. "This was only the first phase, addressing the most stable section of the sigil. Future restorations will involve more damaged areas, which may create greater disturbances in the temporal field."

"And potentially attract more attention," Rowan added, joining them with her monitoring notes in hand. "But today's success is significant. We've proven the restoration is possible, and established a working methodology that can be refined for subsequent phases."

Dylan looked back at the Timewell, where the silver substance now flowed with noticeably greater coherence in the restored section. The golden glow had faded, but a subtle luminescence remained, marking the boundary between restored and still-dormant portions of the sigil.

"How long until we attempt the next section?" he asked, already thinking ahead to the challenges that would entail.

"We should allow at least a week for this restoration to fully stabilize," Thorne advised. "During that time, we'll monitor for any unexpected reactions or adjustments in the sigil's behaviour. The crossing has been damaged for centuries; even positive changes must be integrated carefully."

A week seemed like a reasonable interval to Dylan, fitting well within his summer holiday timeline and allowing him to maintain his carefully balanced schedule between worlds. There was also the matter of his family obligations that he couldn't simply set aside for his Keeper responsibilities.

"That works for me," he confirmed. "And in the meantime?"

"Practice and preparation," Elara replied. "Now that you've experienced actual restoration work, your training can become more focused. We'll concentrate on the specific skills needed for the more challenging sections ahead."

Rowan stepped closer, her expression bright with enthusiasm despite the seriousness of their work. "The data from today's session will be invaluable for refining our approach. I'd like to review it with you when you have time, your perspective on the sigil's responses could help us optimize the mathematical models for the next phase."

There was an eagerness in her voice that went beyond professional interest, a warmth in her eyes that suggested she was looking forward to working with Dylan specifically. Dylan found himself experiencing a similar anticipation, though he wasn't entirely sure why the prospect of reviewing technical data with Rowan should feel so appealing.

"I'd like that," he replied simply.

As they began dismantling the monitoring equipment and preparing to leave the Timewell, Dylan noticed something unexpected, a faint, ghostly reflection in the silver substance of the basin. For just a moment, it seemed to form a face, feminine, with eyes that held ancient knowledge and a smile that suggested recognition.

He blinked, and the image was gone, leaving only the typical swirling patterns. Had he imagined it? A product of fatigue after the intense concentration of the restoration work?

"Did you see that?" he asked Bruno quietly.

Bruno made a soft sound, not quite a whine, not quite a growl, that suggested he had indeed perceived something unusual. His glowing eyes remained fixed on the Timewell for several seconds longer, a thoughtful intensity in his gaze.

Dylan decided not to mention it to the others just yet. Without evidence or a clearer understanding of what he'd seen, it seemed premature to raise concerns. Perhaps it was simply another aspect of the sigil's activation, a visual echo of its original creation, or a manifestation of its awakening consciousness as Elara had described.

After a brief meeting to discuss the next steps, Dylan prepared to return home. His part of the restoration work was complete for now, and he needed to maintain his presence in his own world to avoid raising suspicions.

Creating the gateway back to Blackpool was now almost effortless, the swirling energy forming at his command with precision and stability. As Dylan prepared to step through with Bruno at his side, Thorne offered a final observation.

"What you accomplished today hasn't been done in centuries," he said, his tone conveying both respect and caution. "The crossing has taken its first step toward restoration. But remember, such changes rarely go unnoticed or unchallenged. Be vigilant, even in your world."

"I will," Dylan promised, the weight of responsibility settling more firmly on his shoulders. With a final nod to his mentors, he stepped through the portal, returning once more to the familiar dunes of Blackpool's shore.

The transition between worlds had become smoother with practice, but Dylan still took a moment to reorient himself to the sights and sounds of his home reality. Bruno shook himself, his form returning to normal, eyes shifting from glowing amber back to their usual warm brown.

As they walked home, Dylan found his thoughts alternating between pride in their achievement and questions about what he'd glimpsed in the Timewell. The face in the silver substance had seemed so real, so conscious, not just a random pattern but an intentional manifestation. What could it mean?

When they arrived home, Dylan was surprised to find Mally in the garage, tinkering with his vintage Mini Cooper S. It was unusual to see him there in the middle of the afternoon, he was typically at the record shop until evening.

"You're home early," Dylan observed, pausing in the garage doorway with Bruno at his side.

Mally looked up from the engine he was adjusting, wiping his hands on a rag. "Half day. Delivery cancelled." He studied Dylan for a moment longer than seemed necessary. "Good walk?"

"Yeah," Dylan replied, trying to sound casual despite the lingering mental fatigue from the restoration work. "Just exploring the dunes again."

Mally nodded, his gaze shifting to Bruno, who was acting unusually still and alert beside Dylan. "He seems... different lately. More focused." He put down his wrench and moved closer, kneeling to look Bruno in the eyes. "Almost like he's... I don't know. More present somehow."

Dylan felt a flicker of alarm. This was the second time Mally had commented on changes in Bruno. "He's just maturing, I guess," he offered, hoping it sounded plausible.

"Maybe," Mally agreed, though his tone suggested he wasn't entirely convinced. He stood up, looking directly at Dylan now. "You seem different too. More... centred. Like you've found something that makes sense to you." He smiled slightly. "It's good to see."

There was a perception in his stepdad's observation that caught Dylan off guard. How much was Mally actually noticing? How close was he to suspecting the truth?

"Just enjoying the summer, I guess," Dylan replied, aware of how inadequate the explanation sounded.

Mally nodded, seeming to accept this for now. "Your mum will be home late. Work tea with clients. Thought we might get takeaway from that Indian place you like. Unless you had other plans?"

"No, that sounds good," Dylan agreed, relieved by the change of subject. "I'm going to clean up and maybe rest a bit first. I'm kind of tired."

"I bet you are," Mally said, with something in his tone that made Dylan wonder again just how much his stepdad sensed what was really happening. Then he turned back to his mini, ending the conversation with a casual, "tea around seven, then."

Upstairs in his room, Dylan finally allowed himself to fully process everything that had happened. The restoration had been successful beyond their expectations, a tangible, meaningful step toward repairing the damage that had isolated Dravengate for centuries. He had demonstrated abilities that even Thorne seemed surprised by, working with the sigil's patterns as if he'd been training for years rather than weeks.

And yet, there were new mysteries emerging even as old ones were being solved. The face in the Timewell. Mally's increasing awareness of the changes in both Dylan and Bruno. The question of how the void entities would respond once they realized what had been accomplished.

Bruno watched from his place on the rug as Dylan sat at his desk, automatically opening his Keeper Schedule to update it with notes about today's work and plans for the coming week. Bruno seemed more settled now that they were home, but there was still a watchfulness in his posture that hadn't been there before their journey to Dravengate.

"He knows something's different," Dylan said quietly, glancing toward the door to make sure Mally wasn't within earshot. "Not what, exactly, but he can tell we've changed."

Bruno made a soft sound of acknowledgment, his intelligent eyes fixed on Dylan with what seemed like concern.

"We'll have to be more careful," Dylan continued, thinking aloud. "Maybe... I don't know. Act more normal? Whatever that means now."

He sighed, leaning back in his chair. How did one pretend to be ordinary after successfully restoring part of an ancient magical sigil that maintained connections between worlds? When one's dog was secretly a powerful guardian being? When one had glimpsed a mysterious face in a substance that might contain the essence of previous Keepers?

These weren't questions covered in the typical teenage experience.

Dylan glanced at his calendar, noting that they had a week before their next scheduled visit to Dravengate. A week to practice, to prepare, to maintain his cover as an ordinary boy from Blackpool.

And perhaps most importantly, a week to figure out how to keep Mally from becoming too suspicious.

It was, he reflected wryly, a uniquely complex schedule to maintain, balancing cosmic responsibilities with family takeaway teas, interdimensional magic with everyday teenage life.

But then, wasn't that exactly what being the Keeper of Time was all about? Maintaining balance between worlds, keeping everything in its proper place and flowing in its proper rhythm?

With that thought, Dylan opened his notebook and began carefully documenting everything he'd observed during the restoration process. Whatever challenges lay ahead, he would face them the way he always approached problems, with careful analysis, methodical preparation, and now, with the steady support of his Guardian at his side.

The face in the Timewell could wait. For now, he had notes to organize, patterns to analyse, and an Indian takeaway to look forward to.

Balance in all things, even for the Keeper of Time.

Chapter 13: The Shadow's Response

The week following the successful restoration of the first section of the Time sigil passed in a carefully structured rhythm that Dylan found both productive and comforting. His Keeper Schedule was working brilliantly, with color-coded time blocks ensuring that his magical studies didn't interfere with family obligations or his personal projects.

True to his methodical nature, Dylan had established a precise routine for working with the special crystal Rowan had given him. Each evening, after tea and family time, he would spend exactly forty-five minutes in focused practice, attuning to the complex temporal signature contained within the deep blue stone. Bruno would settle beside him during these sessions, his presence amplifying Dylan's perception in subtle but noticeable ways.

The crystal was unlike any of the training tools he'd worked with previously. Its temporal pattern was intricate beyond anything he'd encountered, with layers of rhythm that seemed to fold back on themselves in fascinating mathematical progressions. Sometimes, when his concentration was particularly deep, Dylan could almost see the structure of the pattern, not with his physical eyes, but with some new sense that was developing alongside his Keeper abilities.

Each night, before sleep, he also reviewed the materials Rowan had provided about historical restoration efforts. The accounts were fragmentary, many dating from centuries before the Cataclysm, but they provided valuable context for understanding the work they were undertaking. Most interesting were Rowan's personal annotations, which connected historical techniques to their current approach with insights that Dylan found both clever and thoughtful.

His aunt's visit had gone more smoothly than expected. Dylan had worried that his preoccupation with Dravengate might make ordinary conversation difficult, but instead he found himself more present and engaged than usual. Perhaps it was because his magical studies provided a productive outlet for his intense focus, leaving him more relaxed in social situations. Or perhaps, as Bruno's knowing eyes sometimes seemed to suggest, he was simply growing.

On the morning scheduled for his return to Dravengate, Dylan woke early, reviewing his notes one final time before packing his backpack with characteristic precision. Today they would evaluate the stability of the restored section and potentially begin preparations for the second phase of the sigil restoration. According to the schedule he and Thorne had established, this would be a relatively straightforward session, assessment and planning rather than active magical work.

"Ready for today?" he asked Bruno, who was waiting patiently by the bedroom door, clearly aware of their plans.

Bruno's tail thumped once against the carpet in what Dylan had come to recognize as affirmation. Since their work with the Timewell, Dylan had noticed subtle changes in Bruno's behaviour even in this world, an increased alertness, more deliberate movements, and an uncanny ability to anticipate Dylan's needs before he expressed them. The Guardian bond was strengthening, even across the boundaries between worlds.

After breakfast and a carefully casual explanation to his mum about their plans for the day ("Just going to explore those rock formations north of town, might be gone most of the day"), Dylan and Bruno set off for their usual portal spot between the dunes. The morning was bright and clear, with just enough cloud cover to keep the summer heat manageable.

Creating the gateway to Dravengate had become almost automatic now. As the swirling portal formed before them, Dylan felt the now-familiar anticipation of crossing between worlds, a mixture of excitement and scientific curiosity that never diminished no matter how many times he made the journey.

They stepped through together, and emerged at the foot of the stone bridge that led to Dravengate. As always, Bruno underwent his transformation as they crossed over, his form enhancing as his Guardian nature expressed itself fully in this realm. The medallion at his collar gleamed in the morning light, its bronze surface catching and reflecting the unique quality of Dravengate's sun.

To Dylan's surprise, Rowan was waiting for them at the bridge, rather than Lysander or one of his Guardian Division members who typically served as escort. She wore practical clothes as always, sturdy trousers and a simple tunic in deep green, but there was something different about her appearance today. Her dark hair was styled differently, braided with small copper beads that caught the light when she moved, and she seemed to stand straighter, more deliberately composed.

"Right on time," she called as they approached, her direct manner unchanged despite the subtle differences in her presentation. "Thought I'd meet you personally today. Thorne and Elara are already at the Timewell, reviewing the monitoring data from the past week."

"Any problems?" Dylan asked, immediately focused on the practical aspects of their work.

"None so far," Rowan replied as they began walking toward the town. "The restored section has remained stable, with temporal coherence actually improving slightly over time as the patterns settle. It's performing better than our models predicted."

There was unmistakable pride in her voice, though whether for the success of their work or for the accuracy of her mathematical frameworks wasn't entirely clear. Perhaps both, Dylan reasoned.

As they made their way through Dravengate's winding streets, Dylan noticed Rowan seemed slightly less focused on their destination than usual, her attention occasionally drifting to him with a thoughtfulness that he couldn't quite interpret.

"You've been practicing with the crystal?" she asked during a brief pause in their conversation.

Dylan nodded. "Every evening. It's fascinating, the patterns are much more complex than the training crystals, but there's an underlying mathematical structure that makes sense once you identify the primary frequencies."

Rowan's face brightened with genuine pleasure. "That's exactly what I hoped you'd notice! Most people get lost in the complexity, but the beauty is in the underlying order. I spent months developing that particular temporal encoding."

"You created it?" Dylan asked, surprised. He had assumed the crystal contained a naturally occurring pattern, perhaps recorded from the Timewell itself.

"It's a synthesis," Rowan explained, her enthusiasm evident. "I combined elements from historical records with observations of the Timewell, then created a harmonized pattern that contains key structural principles of temporal magic." She hesitated, then added with uncharacteristic uncertainty, "It's part of my personal research project, developing new methods for temporal visualization and manipulation."

Dylan was genuinely impressed. Creating such a complex mathematical structure would require not just technical skill but a creative insight that went beyond mere calculation. "That's brilliant," he said with complete sincerity. "The way the secondary frequencies interlace with the primary rhythm, it's like a theorem expressed in temporal energy instead of equations."

Rowan seemed pleased by his understanding, her usually businesslike demeanour softening slightly. "Most people don't get it," she admitted. "Even Thorne thinks it's unnecessarily complex, but complexity isn't the point. It's about finding the elegant solution within the complexity." She glanced at him with a hint of shyness that seemed out of character. "I thought you might understand, given how your mind works."

There was something in her expression, a warmth beyond professional respect, that Dylan wasn't entirely sure how to interpret. Before he could consider it further, they arrived at the Timewell plaza, where Lysander's team had established a less intensive but still vigilant security presence around the perimeter.

The Guardian Captain himself stood near the entrance to the protected area, discussing something with one of his officers. He straightened as Dylan and Rowan approached, offering a formal nod of greeting.

"Keeper Dylan," he said, using the title that still felt slightly strange to Dylan's ears. "Guardian Bruno. We've maintained the temporal isolation field as directed, though at reduced intensity since no active work was scheduled for today."

Bruno's medallion pulsed briefly as they approached the security perimeter, synchronizing with the field as it had during their previous visit. Lysander noticed this with approval. "The integration is excellent," he observed. "The medallion has fully bonded with your Guardian's energy signature."

Dylan nodded, trying to project a confidence he didn't entirely feel about these formal aspects of his role. "Is everything ready for our assessment of the sigil?"

"Yes," Lysander confirmed. "Thorne and Elara are already inside, preparing the monitoring equipment for today's measurements."

As they passed through the security perimeter, Dylan felt the now-familiar sensation of moving through layers of energy, though the resistance was less pronounced than during their previous visit. The Timewell stood as before, but with a noticeable difference in the silver substance within its basin. The restored section now flowed with a smooth, harmonious motion that contrasted sharply with the still-erratic patterns in the untreated areas.

Thorne looked up from his instruments as they approached, his expression one of measured satisfaction. "Ah, excellent. You've arrived. The restoration continues to hold admirably, better than expected, in fact. The repaired section has begun to positively influence adjacent areas, creating a stabilizing effect that extends beyond our initial target zone."

"Like a seed crystal in a solution," Dylan observed, drawing on his knowledge of chemistry. "The restored pattern is providing a template that naturally influences surrounding areas."

"An apt analogy," Elara agreed, joining them from where she had been examining another section of the Timewell. "It suggests our approach is fundamentally sound, working with the sigil's natural tendencies rather than imposing change from outside."

For the next hour, they conducted a thorough assessment of the restored section and its effects on the surrounding temporal field. Dylan found it easier now to attune to the Timewell's patterns, his perception deepening with practice and experience. Bruno remained close, his presence enhancing Dylan's ability to navigate the complex temporal currents without becoming disoriented.

As they worked, Rowan maintained careful records of their observations, occasionally offering insights from her own analysis of the data. Dylan noticed that she seemed to position herself near him more often than strictly necessary, sometimes close enough that their arms would brush when reaching for the same instrument or pointing to a particular feature of the sigil.

During a brief break in their work, while Thorne was recalibrating some of the monitoring equipment, Rowan approached Dylan with an unexpected question.

"Would you like to see something interesting? It's not directly related to today's assessment, but I think you'd appreciate it."

Curious, Dylan nodded, and Rowan led him to a small case she had brought with her, which rested near one of the monitoring stations. From it, she withdrew what appeared to be a journal bound in dark blue leather, its pages filled with diagrams, equations, and notes in her distinctive handwriting.

"This is my personal research," she explained, a hint of vulnerability in her voice that was quite different from her usual confident manner. "I've been working on it since... since my mother died. It's a new approach to understanding how time flows through the crossing, based partly on her unfinished work."

Dylan accepted the journal with care, recognizing that this was not just a professional document but something deeply personal. As he turned the pages, he was immediately struck by the elegance of the mathematical models Rowan had developed, complex, yes, but with an underlying harmony that resonated with his own approach to problem-solving.

"This is remarkable," he said sincerely, examining a particularly intricate diagram that seemed to represent temporal flow as a multi-dimensional network rather than linear pathways. "You're mapping the crossing as a complete system rather than isolated connections."

Rowan's face brightened with genuine pleasure at his understanding. "Yes, exactly! My mother always believed the traditional models were too simplistic, treating each connection as separate rather than part of an integrated whole. She was developing a unified theory when..." she hesitated, then continued more quietly, "when the accident happened."

There was pain behind her words, still fresh despite the years that had passed. Dylan wasn't always adept at responding to emotional cues, but he recognized the significance of Rowan sharing this with him.

"You're continuing her work," he observed. "And expanding it."

Rowan nodded, a mixture of pride and sadness in her expression. "She would have solved it eventually, I'm sure of that. She was brilliant, the youngest Lead Archivist in centuries. Everyone said she would revolutionize our understanding of the crossing." There was a wistfulness in her voice, tinged with determination. "I'm not her, but I can at least try to finish what she started."

"I think what you're doing is impressive," Dylan said with simple honesty. "And from what I can see, you're making significant advances beyond her initial framework."

Rowan looked up at him, surprise evident in her expression. "You really think so?"

"The integration of quantum entanglement principles with classical temporal mechanics?" Dylan gestured to one of her equations. "That's original work. The basis might have come from your mother, but this development is uniquely yours."

Something shifted in Rowan's expression, a softening, a warmth that transformed her features. For a moment, neither spoke, the silence between them charged with a connection that went beyond their shared intellectual interests.

The moment was broken by Thorne's voice calling them back to the main assessment. Rowan carefully returned her journal to its case, her movements deliberate, almost reluctant.

"Thank you," she said quietly. "For understanding."

Before Dylan could respond, Bruno made a sudden alert sound, not quite a bark, but a clear warning. The Rottweiler's attention had shifted abruptly to the perimeter of the plaza, his posture tensing, the medallion at his collar beginning to pulse with increased intensity.

"Something's wrong," Dylan said, immediately picking up on his Guardian's alarm.

Thorne and Elara both looked up from their work, their expressions shifting from inquiry to concern as they registered Bruno's stance.

"Guardian Division reports unusual temporal fluctuations at multiple points around the perimeter," Lysander called from where he stood near the security boundary, hand pressed to what appeared to be a communication device at his collar. "Pattern suggests coordinated activity rather than random disturbances."

Elara moved swiftly to join them, her typically serene expression replaced by focused alertness. "How many locations?"

"Seven distinct points, equidistant around the plaza," Lysander replied, his professional manner intensifying. "All showing the same signature as previous void incursions, but stronger. Much stronger."

Thorne immediately began shutting down certain monitoring instruments, securing others beneath protective coverings. "We need to establish a defensive posture," he said, his voice calm but urgent. "This is not a random probe."

Dylan looked to Bruno, whose attention remained fixed on the perimeter, those glowing amber eyes tracking something invisible to ordinary sight. Bruno's form seemed to be subtly changing, not the full transformation Dylan had glimpsed once before, but a preliminary shifting, muscles becoming more defined, presence more imposing.

"What's happening?" Dylan asked, his hand automatically reaching for the wand in his pocket.

"A coordinated attempt to breach the security perimeter," Thorne explained, moving to stand beside Dylan and Bruno.

"The void entities appear to be working in concert, applying pressure to multiple points simultaneously."

"But why now?" Rowan questioned, quickly gathering her research materials and securing them. "We're not even performing active restoration work today."

"Perhaps that's precisely why," Elara suggested grimly. "They may believe our defences are reduced during assessment phases."

A sudden flare of energy from the perimeter interrupted their discussion. One section of the protective barrier visibly warped, the silvery-blue field stretching inward as if under immense pressure from outside.

"Breach imminent at sector four!" Lysander shouted to his team, already moving toward the threatened section. "Reinforce the field matrix!"

Several Guardian Division members rushed to join their captain, holding their staves toward the distorted section of the barrier. The crystals at the tips of their weapons glowed brightly as they channelled energy into the weakening field, temporarily stabilizing it.

But even as they secured that section, another portion of the perimeter began to distort, the same stretching effect indicating mounting pressure from outside. And then another. And another.

"They're testing our response patterns," Thorne observed, his expression grim. "Learning where we divert resources, then applying pressure elsewhere."

"That suggests coordination beyond anything we've seen from void entities before," Elara said, the concern in her voice evident. "This is not random opportunism."

Dylan watched the Guardian Division scrambling to address each new threat, their disciplined response increasingly strained as more sections of the perimeter came under simultaneous attack. Bruno's growl deepened, the medallion at his collar now glowing with steady intensity as he positioned himself protectively near Dylan and Rowan.

"We should move closer to the Timewell," Thorne decided. "If the perimeter fails, the sigil itself will be their primary target. We must be positioned to defend it directly."

But even as they began moving toward the central platform, a section of the security barrier suddenly collapsed with a sound like shattering glass. Through the gap poured what could only be described as living shadow, amorphous forms darker than mere absence of light, moving with purposeful, flowing grace toward the Timewell.

"Void breach in sector two!" Lysander shouted, already redirecting his team to contain the incursion. "Establish secondary perimeter!"

Another section of the barrier failed almost immediately, then a third, creating multiple points of entry for the shadow entities. The coordinated nature of the attack was now unmistakable, this was not a random opportunity but a calculated strategy.

"To the Timewell!" Thorne commanded, no longer bothering with subtle movement. "We must protect the restored section at all costs!"

They ran toward the central platform, Bruno taking the lead, his body now visibly larger, his movements carrying a power that seemed barely contained within his physical form. The medallion at his collar blazed with golden light, creating a protective aura that pushed back against the encroaching shadows.

As they reached the platform, Dylan could see the void entities more clearly. They were not uniform in size or shape, some were small and quick, darting between larger, more deliberate forms. All shared the same quality of absolute darkness, as if they absorbed light rather than merely blocking it. And all moved with unmistakable purpose toward the Timewell.

"They're targeting the restoration," Rowan said, her voice tight with tension. "If they disrupt the pattern we established, the entire section could collapse."

Dylan felt a surge of protective determination. They had worked too hard, calculated too carefully, to allow their progress to be undone. Without conscious thought, he found himself moving to stand directly before the Timewell, wand raised, Bruno at his side.

"Dylan, wait," Thorne began, but was cut off as another section of the perimeter collapsed, releasing a fresh wave of shadow entities into the plaza.

The situation deteriorated rapidly. Lysander and his team fought valiantly, their weapons projecting beams of concentrated light that seemed to disperse the smaller entities but merely slowed the larger ones. Thorne and Elara had begun weaving some kind of protective enchantment around key monitoring equipment, their movements synchronized from centuries of working together.

In the chaos, Dylan suddenly realized that he and Rowan had become separated from the others, cut off by a stream of shadow entities that now flowed between them and the rest of their group. Bruno remained with them, his protective stance unwavering, but the situation was quickly becoming dire.

"We need to get back to the others," Rowan said, her voice steady despite the clear danger of their position.

But before they could move, a group of larger shadow entities surged forward, surrounding them in a tightening circle of darkness. Bruno's growl became a roar of defiance, his form continuing to shift and expand as he positioned himself between the threats and his charges.

"They're trying to isolate us," Rowan observed, her analytical mind still functioning despite their predicament. She moved closer to Dylan, her shoulder brushing against his as they stood back-to-back, surrounded by advancing shadows.

Dylan raised his wand, focusing his will through it as he had practiced, creating a pulse of energy that pushed the nearest entities back temporarily. But there were too many, and the effect was short-lived. More shadows flowed into the space, their darkness seeming to deepen as they gathered strength.

Across the plaza, he could see Thorne attempting to fight his way toward them, but more void entities continued to pour through the breached perimeter, blocking his path. Lysander and his team were fully engaged defending the other side of the Timewell, unable to provide immediate assistance.

"Dylan," Rowan said urgently, "the Timewell, look!"

He turned to see several smaller shadow entities slipping past their defensive position, flowing directly toward the silver basin at the centre of the platform. As they made contact with the restored section, the harmonious pattern they had so carefully established began to distort, the silver substance darkening where the shadows touched it.

"They're corrupting the restoration," Dylan realized with alarm. "If they disrupt the pattern completely, we'll lose all our progress, and possibly destabilize the surrounding sections as well."

Bruno seemed to understand the threat immediately. With a movement almost too quick to follow, he launched himself toward the Timewell, intercepting the shadow entities before they could penetrate deeper into the silver substance. The medallion at his collar blazed with golden light, creating a barrier between the void entities and the vulnerable sigil.

But this left Dylan and Rowan more exposed, and the remaining shadows closed in around them, their darkness now so thick it was becoming difficult to see beyond their immediate surroundings.

"Stay close to me," Dylan told Rowan, raising his wand again. He focused his perception as he had practiced, identifying the temporal patterns of the void entities, chaotic, discordant rhythms that disrupted the natural flow of time and space.

Drawing on his training, he attempted to create a stabilizing field around them, using mathematical precision to counter the chaos the entities emanated. Rowan pressed closer against his back, and he felt her trembling slightly, not with fear, he realized, but with the effort of channelling her own abilities to reinforce his.

"I can help," she said, her voice strained. "I'm not trained for combat magic, but I understand the theoretical framework. Tell me what pattern you're targeting."

Working together, they managed to establish a small zone of stability around themselves, pushing back the immediate threat. But more shadow entities continued to press in, and Dylan could feel their defensive field weakening under the relentless assault.

Across the plaza, the situation was deteriorating. Lysander's team had been forced to retreat to a tighter perimeter around one section of the Timewell, abandoning their attempt to secure the entire platform. Thorne and Elara were now separated as well, each defending different approaches to the central basin.

And most concerning of all, more shadow entities had reached the Timewell itself, despite Bruno's valiant efforts to hold them back. The silver substance was showing increasing signs of corruption, dark streaks spreading through the carefully restored pattern like ink dropped in clear water.

"We're losing the sigil," Rowan said, her voice tight with frustration. "All our work"

A sudden surge of shadow entities cut off her words as their defensive field finally collapsed. Darkness closed in around them, cold and consuming, dampening sound and light until Dylan could barely make out Rowan's form beside him.

In that moment of near-total isolation, as the shadows pressed in from all sides, Dylan felt something unexpected, not fear, but a strange, calm clarity. Time seemed to slow, his perception expanding beyond normal limitations.

He could sense Bruno across the plaza, still fighting desperately to protect the Timewell. He could feel Rowan beside him, her presence a bright point of determined resistance against the encroaching void. And beneath it all, he could perceive the Time sigil itself, not just the physical manifestation in the silver basin, but it's true nature as a nexus of temporal energy, a critical junction in the vast network of the crossing.

With sudden certainty, Dylan knew what he had to do. Not through calculation or training, but through an intuitive understanding that seemed to rise from some deeper part of his consciousness.

He reached out, not physically but with his perception, connecting directly to the sigil through the wand. Instead of fighting against the corruption spreading through the restored section, he focused on reinforcing its underlying pattern, the mathematical harmony they had so carefully established during the restoration.

It was like holding a musical note against growing dissonance, maintaining the pure tone despite the chaos surrounding it. Dylan poured his will through the wand, visualizing the perfect pattern they had created, refusing to let it be disrupted or destroyed.

Rowan seemed to sense what he was doing. Despite the shadows pressing in around them, she placed her hand over his on the wand, adding her own understanding of the sigil's mathematical structure to his effort. Together, they created a resonance that pushed back against the corruption, stabilizing the restored section even as the void entities continued their assault.

Across the plaza, Bruno had sensed the change as well. The Rottweiler's eyes blazed with golden fire as he fought with renewed determination, his form continuing to shift and expand as he drew on deeper reserves of Guardian energy.

For a moment, balance seemed possible, not victory, perhaps, but at least preservation of what they had accomplished. But then, without warning, a new presence entered the plaza.

Unlike the amorphous shadow entities, this figure had definite form, humanoid in shape, though with proportions that seemed slightly wrong, as if assembled from mismatched parts. It moved with deliberate grace through the breach in the perimeter, darkness swirling around it like a cloak or second skin.

The moment it appeared; the coordinated nature of the attack became clear. The shadow entities responded to its presence, their movements becoming more organized, more purposeful. Some flowed toward it like tributaries joining a river, while others pressed their assault with renewed vigor.

"Who is that?" Rowan whispered, her voice barely audible through the dampening effect of the shadows surrounding them.

Before Dylan could respond, the figure turned toward them, its face, if it could be called that, a void deeper than the shadows it commanded. It made no sound, but Dylan felt its attention fix on him with terrible intensity, as if it had found what it had been searching for all along.

The shadow entities surrounding them surged forward with new purpose, no longer simply containing but actively attacking. Dylan felt a cold pressure against his mind, an alien consciousness attempting to break through his natural defences.

Rowan gasped beside him, clearly experiencing the same invasive presence. Her hand tightened on his, both of them now struggling to maintain their focus on stabilizing the sigil while defending against this new, more personal attack.

And then, across the plaza, something extraordinary happened.

Bruno, surrounded by shadow entities and seemingly on the verge of being overwhelmed, underwent a transformation unlike anything Dylan had witnessed before. The Rottweiler's form expanded dramatically, his size nearly doubling, muscles and bones reconfiguring into something that maintained canine characteristics but with a power and presence that transcended ordinary physical limitations.

His fur took on a golden luminescence that pushed back the surrounding shadows, patterns of light appearing across his body like living sigils. The medallion at his collar seemed to dissolve, its bronze material flowing across his form to create armor-like plates at key points. His eyes blazed like twin suns, no longer merely glowing but radiating a power that cut through the darkness like physical force.

In this fully realized Guardian form, Bruno let out a roar that was felt as much as heard, a sound that resonated on multiple levels of reality simultaneously. The nearest shadow entities recoiled as if struck, some of the smaller ones dissipating entirely under the onslaught of pure Guardian energy.

Even the humanoid figure paused, its attention shifting from Dylan to this new, unexpected threat. There was a moment of what seemed like genuine surprise, an emotion Dylan wouldn't have thought possible from a being of living shadow.

Taking advantage of the distraction, Thorne and Elara finally managed to fight their way through the thinning ranks of shadow entities, reaching the central platform where they immediately began reinforcing Dylan and Rowan's efforts to stabilize the sigil.

"Hold the pattern," Thorne instructed, his voice strained but determined. "We can still preserve the restoration if we maintain coherence at the primary node."

Lysander and his team, seeing Bruno's transformation turn the tide of battle, rallied and began pushing back against the shadow entities with renewed determination. The coordinated attack that had seemed unstoppable just moments before was now faltering, disrupted by the unexpected power of a fully manifested Guardian.

The humanoid figure, sensing the changing momentum of the battle, made a gesture that sent ripples through the surrounding shadows. In response, the void entities began to withdraw, flowing back toward the breaches in the perimeter with the same purposeful movement with which they had entered.

It was not a rout, there was nothing panicked or disordered about their retreat. Rather, it felt like a tactical withdrawal, a cold assessment that continuing the assault would not achieve their objectives.

The figure itself remained a moment longer, its featureless face turned toward Dylan with that same terrible focus. There was communication in that regard, though not in words, a promise, perhaps, or a warning. Then it too flowed backward, melding with the retreating shadows until it was indistinguishable from them.

Within minutes, the plaza was clear of void entities, though the damage they had inflicted remained evident in the shattered security perimeter and the partially corrupted silver substance of the Timewell.

Bruno, still in his fully transformed state, made a circuit of the platform, ensuring no shadow entities remained hidden nearby. His movement had a fluid grace that belied his now-massive size, each step precise and deliberate. The golden light emanating from his form continued to push back the residual darkness left by the void entities, cleansing the space of their influence.

Dylan sagged slightly as the immediate danger passed, the sustained effort of maintaining the sigil's stability taking its toll. Rowan remained beside him, her hand still covering his on the wand, her presence a steady support.

"You did it," she said quietly, genuine admiration in her voice. "You held the restoration intact despite direct corruption attempts. That shouldn't have been possible for someone with your limited training."

"We did it," Dylan corrected, including her in the achievement. "I couldn't have maintained the pattern without your help."

Thorne approached them, his normally impeccable appearance dishevelled from the battle, but his eyes sharp with assessment as he studied Dylan. "Indeed. Your performance was... remarkable. Both of you."

Elara joined them, her silver hair partially undone from its usual careful arrangement, but her expression serene despite the chaos they had just endured. "The Guardian's transformation was equally impressive. Full manifestation is rare, especially in one so newly awakened."

As if hearing his title, Bruno padded over to them, his transformed state still maintained though slightly diminished from its peak during the battle. Up close, the details of his Guardian form were even more impressive, the intricate patterns of light flowing across his golden fur, the intelligence and awareness in those blazing eyes, the sense of barely contained power in each movement.

"Is he... okay?" Dylan asked, uncertain how the transformation might affect Bruno. "This is much more extreme than the partial transformations I've seen before."

"He is as he should be," Elara assured him. "This is the true form of a Guardian, manifested in response to genuine threat. It carries no harm to him, though maintaining it does require considerable energy."

Even as she spoke, Bruno's form began to gradually revert, the golden light dimming, his size reducing, though not completely returning to his normal appearance. It seemed he was finding a middle state, more than his ordinary form, but less than the full manifestation that had turned the tide of battle.

Lysander approached, his uniform torn and singed in places but his bearing still formal despite the evident strain of combat. "The perimeter is secured for now, though several sections will require complete reconstruction. We've established a temporary barrier, but it won't withstand another coordinated assault of that magnitude."

"We should withdraw to the Archives," Thorne decided. "The Timewell is stable enough for now, and we need to assess what just happened in a more secure environment."

Dylan nodded agreement, though his attention remained on Bruno, who had come to stand beside him, those still-glowing eyes watching him with evident concern. Reaching down, Dylan placed his hand on the Rottweiler's head, feeling the residual energy still flowing through his Guardian's form.

"Thank you," he said simply, knowing the words were inadequate but unable to express the depth of his gratitude for Bruno's protection.

Bruno pressed against his leg in familiar reassurance, a gesture that remained unchanged despite his altered appearance. Some things, it seemed, transcended even magical transformation.

As they prepared to leave the Timewell plaza, Rowan moved beside Dylan, her expression troubled. "That wasn't a random attack," she said quietly. "They were specifically targeting the restoration. And that figure, did you see how it controlled the shadow entities?"

"I saw," Dylan confirmed, the memory of that featureless face turned toward him still vivid in his mind. "Do you think it was responsible for the earlier incursions as well?"

"Almost certainly," Thorne interjected, having overheard their conversation. "This level of coordination among void entities is unprecedented in our records. They typically act opportunistically, exploiting weaknesses they encounter. Today's attack was strategy, not opportunity."

"Which suggests intelligence," Elara added grimly. "And purpose beyond mere disruption."

As they made their way through Dravengate's streets toward the Archive Tree, Dylan found himself reviewing the events of the battle, analysing what had worked and what hadn't from a tactical perspective. His naturally methodical mind was already organizing the experience into patterns, looking for weaknesses to address and strengths to build upon.

But beneath this analytical process, a more troubling question persisted: Who or what was the humanoid figure that had directed the shadow entities? And why had its attention fixed so specifically on him?

The mystery added yet another layer to the already complex challenges they faced. The restoration of the Time sigil had just become more than a technical magical working, it was now clearly opposed by forces with intelligence and purpose.

Forces that would almost certainly attack again.

Chapter 14: Guardian Rising

The Archive Tree seemed different as they approached it, more awake somehow, its coppery bark gleaming with a subtle luminescence that pulsed in rhythm with Bruno's still partially-transformed state. The Guardian remained close to Dylan's side as they walked, his enhanced form drawing curious glances from the few Dravengate residents they passed in the streets.

Thorne placed his palm against the massive trunk, and the familiar seam appeared, widening to admit them to the hollow interior. Inside, the central chamber of the Archives had been transformed from its usual scholarly arrangement into something resembling a war room. The large table that normally displayed the crossing map was now covered with monitoring equipment, defensive talismans, and what appeared to be weapons of various designs.

"The second line of defence," Lysander explained, seeing Dylan's surprised expression. "In case the Timewell falls."

The Guardian Captain looked exhausted, his uniform still bearing the marks of battle, but his movements remained precise as he began arranging crystals in a protective pattern around the chamber's perimeter. Several of his division members were already present, setting up additional security measures under Elara's direction.

Rowan moved immediately to one of the monitoring stations, her fingers flying across what resembled mechanical calculating devices as she began analysing data from the attack. Despite the chaos they had just escaped, her focus was absolute, her mind clearly processing the implications of what they had witnessed.

"What exactly happened out there?" Dylan asked, turning to Thorne as the most likely source of answers. "That humanoid figure, it wasn't like the other void entities."

Thorne's expression was grave as he gestured for Dylan to join him near one of the Archive's ancient bookshelves. "No, it wasn't," he confirmed quietly. "And I fear I know what, or rather who, we may be dealing with."

He selected a volume bound in faded black leather, its cover unmarked by any title or symbol. Opening it carefully, he turned to a page showing an illustration that sent a chill through Dylan's spine, a rendering of a figure remarkably similar to what they had seen at the Timewell, surrounded by swirling shadows that seemed to both emanate from and be controlled by it.

"This is from the records of the Cataclysm," Thorne explained, his voice low enough that only Dylan and Bruno, who had moved to stand protectively at his side, could hear. "In the final days before the crossing's collapse, Marwen, the Keeper who betrayed his oath, had an apprentice named Corvus. When the Cataclysm struck, Corvus was believed lost, consumed by the very forces his master had unleashed."

Dylan studied the illustration, noticing details he hadn't been able to discern during the chaotic battle, the slightly elongated limbs, the unnatural fluidity of movement, the absence of distinct facial features replaced by a void-like darkness.

"You think this is the same person?" he asked. "After five hundred years?"

"The void spaces exist outside normal time," Thorne replied grimly. "If Corvus survived by merging with the entities there, as this record suggests he might have, he could have endured in some form all these centuries."

"But why attack now?" Dylan pressed. "The crossing has been damaged for centuries. What's changed?"

"We have," Elara said, joining their conversation. "More specifically, you have. The appearance of a new Keeper, the restoration work beginning on the sigils, these represent the first real threat to the status quo in generations."

Bruno made a soft rumbling sound, his still-glowing eyes fixed on the illustration as if memorizing an enemy's face. The residual transformation continued to flow through him, his form maintaining that middle state between normal dog and full Guardian manifestation.

"If this is truly Corvus," Thorne continued, "then we face a far more dangerous opponent than mere void entities. He was trained in temporal magic by Marwen himself, who, before his betrayal, was one of the most powerful Keepers in Dravengate's history."

The implications were sobering. They weren't just fighting mindless entities drawn to temporal disruption; they were facing an intelligent adversary with knowledge of the very systems they were trying to restore.

"The attack on the Timewell was just the beginning," Elara added. "Now that he knows we have the capability to restore the sigils, he will redouble his efforts to stop us."

Dylan frowned, processing this information with his characteristic methodical approach. "But why would he oppose restoration? If he was a Keeper's apprentice, wouldn't he want the crossing repaired?"

"Perhaps once," Thorne acknowledged. "But after centuries merged with void entities, who knows what motivates him now? The damaged crossing creates instability that void entities thrive on. Full restoration would seal the breaches they exploit to enter our reality."

A sudden commotion from the monitoring station interrupted their discussion. Rowan looked up from her calculations, her expression tense.

"We have a problem," she announced, loud enough for everyone in the chamber to hear. "The attack damaged the temporal isolation field around the Timewell more severely than we realized. The protective array is failing, and without it, the partially restored sigil is vulnerable to direct corruption."

Lysander immediately moved to her side, examining the readings with a frown. "How long until complete failure?"

"Minutes," Rowan replied grimly. "Maybe less. The degradation is accelerating."

"We must return to the Timewell," Thorne decided, already moving toward the Archive's entrance. "If the isolation field collapses completely, the void entities will have direct access to the sigil."

"It could be a trap," Elara cautioned. "The timing is too convenient."

"Nevertheless, we cannot allow the restoration to be corrupted," Thorne countered. "Too much depends on maintaining what progress we've made."

Dylan understood the dilemma immediately. Abandoning the Timewell would preserve their safety but sacrifice their work. Returning risked another confrontation, possibly against greater numbers now that their defensive capabilities had been assessed.

"I'll go," he said, the decision forming with surprising clarity. "Bruno and I can move quickly, assess the situation, and stabilize the sigil if needed."

"Absolutely not," Thorne replied sharply. "You are not yet fully trained, and if this is indeed Corvus, you would be his primary target."

"And I'm also the only one who can directly work with the sigil," Dylan countered, his usual deference to authority momentarily set aside by the urgency of the situation. "We don't have time for debate. The longer we wait, the more likely the restoration will be lost."

Bruno made a determined sound beside him, clearly supporting this decision. His transformed state seemed to intensify slightly, golden light flowing more vigorously through the patterns on his fur.

"I'm going too," Rowan stated firmly, already gathering equipment from the monitoring station. "I understand the mathematical structure of the restoration better than anyone except Dylan. If the sigil needs to be stabilized, you'll need both of us."

Thorne looked as if he wanted to object further, but Elara placed a restraining hand on his arm. "They're right," she said quietly. "Time is against us, and their combined talents offer the best chance of preserving the restoration."

After a moment of internal struggle visible on his face, Thorne nodded reluctantly. "Very well. But not alone." He turned to Lysander. "Captain, assemble your four best. We need a security detail for the Keeper."

"With respect," Lysander replied, "in the current situation, the Guardian provides better protection than my entire division combined. We witnessed that at the Timewell. Better to deploy my people in a perimeter defence, creating a corridor for retreat if needed."

This assessment, coming from the disciplined Guardian Captain himself, carried significant weight. Thorne considered it briefly, then nodded his agreement. "Establish the perimeter. Elara and I will work on reinforcing the Archive's defences in case this is a diversion for a different target."

The plan came together with rapid efficiency. Lysander dispatched his team to create a secure route between the Archive and the Timewell, while Rowan packed essential instruments for assessing and potentially stabilizing the sigil. Dylan found himself impressed by how quickly everyone adapted to the crisis, each person bringing their specific expertise to bear on the problem.

"Take this," Thorne said, handing Dylan a small crystal pendant on a silver chain. "It's a temporal anchor, essentially a stabilized reference point outside normal flow. If the situation becomes untenable, break the crystal. It will create a momentary bubble of suspended time, giving you a few seconds to escape."

Dylan accepted the pendant, recognizing it as a significant safeguard that Thorne wouldn't part with lightly. "Thank you. We'll be careful."

"See that you are," Thorne replied, his stern demeanour softening slightly. "Dravengate cannot afford to lose another Keeper, especially one with your potential."

Within minutes, they were ready to depart. Lysander's team had already moved out to establish the security corridor, and Rowan stood waiting by the Archive's entrance, her bag filled with monitoring equipment and calculation tools. Bruno remained at Dylan's side, his transformed state seemingly stabilized at that middle ground between normal dog and full Guardian manifestation, ready to shift further if threat level increased.

"Stay in constant communication," Elara instructed, handing Rowan a small device that resembled an antique pocket watch. "This is linked to its twin here. If you encounter Corvus or significant void activity, do not engage, report and retreat."

With final nods of acknowledgment, they left the Archive, stepping out into Dravengate's streets which now seemed unnervingly quiet compared to the usual ambient activity. The few residents visible were hurrying about their business with wary glances toward the sky, where unusual patterns of shadow and light played across the normally placid blue. Something about the town's atmosphere had changed, as if the very air were holding its breath in anticipation.

"They sense it," Rowan said quietly as they moved swiftly along the route Lysander's team had secured. "The town itself knows something is wrong."

Dylan had noticed this phenomenon before, the way Dravengate seemed to possess a kind of collective awareness, responding to significant events with subtle environmental changes. Now, with the threat of void corruption looming over the Timewell, that awareness had sharpened into what felt remarkably like anxiety.

Their journey to the central plaza was tense but uneventful. Lysander's team had done their job well, creating a clear path with Guardian Division members stationed at key intersections, monitoring for any sign of void activity. The closer they got to the

Timewell, however, the more Dylan could feel something amiss in the temporal currents flowing through the town.

"Can you sense that?" he asked Rowan, who nodded grimly.

"Temporal disruption, centred on the Timewell," she confirmed. "The isolation field is definitely failing."

Bruno moved ahead of them now, his posture shifting to full alert, those glowing eyes scanning their surroundings with preternatural awareness. The medallion that had merged with his transformed state during the earlier battle now appeared as a golden sigil at the centre of his chest, pulsing in rhythm with his heightened alertness.

As they entered the plaza, the nature of the problem became immediately apparent. The security perimeter Lysander's team had established earlier was visibly deteriorating, sections of the protective barrier flickering like a failing light bulb. Through these unstable sections, wisps of shadow occasionally slipped through, only to be driven back by the Guardian Division members who fought to maintain the integrity of the field.

But more concerning was the Timewell itself. The silver substance in the basin was showing signs of distress, its normally smooth flow disrupted by what looked like ripples of darkness spreading inward from the edges. The restored section that they had worked so hard to establish still maintained its cohesion, but the corruption was approaching it from multiple directions.

"It's worse than I thought," Rowan said, already unpacking her monitoring equipment as they approached the platform. "The void entities aren't just attacking the protective field, they're directly corrupting the temporal medium itself."

Dylan moved to the edge of the basin, extending his perception toward the silver substance as he had learned to do during their restoration work. The patterns were immediately clear to him, the harmonious mathematics of their restored section standing in stark contrast to the chaotic disruption now spreading through the surrounding areas.

"If the corruption reaches the nexus point of the restoration, the entire structure could collapse," he observed, his mind already calculating potential countermeasures. "We need to establish a buffer zone around the restored section, essentially a firebreak to contain the spread."

Rowan nodded, quickly setting up her instruments at strategic points around the basin. "I can model the corruption's spread pattern if you can give me a few minutes to gather readings."

Bruno circled the platform once, then took up position at what appeared to be the weakest section of the remaining security perimeter, his transformed body radiating a golden light that seemed to strengthen the failing barrier wherever he moved close to it.

Working quickly but methodically, Dylan and Rowan established a monitoring network around the Timewell, measuring the corruption's advance and calculating its likely progression. The situation was concerning but not yet critical, the restored section was holding, and the corruption was spreading relatively slowly.

"We have maybe twenty minutes before it reaches the primary node," Rowan reported after analysing the initial readings. "If we can establish a countercurrent along these vectors," she indicated several points on her hastily drawn diagram, ", we should be able to divert the corruption around the restored section."

Dylan studied her calculations, immediately grasping the mathematical elegance of the solution. "That could work. I'll need to use the wand to channel the countercurrent while you monitor the effect and adjust the parameters as needed."

They had just begun preparing for this intervention when Bruno suddenly stiffened, his attention snapping toward the far side of the plaza where the security perimeter was at its weakest. A low, warning growl rumbled from his chest, the golden light around his form intensifying noticeably.

"Something's coming," Dylan said, interpreting his Guardian's alert stance.

No sooner had he spoken than the weakest section of the perimeter collapsed entirely, the protective barrier dissolving like mist before a strong wind. Through the gap poured darkness, not the individual shadow entities they had faced before, but a continuous flow of void-stuff that moved with deliberate, almost liquid grace across the plaza toward the Timewell.

The few Guardian Division members stationed at that section fell back in organized retreat, their weapons projecting beams of light that seemed to do little more than temporarily slow the advancing darkness. One by one, they took up new defensive positions closer to the platform, creating a last line of defence around the Timewell.

And then, emerging from the flowing shadow like a swimmer rising from dark water, came the figure they had seen before, Corvus, if Thorne's identification was correct. In the clearer light of day, without the chaos of full battle surrounding them, Dylan could observe more details of this ancient enemy.

The figure was indeed humanoid, with proportions close enough to human to pass at a distance, but with subtle wrongness that became apparent on closer inspection. The limbs were slightly too long, the movements too fluid, as if the bones beneath the surface, if there were bones at all, had different articulation points than human anatomy. The face remained a void, a darkness deeper than the shadows surrounding it, with no discernible features except for what might have been eyes, points of absolute blackness that somehow managed to convey direction of gaze.

Most disturbing was the way the surrounding shadows responded to its presence, flowing around and through it like extensions of its will, sometimes seeming to emerge directly from its form only to be reabsorbed moments later. The boundary between Corvus and the void entities he commanded was not fixed but fluid, suggesting a symbiotic relationship that had evolved over centuries.

"Fascinating," Rowan whispered beside Dylan, her scientific curiosity momentarily overriding proper caution. "The amalgamation appears conscious across multiple dimensions simultaneously."

Bruno's growl deepened, his form shifting further toward the full Guardian manifestation they had glimpsed during the earlier battle. His size increased noticeably, the golden light flowing through the patterns on his fur brightening until it cast visible illumination across the platform.

The Guardian Division members responded to this new threat by tightening their formation around the Timewell, their weapons trained on the advancing figure. But Corvus seemed unconcerned by this show of force, his attention fixed on Dylan with the same terrible focus as during their previous encounter.

And then, unexpectedly, he spoke.

The voice was not what Dylan had anticipated. Rather than the hollow, echoing sound one might expect from such an otherworldly entity, it was surprisingly normal, pleasant even, with the refined diction of a scholar.

"The new Keeper, I presume," Corvus said, coming to a halt at the edge of the platform. The shadows continued to swirl around him, but maintained a respectful distance from Bruno's golden aura. "How interesting. You're younger than I expected."

Dylan found himself at a loss for words, the normalcy of the voice contrasting so sharply with the entity's appearance that it created a kind of cognitive dissonance. Rowan, however, had no such hesitation.

"What do you want with the Timewell?" she demanded, stepping forward despite Bruno's protective growl suggesting she stay back.

Corvus tilted his featureless head slightly, the gesture somehow conveying mild amusement despite the lack of facial expressions. "Want? Such a simple word for a complex intention. Let's say I wish to preserve the current state of affairs, which your restoration efforts threaten to disrupt."

"The current state is broken," Dylan said, finding his voice at last. "The crossing was meant to connect worlds, not isolate them."

"And who decided this purpose?" Corvus asked, his voice taking on a sharper edge despite maintaining its pleasant tone. "The Architects? The ancient Keepers? Those who established a system that nearly destroyed multiple realities when it failed?" He made a dismissive gesture with one too-long hand. "The Cataclysm revealed the truth, connection is vulnerability. Isolation is safety."

There was a strange conviction in his words, a twisted logic that Dylan could almost follow despite its fundamental wrongness. This wasn't the mindless destruction of chaotic entities; it was a deliberate philosophy grown from centuries of existence in the spaces between realities.

"Safety for whom?" Rowan challenged. "Certainly not for the worlds cut off from each other, deprived of the knowledge and resources they once shared."

"A small price for existential security," Corvus replied with that same eerie calm. "You cannot comprehend what lurks in the deeper void, the entities my kind hold at bay. The damaged crossing is a controlled breach, a monitored wound. Full restoration would tear it wide open, inviting forces beyond your comprehension."

This was unexpected information, suggesting a more complex situation than Thorne had described. Dylan's analytical mind immediately began reassessing their understanding of the void entities and their relationship to the crossing.

"You're saying the void entities serve a protective function?" he asked, genuinely curious despite the danger of their situation.

"In a manner of speaking," Corvus confirmed. "Though 'serve' implies more altruism than is warranted. Let us say our interests temporarily align. They feed on the energies of the damaged crossing, and in doing so, prevent larger breaches that would allow worse things to emerge."

Bruno had been growing increasingly tense during this exchange, his transformation continuing to progress as the conversation extended. He now stood nearly twice his normal size, the golden light emanating from his form pushing back the encroaching shadows wherever it touched them.

"And we're supposed to just take your word for this?" Rowan asked sceptically. "The word of someone who's spent centuries merged with void entities, whose nature we barely understand?"

Corvus made a sound that might have been a laugh, though it held little humour. "Of course not. I expect you to continue your well-intentioned but dangerously misguided efforts to restore the crossing. And I will continue to prevent those efforts from succeeding." He gestured toward the Timewell, where the corruption continued to spread through the silver substance. "Even now, the process is underway."

Dylan glanced at the basin, alarmed to see that the corruption had accelerated during their conversation, dark tendrils now much closer to the restored section than before. This entire exchange, he realized, had been a distraction, keeping their attention focused on Corvus while the void entities continued their work on the Timewell.

"Enough talking," he said firmly, raising the wand. "We're going to stabilize the sigil and continue the restoration, regardless of your warnings."

"Such confidence," Corvus observed, his voice tinged with what might have been genuine regret. "So reminiscent of Marwen before his fall. Very well. Let us proceed to the inevitable conflict."

With a gesture from Corvus, the shadows surrounding him surged forward, flowing around the Guardian Division members despite their attempts to hold the perimeter. Some headed directly for the Timewell, while others moved to encircle Dylan and Rowan, cutting off potential escape routes.

Bruno responded immediately, his form completing the transformation they had glimpsed during the previous battle. In seconds, he stood before them in full Guardian manifestation, massive, powerful, his golden fur radiating light that pushed back the darkness, intricate patterns across his body forming protective sigils that created a barrier between them and the advancing shadows.

In this form, Bruno was magnificent beyond words, no longer simply a larger, glowing version of a Rottweiler, but something that maintained canine characteristics while transcending normal physical limitations. His eyes blazed like twin suns, his presence filling the space around them with a palpable force that even the void entities seemed to respect, keeping their distance from his golden aura.

"Impressive," Corvus acknowledged, observing Bruno's transformation with evident interest. "A Guardian of the old school, manifesting physical form rather than energy projection. Rare in these degenerate times."

Rowan had used the momentary distraction to check her monitoring equipment, her expression growing increasingly concerned. "Dylan, the corruption is less than five minutes from reaching the restoration nexus. If it makes contact, we lose everything we accomplished."

Dylan understood the urgency. Despite the danger Corvus presented, their primary mission had to be preserving the restored section of the sigil. "Can we still establish the countercurrent?"

"Yes, but I'll need to adjust the calculations to account for the accelerated corruption rate," Rowan replied, already making rapid adjustments to her equipment. "And we'll need a defensive perimeter to work within."

Bruno seemed to understand their needs without verbal explanation. The transformed Guardian moved to position himself between them and Corvus, creating a protective space around the section of the Timewell that contained the restored sigil. The remaining Guardian Division members rallied to his position, forming a secondary perimeter that reinforced Bruno's golden barrier.

"Work quickly," one of Lysander's lieutenants advised as he took up position nearby. "We can hold this formation for a few minutes at most."

Dylan and Rowan wasted no time, moving to the edge of the basin where the silver substance continued to darken with spreading corruption. Using the wand as a focus, Dylan extended his perception into the Timewell, identifying the mathematical patterns they had established during the restoration.

"I need to counter the corruption by reinforcing the harmonic frequency of the restored section," he explained to Rowan as they worked. "If you can monitor the response and guide me to the critical junction points, I can create a buffer that should repel the void energy."

Rowan nodded, setting up her instruments at key positions around the basin. "I'll track the corruption flow and identify optimal intervention points. Just follow my guidance on where to focus your energy."

Beyond their protective perimeter, Corvus watched their efforts with that same terrible focus, occasionally directing the shadow entities to probe for weaknesses in Bruno's golden barrier. The void entities flowed around the perimeter, seeking entry points, only to be driven back by the combined efforts of Bruno and the Guardian Division members.

"You cannot maintain this defence indefinitely," Corvus observed, his voice still unnervingly calm despite the escalating conflict. "The void entities are limitless, while your energies are finite."

Dylan ignored the taunt, focusing entirely on his work with the Timewell. Under Rowan's precise guidance, he used the wand to project stabilizing energy into the silver substance, creating currents that diverted the corruption away from the restored section. It was delicate, precisely calibrated work, too much force would disrupt the restoration itself, too little would fail to repel the corruption.

"The eastern quadrant is holding," Rowan reported after several minutes of intensive effort. "But the corruption is adapting, finding new vectors of approach. Shift your focus to coordinates seven through nine."

Dylan adjusted accordingly, redirecting his energy through the wand to reinforce the threatened sections. The work was mentally exhausting, requiring constant concentration and fine adjustments based on Rowan's ongoing analysis. But gradually, they began to see results, the corruption's advance slowed, then halted at the boundaries they had established.

"It's working," Rowan confirmed, a note of cautious optimism in her voice. "The buffer zone is holding. If we can maintain this for another few minutes, the restored section should stabilize against the corruption."

Corvus, sensing the changing tide of the conflict, intensified his assault on their protective perimeter. More shadow entities poured through the collapsed section of the outer barrier, joining those already attacking Bruno's golden shield. The transformed Guardian held firm, but Dylan could sense the strain this sustained defence was placing on his energy reserves.

"We need to finish this quickly," he told Rowan, casting a concerned glance toward Bruno. "He can't maintain full manifestation indefinitely."

Rowan nodded grimly, making rapid adjustments to her calculations. "I'm detecting a pattern in the corruption's flow, it's not random, but following specific pathways that correspond to the sigil's original design. If we can identify the control points, we might be able to purge the corruption entirely rather than just containing it."

This was a more ambitious goal than their original plan, but Dylan immediately grasped the potential. Instead of merely defending the restored section, they could potentially cleanse a larger portion of the Timewell, setting the stage for accelerated restoration work in the future.

"Show me the pattern," he requested, and Rowan quickly sketched a diagram based on her instrument readings.

Dylan studied it briefly, his mathematical mind immediately recognizing the underlying structure. "It's following the fracture lines from the Cataclysm," he realized. "Using the existing damage as channels for spreading."

"Exactly," Rowan confirmed. "And if we can establish counter currents along these same channels,"

"We can flush the corruption back out through its own pathways," Dylan finished, already adjusting his approach to implement this new strategy.

Working in perfect synchronization, they established new energy flows through the Timewell, using the wand to channel precisely calculated currents that followed the ancient fracture lines in reverse. The silver substance responded beautifully, the natural mathematics of the sigil amplifying their efforts as if eager to be cleansed of the invading corruption.

Outside their protective bubble, the battle intensified. Corvus, perhaps sensing the changing dynamics within the Timewell, directed a concentrated assault against one section of Bruno's barrier. Shadow entities flowed together into larger, more substantial forms that hammered against the golden shield with increasing force.

Bruno stood firm, his transformed body absorbing the impact, but Dylan could sense his Guardian's energy beginning to falter under the sustained assault. The golden light flickered briefly in one section of the barrier, causing the Guardian Division members to quickly reinforce that area with their own defensive capabilities.

"Almost there," Rowan reported, monitoring the cleansing process within the Timewell. "The corruption is retreating along all primary channels. Just a few more minutes and the sigil should stabilize."

But they didn't have a few more minutes. With a surge of concentrated effort, Corvus directed a massive wave of shadow entities against Bruno's weakening barrier. The golden shield held initially, then began to crack in multiple places, thin tendrils of darkness seeping through the fractures.

"Dylan!" one of the Guardian Division members shouted in warning as the barrier began to fail.

Faced with an impossible choice between maintaining their work with the Timewell and addressing the immediate threat, Dylan made a split-second decision. Keeping one hand on the wand to sustain the cleansing process, he reached for the temporal anchor Thorne had given him with the other.

"Rowan, can you maintain the current flow for thirty seconds on your own?" he asked urgently.

She glanced at the monitoring equipment, then nodded with determined confidence. "Go. Help Bruno. I can hold this."

Without hesitation, Dylan moved toward the failing barrier, the temporal anchor clutched in his free hand. Bruno was visibly struggling now, his massive form trembling with the effort of maintaining the golden shield against Corvus's relentless assault. The medallion at the centre of his chest, which had merged with his transformed state, was pulsing erratically, its light flickering as energy reserves depleted.

Dylan acted on instinct rather than calculation, raising the wand toward the weakest section of the barrier. Drawing on everything he had learned about temporal manipulation, he focused his will through the ancient tool, not fighting against the void entities directly but rather stabilizing the time flow around them, creating a zone where their chaotic energy found it difficult to maintain coherence.

It wasn't an attack in the conventional sense, but rather a reinforcement of natural order against entropy, an approach perfectly suited to his mathematical mind and the wand's fundamental purpose. Where his influence touched, the shadow entities slowed, their amorphous forms becoming sluggish and less responsive to Corvus's direction.

Sensing the support, Bruno rallied, the golden light of his barrier strengthening once more. The transformed Guardian gave Dylan a look of such intelligence and gratitude that it momentarily took his breath away, a clear acknowledgment from one sentient being to another, transcending the normal boundaries of human-animal communication.

Together, they established a new rhythm of defence, Bruno providing the raw power of the barrier, Dylan selectively applying temporal stabilization to critical areas when shadow entities concentrated their assault. It wasn't a permanent solution, but it bought precious time for Rowan to complete her work with the Timewell.

Corvus observed this development with evident frustration, his featureless face somehow conveying displeasure despite the absence of normal expressions. "Clever," he acknowledged, his pleasant voice taking on a harder edge. "But ultimately futile. You cannot maintain this defence forever, and I have all the time in the world."

As if to emphasize this point, he made a new gesture, and the shadows around him began to coalesce into something larger and more substantial than previous manifestations, a form that resembled a massive serpent composed entirely of void-stuff, its body thick as a tree trunk, its length extending in coils around much of the platform.

"Dylan, I'm almost finished," Rowan called from her position at the Timewell. "The corruption is nearly purged from all major channels."

"Hurry," Dylan replied, eyeing the growing shadow-serpent with alarm. "I don't think our defences will hold against that thing."

The shadow-serpent completed its formation, its head rising above the platform, featureless except for a mouth-like opening that seemed to absorb light rather than simply blocking it. At a signal from Corvus, it struck with shocking speed, its massive form crashing against Bruno's barrier with force that sent visible shockwaves across the golden shield.

Bruno roared in pain and defiance, his transformed body absorbing the impact but clearly damaged by its intensity. The golden barrier flickered violently, sections disappearing entirely before reforming with visible effort.

Dylan didn't hesitate. Seeing his Guardian in genuine danger, he activated the temporal anchor, crushing the crystal in his hand as Thorne had instructed. The effect was immediate, a bubble of suspended time expanding outward from the broken crystal, encompassing Dylan, Bruno, and the section of barrier under direct attack.

Within this bubble, everything moved at a fraction of normal speed. The shadow-serpent's attack appeared almost frozen, giving Dylan precious seconds to assess and respond. Bruno's eyes met his, communication flowing between them without need for words, a shared understanding of what needed to be done.

Using the wand, Dylan channelled his energy directly into Bruno's golden barrier, reinforcing it at the exact point of the serpent's attack. The Guardian accepted this support, incorporating Dylan's contribution seamlessly into his own defensive structure. When the temporal bubble collapsed seconds later, returning them to normal time flow, the strengthened barrier held against the serpent's strike.

"It's done!" Rowan shouted triumphantly from the Timewell. "The corruption is purged from all primary channels, and the restored section is fully stabilized."

Her timing couldn't have been better. Bruno was reaching the limits of his endurance, the golden light of his barrier noticeably dimmer despite Dylan's support. The Guardian Division members were similarly exhausted, their weapons projecting weaker beams as energy reserves depleted.

Corvus sensed this turning point as well. With a gesture that conveyed both frustration and reluctant acceptance, he dissolved the shadow-serpent back into its component entities. "This battle is concluded," he announced, his voice betraying little emotion despite the setback. "But the war for the crossing's future continues."

The shadow entities began to withdraw, flowing back toward the breached section of the outer perimeter in that same organized retreat they had witnessed during the previous encounter. Corvus himself remained a moment longer, his featureless face turned toward Dylan.

"Consider carefully what I told you, young Keeper," he said, his voice once again taking on that scholarly tone that seemed so at odds with his appearance. "Not all restoration is beneficial. Some broken things should remain broken."

With those parting words, he too flowed backward, melding with the retreating shadows until he was indistinguishable from them. Within minutes, the plaza was clear of void entities, though the damage they had inflicted remained evident in the breached security perimeter and the lingering traces of corruption in the Timewell's silver substance.

Bruno's transformation began to recede as the immediate threat passed, his massive form gradually shrinking, the golden light dimming to a subtle glow. Despite returning toward his normal appearance, he remained larger and more imposing than his usual self, the medallion at his chest still visible as a golden sigil embedded in his fur.

Dylan moved to his Guardian's side, placing a steadying hand on Bruno's shoulder as the Rottweiler seemed to momentarily struggle with the transition. "Are you okay?" he asked quietly, with genuine concern in his voice.

Bruno leaned against him, a familiar gesture of reassurance despite his altered state. His eyes had dimmed from their sun-like brilliance but retained a golden glow that suggested his Guardian nature remained close to the surface.

"He'll be fine," Rowan said, joining them after securing her monitoring equipment. "Guardian transformations are physically demanding but not harmful. He just needs rest to replenish his energy reserves."

She looked tired herself, the sustained effort of maintaining the cleansing process in the Timewell having taken a visible toll. Despite this, there was a brightness in her eyes, pride in what they had accomplished against seemingly impossible odds.

"You did brilliantly," she told Dylan, genuine admiration in her voice. "Both of you. That temporal stabilization technique when the barrier was failing, I've never seen anything like it."

Dylan shrugged slightly, uncomfortable with direct praise despite the warmth it created. "It wasn't planned. Just... intuition, I guess."

"The best Keepers balance calculation with intuition," came Thorne's voice as he and Elara hurried into the plaza, accompanied by a fresh contingent of Guardian Division members. "When we received word of the escalated attack, we feared the worst."

His gaze swept over the scene, the damaged security perimeter, the exhausted but intact defenders, the Timewell where the silver substance now flowed with remarkable clarity throughout the cleansed channels.

"But it seems our fears were misplaced," he continued, genuine pride evident in his voice. "You've done more than defend the restoration, you've actively advanced our work."

Elara moved directly to Bruno, kneeling beside the still partially-transformed Guardian with gentle concern. She placed her hands on either side of his massive head, studying the golden glow that continued to emanate from his form.

"Such a complete manifestation," she murmured, clearly impressed. "And maintained for so long against direct assault. Your Guardian has remarkable reserves of strength, Dylan."

Bruno made a soft rumbling sound that might have been pleasure at the recognition, leaning slightly into Elara's touch as she examined him.

"Will he fully return to normal?" Dylan asked, watching his transformed companion with a mixture of awe and concern.

"Yes, though it may take time," Elara explained, rising from her examination. "The first full manifestation often leaves an imprint that lingers, especially after such an intense engagement. He may maintain some enhanced characteristics for several days."

Lysander approached, looking battered but resolute after receiving reports from his division members. "The plaza is secure for now, but our defensive capabilities are severely compromised. The outer perimeter will require complete reconstruction, and my team needs recovery time before they can resume full protective duties."

"We should withdraw to the Archives," Thorne decided. "Take what we need from the monitoring stations and secure the rest. The Timewell is stable enough to leave unattended for now, especially with the cleansed channels providing natural resistance to further corruption."

As they gathered equipment and prepared to depart, Dylan found himself drawn back to the Timewell for a final look. The silver substance flowed with newfound clarity, the patterns within it more distinct and harmonious than he had seen before. Their defensive action had turned into an unexpected advance, not just preserving the restoration but actively expanding its influence.

And yet, Corvus's parting words lingered in his mind. Not all restoration is beneficial. Some broken things should remain broken. Was there truth to that warning, or merely the self-serving philosophy of an entity that thrived in the damaged crossing's instability?

"Troubled thoughts?" Rowan asked, joining him at the basin's edge.

"Just... considering perspectives," Dylan replied. "What Corvus said about worse things in the deeper void, about the damaged crossing acting as a controlled breach, could there be any truth to that?"

Rowan considered this seriously, her analytical mind never dismissing a hypothesis without examination. "It's possible," she acknowledged. "The crossing connects to multiple realities, some potentially very different from our own. The Cataclysm could have created a specific type of damage that, paradoxically, prevents worse breaches."

She gestured toward the cleansed channels in the silver substance. "But that doesn't mean restoration is wrong. It means we need to understand the full system before making irreversible changes. Repair with comprehension, not blind reconstruction."

Her perspective resonated with Dylan's methodical approach to problems. It wasn't a question of whether to restore the crossing, but how to do so with proper understanding of all potential consequences.

"We'll research it," he decided. "Before we activate more sigils, we should explore Corvus's claims, see if there's any historical evidence supporting his warning."

Rowan nodded, a hint of admiration in her eyes. "That's why the wand chose you," she said quietly. "You question. You don't just accept the established narrative."

There was something in her expression, a warmth that went beyond professional respect, that caught Dylan off guard. Before he could formulate a response, Bruno padded over to them, his transformation continuing to recede though still noticeably larger than his normal form. Bruno nudged Dylan's hand with his nose, a familiar gesture that seemed to suggest it was time to go.

"Right," Dylan acknowledged, patting Bruno's head. "We should join the others."

As they made their way back through Dravengate's streets toward the Archive Tree, Dylan found himself walking between Bruno and Rowan, the three of them forming a natural unit after their shared experience at the Timewell. The Guardian Division members formed a protective perimeter around their group, though the immediate threat appeared to have passed.

The town itself seemed to be recovering from the shadow incursion, the unnatural patterns in the sky gradually returning to normal, residents cautiously emerging from wherever they had sought shelter during the disturbance. There was a resilience to Dravengate that Dylan found reassuring, this was not the first crisis the town had weathered, and it would not be the last.

At the Archive Tree, they found additional security measures had been implemented during their absence. New crystals embedded in the coppery bark glowed with protective energy, and several Guardian Division members stood at attention nearby, creating a layered defence against potential attack.

Once inside, the central chamber had been further transformed into a secure operations centre. Maps and monitoring equipment covered most available surfaces, and additional Archive staff had been called in to assist with analysing the data from the shadow incursion.

"We need to debrief while everything is still fresh," Thorne said, gesturing toward a quiet corner where they could speak privately. "Particularly regarding your direct interaction with Corvus. Any information about his capabilities and intentions could be crucial."

For the next hour or so, Dylan and Rowan recounted the confrontation in detail, describing Corvus's appearance, abilities, and most importantly, his statements about the crossing and void entities. Thorne and Elara listened intently, occasionally asking clarifying questions but mostly allowing them to provide a complete account without interruption.

"His claim about the deeper void is concerning," Elara acknowledged when they had finished. "There are references in our oldest records to entities beyond the void entities we currently encounter, things that the original Architects specifically designed the crossing to exclude."

"Could the damage from the Cataclysm actually be functioning as Corvus described?" Dylan asked. "A controlled breach that prevents larger incursions?"

Thorne looked troubled by this possibility. "It's not inconsistent with certain theoretical models of the crossing's structure.

The current damage might be creating a specific type of instability that paradoxically prevents more catastrophic failures."

"But that doesn't mean restoration should be abandoned," Elara added firmly. "It means we need to incorporate this understanding into our approach, restore the crossing while maintaining whatever protective function the current configuration provides."

This aligned with the conclusion Dylan and Rowan had reached at the Timewell. Not a question of whether to proceed, but how to do so with complete understanding.

"We should consult the oldest records," Thorne decided. "There may be information about these deeper void entities and how the original crossing was designed to contain them." He turned to Rowan. "Your expertise in archival research will be invaluable for this task."

She nodded, obvious satisfaction in her expression at being trusted with such a crucial assignment. "I'll start immediately. There are some pre-Cataclysm texts in the sealed section that might contain relevant information."

As the debriefing concluded, Dylan became aware of his growing exhaustion. The sustained magical effort at the Timewell, combined with the emotional intensity of direct confrontation with Corvus, had depleted his energy reserves more than he had realized. Bruno appeared similarly tired, the continued partial transformation clearly requiring ongoing effort to maintain.

Elara noticed their condition with her characteristic perceptiveness. "You both need rest," she said gently but firmly. "Keeper and Guardian alike require recovery time after such intensive energy expenditure."

"I should return home soon anyway," Dylan acknowledged, checking his watch to find that several hours had passed since their arrival in Dravengate that morning. "My parents will be expecting me for tea."

"Before you go," Thorne said, "there's something you should know." His expression was serious but not grim. "What you accomplished today, not merely defending but actively advancing the restoration despite direct opposition, it confirms what the wand's choice suggested. You are truly the Keeper of Time, Dylan Bennett. Not a candidate or potential, but the actual successor to the lineage."

This formal acknowledgment fell heavily in the quiet corner of the Archives. Dylan had been operating under the assumption that he was still in a probationary phase, learning, testing, proving his capability. To be recognized as the actual Keeper, with all the responsibility that entailed, was both an honour and a sobering realization.

"I don't know what to say," he admitted honestly.

"No response is necessary," Thorne assured him. "The title is not bestowed by us, but confirmed by your actions and the wand's continued acceptance of your wielding. I simply thought you should be aware of your standing before returning to your world."

Bruno made a soft sound, pressing against Dylan's leg in what felt like both congratulation and support. Bruno's eyes, still maintaining their golden glow despite his otherwise normalizing appearance, held a clear pride in his Keeper's recognition.

As they prepared to depart, Rowan approached Dylan once more. "I'll begin the research immediately," she promised. "By the time you return, I should have preliminary findings about these deeper void entities and what they might mean for our restoration approach."

"Thank you," Dylan said, genuinely appreciative of her dedication. "For everything today, not just the research, but at the Timewell. We couldn't have succeeded without your mathematical insights."

A slight flush coloured Rowan's cheeks at the praise. "We make a good team," she said, her voice carrying a warmth that seemed to go beyond professional courtesy. Then, in a move that caught Dylan completely by surprise, she quickly leaned forward and pressed a kiss to his cheek. "For luck," she added hastily, stepping back immediately, her flush deepening.

Dylan froze, completely unprepared for this gesture. His mind, usually so quick with calculations and patterns, seemed temporarily unable to process this unexpected social interaction. He was vaguely aware of Elara turning away to hide a smile, and even Thorne seemed to be suppressing a look of amusement.

"I... thank you?" he managed eventually, the phrase coming out more as a question than a statement.

Bruno made a sound that, even in his semi-transformed state, was unmistakably the canine equivalent of a snicker.

Still flustered, Dylan focused on the practical task of creating their return portal, if only to have something concrete to concentrate on rather than trying to decipher Rowan's unexpected gesture. The wand responded to his intent as always, though he noticed the portal formed more quickly and with greater stability than in previous attempts, perhaps another sign of his growing capability as Keeper.

"We'll expect you in three days' time," Thorne said as they prepared to step through. "Sooner if circumstances require it. The communication crystal can be used in emergencies."

With final nods of farewell, Dylan and Bruno stepped through the portal, returning once more to the familiar dunes of Blackpool's shore. The transition between worlds had become almost comfortable now, though Dylan noticed that this particular crossing left him with a lingering awareness of temporal currents that he hadn't experienced previously.

Bruno shook himself as always, his form continuing to normalize though not completely returning to his ordinary appearance. He remained slightly larger, his muscles more defined, and a subtle glow still emanated from his eyes, though muted enough that it might not be immediately obvious to casual observation.

"You should probably try to look as normal as possible before we get home," Dylan suggested as they began walking back toward town. "Mum might notice if you're still... enhanced."

Bruno huffed softly, and with what appeared to be conscious effort, dimmed the glow in his eyes to nearly imperceptible levels. His size remained somewhat increased, but not so dramatically that it couldn't be explained away as a trick of the light or faulty memory.

As they walked, Dylan found his mind returning repeatedly to the moment in the Archives, Rowan's unexpected kiss, the warmth in her eyes, the flush in her cheeks afterward. He had limited experience with social cues, particularly those related to romantic interest, but even he recognized that this gesture likely went beyond mere friendship or professional courtesy.

The realization was both flattering and mildly terrifying. At sixteen, Dylan had given little thought to romance, finding the complex and often unspoken rules of dating to be an incomprehensible maze compared to the clean logic of mathematics. But there had been something about Rowan, her direct manner, her brilliant mind, her ability to see patterns as he did, that resonated with him in a way few people ever had.

Bruno glanced up at him as they walked, those still-faintly-glowing eyes holding what looked remarkably like amusement at his Keeper's obvious confusion.

"You're not helping," Dylan told him dryly.

Bruno made a sound that was unmistakably the dog equivalent of laughter.

The Keeper of Time

By the time they reached home, Dylan had managed to push the confusing social aspects of the day to the back of his mind, focusing instead on the practical challenges they had overcome and the new questions raised by Corvus's warnings. Bruno had successfully suppressed most visible signs of his transformation, though he still moved with a fluidity and power that wasn't quite normal for an ordinary dog.

Tea that evening was a mercifully straightforward affair, his mum chatting about a new design commission she was excited about, Mally recounting an amusing story about a customer at the record shop. Dylan found himself genuinely engaged in the conversation, the intensity of his experiences in Dravengate somehow making these ordinary family interactions more precious rather than less interesting.

Later, in the quiet of his room, Dylan sat at his desk reviewing his notes from the day's events. Bruno lay on the rug beside him, finally back to his normal appearance except for a very faint glow still visible in his eyes if one looked closely in the right light.

"Officially the Keeper of Time now," Dylan murmured, the title still feeling strange when applied to himself. "Quite the summer job, isn't it?"

Bruno huffed softly in agreement, his tail thumping once against the carpet.

As Dylan prepared for bed, his phone chimed with an incoming text message. The number was familiar now, Rowan, messaging from whatever research outpost she was using in his world.

"Found references to 'Deep Void Entities' in pre-Cataclysm texts. Architects specifically designed crossing to exclude them. Corvus may be partially right. Will have more details when you return. Stay safe. -R"

There was a brief pause, then a second message appeared:

"Sorry about earlier. Was impulsive. Hope it wasn't uncomfortable. -R"

Dylan stared at the messages, unsure how to respond, particularly to the second one. After careful consideration, he typed:

"Looking forward to hearing about your research. Don't worry about earlier. It was... nice. See you in three days."

He hesitated over the final sentence, then added:

"Thank you for your help today. We make a good team."

Satisfied that this response acknowledged both the professional and personal aspects of their interaction without overcommitting in either direction, he sent the message and put his phone away.

Bruno watched this process with evident interest, those intelligent eyes following Dylan's movements as he finished his nightly routine and finally climbed into bed.

"It's been quite a day," Dylan said to his Guardian as he switched off the lamp. "Official Keeper recognition, full transformation, void entity battle, cryptic warnings from ancient shadow-merged apprentices, and..." he paused, still processing the last part, "...whatever that was with Rowan."

Bruno made a soft sound that somehow managed to convey complete understanding despite coming from a supposedly ordinary dog.

As Dylan drifted toward sleep, his mind continued to process everything that had happened. The successful defence of the Timewell, Bruno's magnificent transformation, Corvus's warnings about the deeper void, Rowan's unexpected gesture of affection, all swirled together in his thoughts, gradually organizing themselves into the patterns his mathematical mind naturally created.

One conclusion emerged clearly from this mental organization: their work in Dravengate was becoming more complex and more dangerous than he had initially understood. This wasn't just about restoring magical connections between worlds, it was about maintaining a delicate balance between restoration and protection, between repairing damage and preserving necessary barriers.

And he, Dylan Bennett, sixteen-year-old from Blackpool with a love of mathematics and routine, was now officially the Keeper of Time, responsible for navigating these impossible complexities.

It should have felt overwhelming. But as Bruno's steady presence anchored him in the darkness, Dylan found himself facing this new reality with unexpected calm. One step at a time. One calculation after another. One pattern connected to the next.

That was how he had always approached problems. That was how he would approach this one. Even if some of those problems, like deciphering exactly what Rowan's kiss might mean, were considerably more bewildering than temporal mathematics.

Chapter 15: Two Worlds

The next three days passed with an almost startling normalcy, as if the ordinary world was determined to counterbalance the extraordinary events Dylan had experienced in Dravengate. He attended a family barbecue at his aunt's house, helped Mally organize his vinyl collection using a cataloguing system Dylan had developed, and spent a rainy afternoon baking biscuits with his mum, all perfectly normal activities that now felt somehow different, viewed through the lens of his expanding awareness.

Bruno had fully returned to his ordinary appearance by the morning after their battle with Corvus, though Dylan occasionally caught hints of that golden glow in the Rottweiler's eyes when they practiced their connection exercises in the privacy of his bedroom. The medallion remained invisible in this world, but Dylan could sense its presence when he extended his perception in the way Elara had taught him, a subtle warmth at Bruno's collar that pulsed with protective energy.

Though he tried to focus on his regular summer activities, Dylan found his thoughts continually returning to the questions raised during their confrontation with Corvus. The warning about "deeper void entities" seemed particularly significant, especially after Rowan's text confirming historical references to these beings. If the current damaged state of the crossing was actually serving a protective function, their restoration efforts would need to be carefully reconsidered.

And then there was the matter of Rowan herself. Her impulsive gesture in the Archives had awakened feelings Dylan wasn't entirely sure how to process. Their text exchanges since that day had remained primarily focused on research findings and theoretical questions about the crossing, but there was an undercurrent of something warmer in their communication, a personal connection that went beyond their shared intellectual interests.

On the evening before their scheduled return to Dravengate, Dylan sat at his desk reviewing his notes and preparing questions for their next session. His Keeper Schedule had been updated with a new color-coded section specifically for researching the deeper void entities and their relationship to the crossing's current structure. If they were going to continue the restoration work, they needed to fully understand the potential consequences.

Bruno lay nearby, watching Dylan's preparations with his usual attentiveness. The Rottweiler had been somewhat subdued since their return from Dravengate, as if conserving energy after the tremendous expenditure of his full transformation. Despite this, he remained alert and protective, occasionally rising to check the window or doorway before returning to his post.

"Something feels different," Dylan said quietly, not really expecting a response but finding it natural to share his thoughts with Bruno. "Not just with us, but with... everything."

Bruno raised his head, those intelligent eyes fixed on Dylan with clear understanding. There was something in his gaze that suggested agreement, he too had sensed the subtle shifts occurring around them.

Dylan's phone chimed with an incoming text message:

"Found significant information about Deep Void Entities. Original crossing design included specific barrier functions. Sending full report to Archives for tomorrow's meeting. Also, my field assignment here ends tonight. Returning to Dravengate permanently. See you tomorrow. -R"

The message was primarily professional, but the fact that Rowan had thought to inform him personally about her return to Dravengate suggested a consideration that went beyond their working relationship. Dylan found himself unexpectedly pleased by this small courtesy, though he wasn't entirely sure why it should matter where Rowan was based.

He sent a brief acknowledgement, then returned to his preparations. Tomorrow promised to be significant, not just continuing the restoration work, but potentially redefining their entire approach based on this new information about the crossing's original design.

As he organized his notes, Dylan became aware of a subtle disturbance in the air, not a physical sensation, but something perceived through that other sense he had been developing. It was as if the temporal currents flowing through ordinary reality had momentarily rippled, like a stone dropped into still water.

Bruno noticed it too, rising immediately to full alertness, his gaze fixed on a point near Dylan's bedroom window. For a brief moment, Bruno's eyes flashed with that golden glow, responding to whatever disturbance had occurred.

Dylan moved to the window, peering out at the ordinary Blackpool evening. Nothing seemed visibly amiss, the street was quiet, a few neighbours returning home from work, the sky beginning to dim toward sunset. And yet, something felt undeniably wrong, as if the fabric of reality had briefly thinned.

"You felt it too, didn't you?" he asked Bruno, who had come to stand beside him at the window.

Bruno made a soft sound of confirmation, his attention still focused outward, scanning for potential threats.

Dylan extended his perception as he had practiced, trying to sense the temporal currents flowing through the world around him. There, another ripple, subtle but distinct, like a brief fluctuation in the normally steady flow of time. It wasn't centred on any particular location but seemed to permeate the entire area, as if the boundary between worlds had momentarily wavered.

His phone chimed again, this time with a message from an unknown number:

"Temporal disturbances detected in your vicinity. Activity consistent with boundary thinning. Exercise caution. Lysander has dispatched monitoring team to your area. -Thorne"

So Dravengate had sensed it too. Whatever was happening wasn't just his imagination or an overactive Keeper sensitivity.

Before Dylan could respond, his mother called from downstairs:

"Dylan! Tea's ready!"

The contrast of ordinary family routine with interdimensional disturbances was still something Dylan was adjusting to. With a final glance at the seemingly normal world outside his window, he headed downstairs with Bruno following closely behind, his Guardian's senses still clearly on alert.

Tea was pizza, a Friday tradition in their household that predated even Dylan's most established routines. His mum had made it from scratch as she always did, with separate sections for each family member's preferred toppings. The familiar ritual of their Friday meal should have been comforting, but Dylan found his attention repeatedly drawn to subtle abnormalities he would never have noticed before his Keeper training.

The shadows in the corners of the dining room seemed slightly too deep, as if extending beyond their natural boundaries. Occasionally, objects appeared to momentarily shift position when viewed from the corner of his eye. And most disturbingly, there were brief instances where the ambient sounds of the house, the refrigerator's hum, the tick of the wall clock, his parents' voices, seemed to fade and distort before returning to normal.

"You're quiet tonight," his mum observed as they finished eating. "Everything okay?"

Dylan pulled his attention back to the table, trying to project normalcy despite his growing concern about the disturbances. "Just thinking about a maths problem," he replied, defaulting to his standard excuse for periods of abstraction.

"Always working, that brain of yours," Mally said with affectionate understanding. "Even during summer holiday."

Bruno, who had remained unusually vigilant throughout tea, suddenly rose from his place beside Dylan's chair, his attention fixed on the living room doorway. A low growl rumbled in his chest, not aggressive, but clearly responding to something that concerned him.

"What's got into him?" Dylan's mum asked, looking toward the apparently empty doorway.

Dylan followed Bruno's gaze and felt his breath catch. For just a moment, the doorway seemed to shimmer, the view beyond it flickering briefly to show not their familiar living room, but what appeared to be a stone-walled chamber lit by crystalline lights, a space that strongly resembles one of the Archive's lower levels.

The vision lasted only seconds before reality reasserted itself, the ordinary living room returning to view. But there was no mistaking what he had seen, a momentary overlap between worlds, exactly as Thorne's message had warned.

"Probably heard the neighbour's cat," Dylan suggested, trying to sound casual while his mind raced to process the implications. "He's been a bit jumpy today."

His mum seemed to accept this explanation, but Mally gave Dylan a thoughtful look, his gaze shifting between him and Bruno with an expression that suggested he might have noticed something unusual as well. Before any questions could be asked, however, Dylan's phone vibrated in his pocket.

"May I be excused?" he asked. "I want to finish that problem before bed."

With permission granted, he hurried back upstairs, Bruno following close behind. Once safely in his room with the door closed, Dylan checked the message:

"Boundary fluctuations are increasing. Multiple overlaps detected in your area. Temporal integrity compromised. Return to Dravengate immediately if possible. -Thorne"

This was escalating faster than anyone had anticipated. Dylan glanced at Bruno, who stood at attention near the door, clearly sensing the growing disturbances. Bruno's eyes now showed distinct traces of that golden glow, his Guardian nature responding to the potential threat.

"We need to go," Dylan said quietly. "But I can't just disappear without explanation, especially with whatever's happening getting worse."

He considered his options quickly. His parents were accustomed to his independent nature and frequent walks with Bruno, but disappearing for potentially hours during a strange event might cause unnecessary worry. A compromise was needed.

Heading back downstairs, Dylan found his parents cleaning up after tea. "Bruno's restless," he explained. "I'm going to take him for a quick walk before it gets completely dark."

"Don't go far," his mum advised. "Looks like there might be a storm coming. Sky's gone a bit strange."

Dylan glanced out the kitchen window and felt a chill run through him. The evening sky did indeed look unusual, not with the normal cloud patterns of an approaching storm, but with subtle ripples of colour that shouldn't be there, like oil on water.

"We'll stay close," he promised, knowing it was at least partially true. Physically, he would remain nearby, even if he was temporarily in another dimension.

Once outside, Dylan and Bruno moved quickly to their usual portal spot between the dunes. The evening air felt charged with an unnatural energy, and twice more during their brief walk, Dylan witnessed momentary overlaps, a Dravengate street lamp briefly appearing at the corner of the road, a flash of coppery bark replacing an ordinary tree trunk before fading back to normal.

"It's getting worse," he murmured as they reached the secluded area that had served as their transition point. "The boundaries between worlds are definitely weakening."

Bruno's eyes now glowed openly with golden light, his form beginning to shift slightly toward his Guardian state even before they crossed over. The medallion at his collar became visible, no longer hidden by the transition between worlds but actively manifesting in response to the growing disturbance.

Creating the portal was both easier and harder than usual, easier because the boundary between worlds had thinned, requiring less energy to breach, but harder because the instability made it difficult to maintain control over the gateway's form. When it finally stabilized enough for safe passage, Dylan and Bruno stepped through immediately, not knowing how long the deteriorating conditions would allow for safe transit.

They emerged not at the foot of the stone bridge as usual, but directly in the central plaza of Dravengate, only meters from the Timewell itself. Dylan stumbled slightly, disoriented by this unexpected arrival point. Bruno steadied him with his body, the Rottweiler already fully transformed into his enhanced Guardian state, clearly responding to the emergency conditions.

Dravengate was in a state of controlled chaos. Guardian Division members moved with urgent purpose throughout the plaza, establishing defensive positions around the Timewell and other key structures. Ordinary residents were being directed toward designated shelter areas, the evacuation proceeding with remarkable order despite the obvious tension in the air.

Thorne spotted them almost immediately, hurrying over with uncharacteristic haste. "Thank the Architects you've arrived safely," he said, relief evident in his voice. "The boundary degradation is accelerating beyond our most pessimistic projections."

"What's happening?" Dylan asked, taking in the emergency preparations around them. "I saw overlaps between worlds, parts of Dravengate appearing briefly in Blackpool."

"The cleansing of the Timewell had an unexpected consequence," Thorne explained as he led them toward a command post that had been established near the sigil. "When we purged the corruption from the channels, we apparently disrupted whatever makeshift barrier had been established after the Cataclysm. The boundaries between connected worlds are becoming increasingly permeable."

At the command post, they found Elara coordinating with Lysander on defensive deployments, while a team of Archivists worked with complex instruments monitoring the temporal field. Rowan was among them, her expression intensely focused as she analysed incoming data. She looked up as they approached, her face brightening momentarily at the sight of Dylan before professional concern reasserted itself.

"The boundary integrity is failing at an exponential rate," she reported without preamble. "Current projections suggest complete collapse of the separation between Dravengate and your world within twelve hours if the degradation continues unchecked."

"What does 'complete collapse' mean exactly?" Dylan asked, trying to envision the consequences of such an event.

"A merging of realities," Elara said gravely. "Dravengate would begin to physically manifest in your world, and portions of your world would appear here. The results would be catastrophic for both realms, physical laws in conflict, temporal desynchronization, spatial overlaps resolving in unpredictable ways."

"And that's not the worst of it," Rowan added, gesturing toward a diagram that displayed energy patterns flowing through the crossing. "The boundary weakening isn't limited to just our two worlds. All remaining connections are affected, including whatever barriers are holding back the Deep Void Entities Corvus warned about."

Dylan studied the diagram, his mathematical mind immediately grasping the patterns of degradation. "It's following the fracture lines from the Cataclysm," he observed. "The same channels we used to purge the corruption are now serving as conduits for boundary dissolution."

"Precisely," Thorne confirmed. "Our cleansing action removed the corruption but also dissolved the makeshift barriers that had formed along those same pathways. It's as if we removed a scab, only to find the wound beneath still unhealed."

Bruno moved to the edge of the command post, his transformed form alert and watchful, those glowing eyes scanning the plaza with protective intensity. The medallion at his chest pulsed with golden light, seemingly responding to the fluctuations in the temporal field around them.

"So what do we do?" Dylan asked, focusing on solutions rather than dwelling on the unintended consequences of their previous work. "How do we restabilize the boundaries?"

"That's why we needed you here urgently," Elara explained. "As Keeper, you have the ability to directly influence the temporal fabric of the crossing. The wand can be used to reestablish boundaries along the cleansed channels, not the corrupted barriers that existed before, but proper, stable separations as originally designed."

"But I've never done anything like that," Dylan pointed out. "All our work so far has been about restoration, not establishing new boundaries."

"Which is why you'll need this," Rowan said, bringing over a large, ancient-looking book bound in what appeared to be silver-infused leather. "My research into the Deep Void Entities led me to this, the original Architect's manual for the crossing's boundary systems. It contains the mathematical framework for proper world separation without compromising controlled connection."

Dylan accepted the book, immediately recognizing its significance. This wasn't just historical information but practical instruction, the actual specifications for how the crossing was meant to function. "This could take days to fully understand," he said, daunted by the complexity evident even from a brief glimpse of the open pages.

"We don't have days," Thorne acknowledged grimly. "But you don't need to master the entire system immediately. Focus on the primary boundary equations in chapter three. They contain the foundational patterns that should allow you to stabilize the most critical junctions."

The Keeper of Time

Looking around at the increasingly urgent activity in the plaza, Dylan felt the weight of responsibility settling firmly on his shoulders. This wasn't a training exercise or a carefully controlled restoration sequence. This was a genuine emergency requiring immediate action from the Keeper of Time.

"I'll need space to work," he said, decision made. "And Rowan's help with the mathematical translations. Bruno will provide protection while we focus on the boundaries."

The command post quickly reorganized to accommodate this plan. A workspace was cleared for Dylan and Rowan near the Timewell, with Bruno taking up position beside them, his transformed state creating a natural perimeter of golden light that pushed back against the growing temporal disturbances in the plaza.

As they settled into their work, Dylan could feel the boundary between worlds continuing to weaken. Momentary overlaps similar to what he had witnessed in Blackpool were now occurring throughout Dravengate, brief glimpses of ordinary streets, buildings, even people from his world appearing and disappearing like ghosts. The effect was disorienting, reality itself seeming to flicker and stutter as the two worlds began to bleed into each other.

"We need to hurry," Rowan said, her voice tense as she helped Dylan navigate through the ancient text. "The degradation rate is increasing."

Together, they focused on the primary boundary equations, Dylan's mathematical mind quickly grasping the elegant patterns described in the Architect's manual. These weren't simplistic divisions but complex interrelationships, boundaries that separated while still allowing for controlled connection, filters that distinguished between beneficial exchange and dangerous incursion.

"It's brilliant," Dylan murmured, genuine appreciation in his voice despite the pressure of their situation. "The original design wasn't about isolation but selective permeability, like a cell membrane that allows nutrients in while keeping toxins out."

"Exactly," Rowan agreed, her own admiration evident. "And the key is this harmonic frequency pattern, it creates resonance between connected worlds while maintaining distinct separation."

As they worked through the mathematical framework, Dylan began to understand not just how to reestablish boundaries, but why Corvus's warning held partial truth. The damaged crossing had indeed been functioning as a kind of barrier against deeper threats, but in a crude, unstable way compared to the sophisticated system originally designed by the Architects.

"We can restore the proper barriers," he realized, the solution taking shape in his mind. "Not just patching the current degradation, but implementing the original filtration design. It would allow for controlled connection while specifically blocking the Deep Void Entities."

Rowan's eyes lit up with understanding. "That's it! Instead of just stopping the current crisis, we rebuild according to original specifications. The math supports it, look here." She pointed to a section of equations that detailed the selective permeability functions.

Their breakthrough came just in time. Beyond their working area, the boundary degradation was accelerating visibly. Larger, more persistent overlaps were occurring throughout the plaza, some lasting several minutes before fading. Guardian Division members were struggling to maintain order as confused residents of both worlds occasionally found themselves temporarily transported across the weakening divide.

"We need to implement this now," Dylan said, the completed mathematical framework clear in his mind. "I'll need to work directly with the Timewell."

Bruno moved with them as they approached the central basin, his protective aura expanding to create a stable workspace amid the increasing chaos. The silver substance within the Timewell was visibly disturbed, its normally smooth flow disrupted by ripples and eddies that corresponded to the boundary failures occurring throughout Dravengate.

Dylan removed the wand from his pocket, feeling the familiar warmth against his palm as it responded to his intent. With Rowan beside him providing reference points from the Architect's manual, he extended his perception into the Timewell, identifying the cleansed channels that were now serving as conduits for boundary dissolution.

"I need to establish the harmonic pattern along each major channel," he explained, as much to organize his own thoughts as to inform Rowan. "The resonance will create stable boundaries that allow for controlled connection while filtering out disruptive elements."

"Start with the primary junction," Rowan suggested, indicating a specific point in the silver substance where multiple channels converged. "If we can stabilize that, the effect should propagate outward along the connected pathways."

Dylan nodded, raising the wand toward the indicated junction. Drawing on everything he had learned about temporal manipulation, combined with the mathematical framework from the Architect's manual, he focused his will through the ancient tool. This wasn't like the previous restoration work, which had been about repairing existing structures. This was creative work, establishing new patterns based on original design principles but implemented through his own understanding and intent.

The wand grew warmer in his hand, channelling his purpose into the Timewell with remarkable precision. The silver substance responded immediately, the disrupted flow at the primary junction beginning to stabilize into a complex but harmonious pattern that matched the equations they had studied.

"It's working," Rowan confirmed, monitoring the effect through instruments set up nearby. "Boundary integrity increasing at the primary junction. The resonance is beginning to propagate along connected channels."

Dylan maintained his focus, guiding the stabilizing effect outward from the central point, establishing the harmonic pattern in each major channel as it was reached. It was delicate, demanding work, each section required slight adjustments to account for its specific position in the overall network, like tuning individual strings in an impossibly complex instrument.

Bruno remained vigilant beside them, his transformed state seemingly in harmony with Dylan's work, the golden light of his Guardian aura pulsing in rhythm with the stabilizing patterns being established in the Timewell. Occasionally, when boundary failures brought particularly disruptive overlaps near their position, Bruno would intensify his protective field, creating a bubble of stable reality within which Dylan could continue his work undisturbed.

The process took nearly an hour of intense concentration, but gradually, the effects became visible throughout Dravengate. The random, chaotic overlaps between worlds began to diminish in both frequency and duration. Where they did occur, they now followed more predictable patterns, as if being channeled through controlled points rather than breaking through randomly.

"The boundary integrity is stabilizing," Thorne reported from the command post, visible relief in his voice. "Random incursions are down by sixty percent and continuing to decrease."

"And the Deep Void access points?" Elara asked the question that concerned them all.

"Fully contained," Rowan confirmed, checking readings from specialized instruments set up specifically to monitor those particular boundaries. "The filtration function is working exactly as described in the manual. Controlled connection maintained; dangerous incursions blocked."

As the immediate crisis subsided, Dylan finally lowered the wand, the extended effort leaving him tired but satisfied. The Timewell now displayed a beautiful complexity of flow, the silver substance moving in patterns that reflected the selective permeability they had established, boundaries that separated while still allowing for controlled connection.

"You did it," Rowan said, with genuine admiration in her voice. "Not just emergency patching, but actual implementation of the original design. This is... remarkable."

Bruno pressed against Dylan's leg, offering his solid presence as support. Bruno's transformation remained active, but his protective stance had relaxed somewhat as the immediate threat diminished.

"We did it," Dylan corrected, including both Rowan and Bruno in the achievement. "I couldn't have understood the mathematical framework without your research, and Bruno's protection gave us the stable space to work."

As the emergency response throughout the plaza transitioned from crisis management to recovery operations, Thorne and Elara joined them at the Timewell.

"Extraordinary work," Thorne said, studying the new patterns flowing through the silver substance with evident appreciation. "You've implemented functioning boundary protocols that haven't been seen since before the Cataclysm."

"And potentially solved the dilemma Corvus presented," Elara added thoughtfully. "These new boundaries maintain controlled connection while specifically filtering out the deeper threats he warned about. The crossing can be restored without sacrificing the protective function of the current configuration."

The implications were significant. Their restoration work could continue without fear of inadvertently releasing worse entities than those they currently faced. The balance Corvus had spoken of, between restoration and protection, could be maintained through proper implementation of the original design rather than preserving the damaged state.

"We should expect continued resistance," Thorne cautioned, ever practical despite their success. "Corvus and the void entities may not appreciate the elegance of this solution if it threatens their established position."

"We'll be ready," Dylan said with newfound confidence. His first major crisis as official Keeper had been successfully resolved, not through combat but through understanding and implementation of the crossing's true design. It felt right, using knowledge and pattern recognition rather than force to address the fundamental problems.

As the immediate work concluded and the plaza began returning to something resembling normal operations, Dylan became aware of just how long they had been in Dravengate. According to his watch, nearly three hours had passed since he had left home for what he had told his parents would be a "quick walk" with Bruno.

"I should return soon," he said, concerned about potential worry his extended absence might cause. "My parents will be wondering where I am."

"Of course," Thorne agreed. "The crisis is contained for now, and you've established a framework that can be monitored and maintained while you're away."

"I'll compile complete documentation of today's work," Rowan promised. "With your boundary implementation as a foundation, we can develop a revised restoration plan that incorporates these protective functions into all future sigil work."

As Dylan prepared to depart, creating the return portal with Bruno at his side, Rowan approached once more. There was a moment of awkward hesitation between them, the memory of her impulsive gesture from their previous parting clearly in both their minds.

"Thank you," she said finally, settling for professional gratitude though her eyes suggested more complex feelings. "What you did today wasn't just impressive, it was brilliant. A true Keeper solution."

"I couldn't have done it without your research," Dylan replied honestly. "You found exactly what we needed when we needed it most."

Another moment of hesitation, then Rowan stepped forward and gave him a quick hug, brief but deliberate, less impulsive than her previous gesture but perhaps more meaningful for being consciously chosen.

"Be careful," she said as she stepped back. "The boundaries are stabilizing, but there may still be echoes of the disruption in your world. If anything unusual happens, use the communication crystal immediately."

Dylan nodded, somewhat flustered by the hug but managing a coherent response. "I will. See you in three days for the regular session?"

"I'll be here," she confirmed with a smile that transformed her usually serious expression. "With comprehensive notes on everything we've learned today."

With final farewells to Thorne and Elara, Dylan and Bruno stepped through the portal, returning once more to the dunes of Blackpool. The transition was smoother than Dylan had feared given the recent boundary issues, suggesting their work had successfully stabilized the connection between worlds.

Evening had fully settled during their absence, the sky dark except for scattered stars visible between passing clouds. Bruno shook himself as always, his Guardian transformation receding though not completely disappearing, subtle traces of that golden glow remained in his eyes, and his overall presence seemed somehow larger than his physical form would suggest.

As they walked home, Dylan was alert for signs of continued boundary weakening, but the overlaps appeared to have ceased. Occasionally, he thought he caught glimpses of something not quite normal from the corner of his eye, shadows that moved independently of their sources, lights that flickered with colours not found in ordinary streetlamps, but these could have been tricks of tired eyes rather than actual manifestations.

When they reached home, Dylan was relieved to find his absence hadn't caused undue concern. His parents were watching television in the living room, his mum looking up with a smile as they entered.

"Good walk?" she asked casually.

"Yes," Dylan replied, grateful for the simple question that required no elaborate explanation. "Bruno seemed to need the exercise."

Mally glanced at them over the rim of his coffee mug, his gaze lingering on Bruno in a way that made Dylan wonder if his stepdad noticed something different about the dog. But if he did, he made no comment, simply nodding acknowledgment before returning his attention to the program they were watching.

Upstairs in his room, Dylan finally allowed himself to fully process everything that had happened. In the space of one evening, they had faced a major interdimensional crisis, implemented original Architect designs for the crossing's boundary systems, and potentially resolved the core dilemma of their restoration work. It was a lot to absorb, even for a mind as adept at pattern recognition as his.

Bruno settled on his usual spot on the rug, though his attention remained unusually active, those still-faintly-glowing eyes occasionally moving to the window or doorway as if continuing to monitor for potential disturbances. The medallion had disappeared from view again in this world, but Dylan could sense its presence when he extended his perception, a warm pulse of protective energy that remained active despite their return.

His phone chimed with an incoming message:

"Boundary systems holding stable. Minor fluctuations but within acceptable parameters. Your implementation is functioning exactly as designed. Rest well, Keeper. -Thorne"

A second message followed almost immediately:

"The selective permeability equations you implemented are beautiful. Looking forward to exploring applications for future restoration work. Thank you again for today. -R"

The formal update from Thorne was reassuring, but Dylan found himself more pleased by Rowan's personal message than he might have expected. There was something genuinely satisfying about having someone who appreciated the mathematical elegance of his work, who saw beauty in equations and patterns as he did.

As he prepared for bed, Dylan found himself reflecting on how dramatically his summer had changed from his original carefully structured plans. Instead of quiet days of mathematical study and gaming, he had become the Keeper of Time, responsible for maintaining the boundaries between worlds while gradually restoring an ancient magical crossing.

And somehow, despite the enormous responsibility and occasional danger, it felt right. The patterns and structures of temporal magic resonated with his mathematical mind in ways that ordinary life rarely had. Even the social complexities, like his evolving connection with Rowan, seemed somewhat more navigable within the context of their shared work and mutual understanding.

Bruno watched from his place on the rug as Dylan completed his nightly routine, those intelligent eyes following his movement with faithful attention. Their bond had deepened tremendously through these experiences, evolving from the ordinary connection between boy and dog into something far more profound, Keeper and Guardian, linked across worlds by purpose and magic.

Just as Dylan was about to turn off his lamp, he noticed something unusual outside his window. At first, he thought it was just stars visible through a break in the clouds, but there was something odd about their arrangement, patterns that didn't match any constellation he recognized.

Moving to the window, he peered out at the night sky and felt a chill run through him. Overlaid on the familiar stars were others that shouldn't be there, brighter, with colours rarely seen in Earth's night sky, arranged in formations he had only ever seen while standing in Dravengate's central plaza.

Bruno joined him at the window, a soft rumble in his chest suggesting he too saw the anomaly. The Rottweiler's eyes glowed more distinctly now, responding to this evidence that despite their best efforts, some blending of the worlds continued.

Dylan reached for his phone to report this development, then hesitated. The overlapping stars weren't causing any immediate harm, and Thorne had mentioned "acceptable parameters" for minor fluctuations. Perhaps this was simply one of those, a harmless echo that would resolve itself as the new boundary systems fully settled.

Instead of sending an urgent alert, he took a photo of the phenomenon and attached it to a more measured message:

"Seeing these overlapping stars in Blackpool sky. Stable, not expanding. Worth monitoring but doesn't seem to be causing problems. Will check again in the morning."

He sent the message to both Thorne and Rowan, then returned to bed, though his gaze periodically drifted back to the window where those impossible stars continued to shine alongside the familiar ones of Earth's night sky.

Bruno settled once more on his rug, but positioned himself facing the window, his Guardian instincts clearly maintaining watch over this minor but significant anomaly.

As Dylan drifted toward sleep, he found himself not troubled but oddly comforted by those overlapping stars. They were a reminder that the worlds were not truly separate but connected, distinct realities that nonetheless shared fundamental patterns and could communicate through properly established channels.

Like the mathematical harmonics they had implemented in the Timewell, there was a beauty to this controlled connection, this selective permeability between worlds that allowed for exchange without chaos.

The Keeper of Time

Summer was coming to an end, and everything had changed. His carefully structured plans had given way to something far more complex and challenging, yet also more fulfilling than he could have imagined.

He was Dylan Bennett, sixteen years old, from Blackpool, England. He liked mathematics and gaming and keeping to carefully constructed routines.

And he was also the Keeper of Time, guardian of the boundaries between worlds, protector of the crossing that connected realities.

Two identities. Two worlds. Both equally real, both equally his.

As sleep finally claimed him, the starlight from two different skies cast gentle patterns across his room, ordinary and extraordinary illumination overlapping in perfect harmony.

To be continued ....

Printed in Dunstable, United Kingdom

66213593R00178